8

POSTMAN'S KNOCK

Inspector Pitt has a problem. The postman in Grange Road has mysteriously vanished. Had he absconded with the mail? Been kidnapped or perhaps murdered? And why had he delivered only some of the letters? The people of Grange Road seem averse to police inquiries. Was there a conspiracy to remove the postman? Before any questions are answered, assault, blackmail and sudden death disturb the normal peace of Grange Road.

Books by J. F. Straker
in the Linford Mystery Library:

A CHOICE OF VICTIMS
SWALLOW THEM UP
DEATH ON A SUNDAY MORNING
A LETTER FOR OBI
COUNTERSNATCH
ARTHUR'S NIGHT
A PITY IT WASN'T GEORGE
THE GOAT
DEATH OF A GOOD WOMAN
MISCARRIAGE OF MURDER
SIN AND JOHNNY INCH
TIGHT CIRCLE
A MAN WHO CANNOT KILL
ANOTHER MAN'S POISON
THE SHAPE OF MURDER
A COIL OF ROPE
MURDER FOR MISS EMILY
GOODBYE, AUNT CHARLOTTE
FINAL WITNESS
PICK UP THE PIECES

J. F. STRAKER

POSTMAN'S KNOCK

Complete and Unabridged

LINFORD
Leicester

First published in Great Britain

First Linford Edition
published 2005

British Library CIP Data

Straker, J. F. (John Foster)
  Postman's knock.—Large print ed.—
  Linford mystery library
  1. Detective and mystery stories
  2. Large type books
  I. Title
  823.9'14 [F]

ISBN 1–84617–075–3

Published by
F. A. Thorpe (Publishing)
Anstey, Leicestershire

Set by Words & Graphics Ltd.
Anstey, Leicestershire
Printed and bound in Great Britain by
T. J. International Ltd., Padstow, Cornwall

This book is printed on acid-free paper

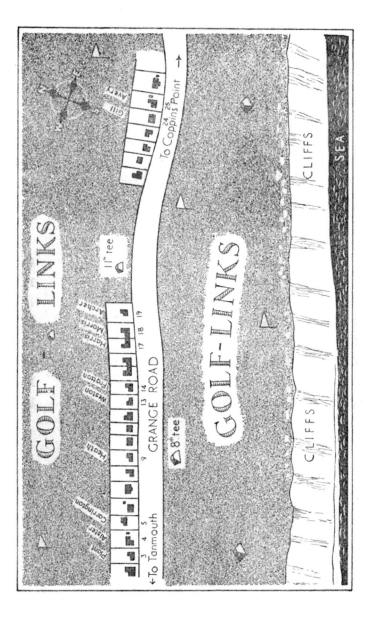

1

The Postman's Late

Miss Plant deposited her wet umbrella in the hall-stand of No. 24 Grange Road, stripped from her squat figure the transparent plastic mackintosh that enveloped it, and implanted a damp kiss on the proffered cheek of her friend.

'What a wretched afternoon, Hermione!' she exclaimed breathlessly, peering in the narrow mirror at her straggling grey locks. 'I ran all the way. And just look at my hair! It was so nice this morning, too.'

It did not occur to Mrs Gill to query whether it was the hair or the weather that had been nice that morning. Ethel Plant's hair was never nice. She steered her guest into the front parlour, gave the fire an expert poke, and carefully balanced a fresh lump of coal over the solitary flame.

'I thought we would have our tea in the window,' she said. 'I know it's dark, and one can't see much on a day like this, of course. But I like it in the window. You aren't cold, are you? You don't want to sit by the fire?'

Miss Plant, warm from her unwonted exercise, raised no objection. She knew that her friend never moved far from the front window, from which vantage-point she could observe the comings and goings of her neighbours. And if she herself lacked the inquisitiveness that possessed Mrs Gill, she had no desire to spoil the other's pleasure.

She settled herself comfortably and waited for the tea.

It was, as Miss Plant had said, a wretched afternoon. The rain that had begun to fall shortly after lunch had turned to sleet, and was being driven in fierce gusts against the windows. Although the curtains were still undrawn, Miss Plant found no pleasure in gazing out at that small portion of Grange Road made visible by the street-lamp outside No. 24. She preferred to think of her tea.

Only the knowledge that it would be a good one had brought her the length of Grange Road in such weather.

She tucked in zestfully when the tea arrived, begrudging the pauses necessitated by conversation. With Hermione there was always plenty of the latter.

'The postman's late,' said Mrs Gill. 'It must be this awful weather that's delayed him. Never after 4.30, as a rule. Had he called at your place when you left, Ethel?'

Miss Plant shook her head and swallowed rapidly. 'There was nothing for me,' she said. 'But I saw him outside No. 5 — Mr Carrington's bungalow. He was just going in as I passed. Only it wasn't our usual postman. Not Mr Gofer. A little man — rather surly, I thought. He just grunted when I said good-evening.'

'They take on lots of extra postmen at Christmas,' said her friend. 'I hope we haven't seen the last of Mr Gofer. Such a nice young man, I always think.' She frowned. Miss Plant had unwittingly reminded her that there were some inhabitants of Grange Road with whom she was unfamiliar. It was a state of affairs

Mrs Gill always sought to rectify. 'I suppose you still haven't got to meeting Mr Carrington, Ethel?' she asked. 'It seems odd, you being such a close neighbour and yet knowing so little about him.'

'It's not odd at all, Hermione,' Miss Plant retorted. 'Mr Carrington's not a friendly type. I doubt if he's ever spoken to a soul in the road. Except Dorothy Weston, of course. Maybe he's shy, or maybe he thinks we're not good enough for him. Or perhaps it's just because he's an artist.'

'I never did trust artists,' declared Mrs Gill. 'Quite unreliable. And all those nudes — disgusting, I call it. I shouldn't be surprised if *she* poses for him like that.'

'I don't think he paints people,' said Miss Plant. 'Just scenery and things.'

'That's what he says, I've no doubt. But they're all tarred with the same brush. And that reporter from the *Chronicle* — a Mr Bullett, wasn't it? He was no better, if you ask me. Just like his friend, never spoke to anyone. Does he still visit there, by the way?'

'I don't know, Hermione.' Miss Plant helped herself absently to the last muffin and wiped her fingers on the paper napkin. 'The bungalow is so far back from the road; and all those trees and bushes, they quite shut it off. And there's the Alsters between us, you see. I really know very little of what goes on at No. 5.'

Mrs Gill regarded her friend with tolerant contempt. Such hindrances as Miss Plant had enumerated would not have prevented *her* from obtaining the information she desired. 'I have an idea,' she said slowly, 'that there may be trouble brewing for your friend Carrington.'

Miss Plant bit squelchily into the muffin and munched contentedly.

'Because of Miss Weston?'

'Yes, Ethel. I may be old-fashioned, and I know artists have a different code of morals from other people — and Dorothy Weston *does* earn her living in the chorus (or did; I imagine Carrington is now her main source of income. They say he's very well off). So I'm saying nothing about the way they carry on together — her being so brazen about it, and spending half the night at the bungalow. But when she's practically engaged to another man it — well, I know what I'd do if I were her fiancé.'

'But Donald Heath isn't her fiancé,' Miss Plant protested.

'Maybe not. But it's an understood thing that they're to be married as soon as the firm gives him a rise. I had that from Mrs Heath herself. And you can't say it's wishful thinking on her part, for she can't stand the girl. No, Ethel. If I were Carrington I wouldn't sleep too easy in my bed. Donald Heath is a quick-tempered young man, and he's quite infatuated with the girl. He won't take it lying down, her getting involved with another man. It's my belief he'll warn Carrington to keep away from her — or else! . . . '

'I don't think Mr Carrington would be easily frightened,' said Miss Plant. 'And although he isn't very tall he's quite broad. I should say he could give as good as he got.'

'I've no doubt he could — in a fair

fight.' Mrs Gill looked solemn. 'But there are other ways of disposing of a rival, Ethel. And Donald Heath has a lot of his father in him, or I'm no judge. There's a mean streak somewhere. If he hated someone bad enough I wouldn't put even murder past him.'

★   ★   ★

'It's getting on for five, Donald,' Mrs Heath called from the kitchen. 'Come and have your tea.'

Donald Heath shook his head irritably and continued to stare at where he knew the garden gate to be. For over half an hour he had stood in the dark parlour gazing out of the window, so that his eyes were now attuned to the gathering gloom. Half an hour ago he could see the gate clearly; could pick out through the scurrying rain and sleet the white sandbox on the eighth tee across the road, the haze of the sea beyond. But sea and links, even Grange Road itself, were now engulfed in the darkening night. Only his long vigil enabled him still to distinguish

7

the white blur that marked the garden gate of No. 9.

Mrs Heath, annoyed at her son's lack of response, came shuffling into the room, her feet encased in the habitual carpet slippers that had once belonged to her late husband. 'Standing there in the dark!' she scoffed, switching on the electric light. 'If you've nothing better to do than — '

'Turn it off!' he said sharply. When she did not move he lunged past her and snapped up the switch, plunging them once more into gloom. 'I wish you wouldn't interfere, Mother. I know what I'm doing.'

'So do I,' she retorted. 'You're waiting for the postman — though goodness knows why you have to wait in the dark. Anyway, he must have passed the house ages ago; it's well after his usual time. Don't be a fool, Donald. Come and have your tea, there's a good lad.'

'It's easier to look out with the lights off,' he said. 'And he hasn't passed — I'd have seen him. I expect he's late because of the Christmas mail.'

8

He moved closer into the bay-window. Even the white blur of the gate was gone now, thanks to his mother's interference. Because of the strain under which he was labouring the incident annoyed him unduly. He said angrily, 'You know as well as I do how important it is that we should get Aunt Ellen's letter. Where else should we raise two hundred quid?'

'Where indeed?' she said wearily. 'But a watched pot never boils. If there's a letter your standing there won't bring it any quicker. You might just as well have your tea. And you said yourself they most likely won't check the cash until they close for Christmas. There's time enough.'

'You don't understand,' he said. 'If the money doesn't come by this post it may not come at all. I told her I'd got to have it before the week-end, and she's had bags of time to make up her mind. That's what scares me — that she may not send it.'

'She'll send it,' said his mother. She said it to reassure him, and then realized that she believed it. 'Today's only Friday. If it doesn't come by this post it'll come tomorrow. You'll see.' There was bitterness in her voice as she went on. 'While your father was alive we could have starved to death, for all she cared. She wouldn't help her own sister then for fear he'd benefit, she hated him that bad. But it's different now. All that money, and you her only nephew — and your father dead. Oh, yes, she'll send it, if only to salve her conscience for the way she's neglected us in the past.'

'Well, I hope to blazes you're right,' he answered, slightly cheered by the conviction in her tone. 'And in that case it'll come tonight. It *must* do. You know, Mother, I can't say I blame Aunt Ellen for not wanting Dad to get his hands on her money. A fat lot we'd have seen of it if he had.'

'That'll do, Donald,' she said sharply. 'I'll not have you speak like that about your father. And you're a nice one to malign him, I must say! At least he never stole money from his own firm.'

It was not meant as a defence of the late Mr Heath. She was annoyed at Donald's smug criticism of his father, embittered by the further worry and disgrace he had brought to her. She had thought she had become hardened to both; but that was before she knew her son to be a thief.

Donald shivered. Even to himself he had not cared to think of it as stealing.

'Maybe I shouldn't have told her why I needed the money,' he said, his fears returning. 'My borrowing it from the firm, I mean. Only how else could I make her realize the urgency? She might have held it up and sent it as a Christmas present. And a fat lot of use it would have been to me in gaol.'

Mrs Heath did not wince at the thought of this possibility. Gaol or the threat of gaol had loomed large in her married life. 'It's as well you didn't tell her how you spent the money,' she said. 'If she knew it had all gone on that woman she wouldn't send you a penny. Your father all over again, she'd think.'

'I've told you before, Mother, I won't have you referring to Dorothy as 'that woman.' '

'Hussy, then, if you prefer it. It's nearer

the truth,' said his mother. 'No, Donald, I won't be shut up. She *is* a hussy, and if you weren't an infatuated fool you'd know it. Look at her hair! It wasn't always red, I'll be bound. And the way she wears it, the way she dresses; trying to pass herself off as twenty, when she's at least thirty-five. And that's eight years older than you, Donald. A nice wife *she'll* make you!'

'I don't care how old she is. I love her, and that's that.'

'The more's the pity,' answered his mother. 'However, from what I hear there's no need for me to put you against her. She'll not marry you with Carrington around. Carrington's got money. And money speaks louder than love to a girl like Dorothy Weston.'

He was silent, realizing the truth of her remarks. Much as he loved Dorothy, he was not blind to her faults. Money was Dorothy's god. If Carrington was in earnest about her . . .

'I'll deal with Carrington,' he said viciously, clenching his fists. 'I'll not have him — '

The click of the garden gate, the faint crunch of feet on gravel, caused him to break off and rush to the front door, ready to open it against the expected knock. Aunt Ellen was a careful woman. The letter would be registered.

But no knock came. There was the sound of feet shuffling on the step outside, and two envelopes fell with a plop into the wire cage. Donald fished them out hastily. A circular and a Christmas card. Nothing from Aunt Ellen.

Panic seized him. He flung open the door and stepped out into the driving sleet.

'Hey, postman!' he shouted.

The white beam from the man's torch paused in its jerky progress down the path and then swung back towards him.

'There should be another letter for me,' Donald said desperately. 'A registered letter. Are you sure you haven't mislaid it?'

'Sorry. That's all,' came the disembodied voice from behind the torch.

He watched the beam move on down

the path, shine momentarily on the white gate, and then pass through it and disappear into the night.

'Any luck, dear?' Mrs Heath asked anxiously.

He showed her the two envelopes, his mind in a turmoil. She had been so certain that the money would come — and didn't she know her own sister? It was inconceivable that Aunt Ellen could have failed him. The money was there: it just *had* to be there, somewhere in the postman's possession. The man was lying. Either he was a thief, or he was too damned careless to sort the mail properly. And with every second the precious cheque was going farther and farther away . . . going . . . going . . .

'Donald! Donald, come back!'

If he heard her he took no heed. His slippers splashed in the puddles as he ran down the uneven path and out through the gate. A few yards up the road the white beam danced ahead of him. With no thought in his mind but that he must get the letter at any cost, Donald Heath went after it.

'I can't say I'm over-keen on Mrs Heath either, come to that,' said Miss Plant, her plump fingers hovering indecisively over the cakes. 'If Donald gets his meanness from his father he gets his bad temper from his mother, I'd say.'

'She went through enough to sour any woman, while that husband of her's was alive,' said Mrs Gill. 'I'm sorry for her. But she hasn't managed to knock any sense into Donald, for all the lesson her husband taught her. He's got his father's itch for flashy women, has that young man. What sort of a wife will Dorothy Weston make him? Apart from being years older, she's got the typical chorus-girl's attitude to life.'

Miss Plant wondered vaguely how her friend could consider herself an authority on chorus-girls. But she was not sufficiently interested to seek enlightenment.

From some motive she could not explain, she was moved to speak in Dorothy Weston's defence.

'She dresses smartly, Hermione. And

she doesn't *talk* common. I don't think she's so bad really, even if she does rather throw herself at Mr Carrington.'

'Nonsense, Ethel. She dresses like a tart — and behaves like one, too. I'm surprised at your sticking up for her.'

'I met her mother in the High Street this morning,' said Miss Plant. 'Apparently today is Dorothy's birthday, and they are having a small family party to celebrate. Her married sister's coming down from Town. That doesn't sound very immoral, does it?'

Mrs Gill snorted.

'It doesn't sound like Dorothy Weston, you mean. If it's a tea-party this afternoon it'll be something very different this evening.'

★ ★ ★

'Whose idea was the family get-together, Dolly? Not yours, surely? So out of character,' said Mrs Gault. 'And what has happened to the new boy friend you told me about? The wealthy artist? Why isn't he devising something gayer in the way of

16

a birthday celebration? Something with a drop of sparkle?'

Dorothy Weston frowned.

'I'm worried about him, Sue. I think he's cooling off, blast him! He rang up this morning to wish me a happy birthday and to ask if I'd had his present (which I haven't. I'm hoping it will come by this afternoon's post). But he said nothing about our getting together. In fact, he talked of going to Town.' She sighed. 'Oh, well. It was fun while it lasted.'

'In love with him?' asked her sister.

'No, I don't think so. But he's such good fun. He and I have the same ideas about life.'

'H'm! I can imagine what *they* are,' said Susan dryly. 'Well, don't let him go without a struggle, my dear.'

'I don't intend to. All the same, I'm becoming more and more convinced that I'm destined to be Mrs Donald Heath. I can't say the prospect thrills me; Jock's at the top of the list and Donald's at the bottom. But Donald's the only one I can really count on.'

'He doesn't sound wildly exciting,' her

sister commented. 'And why this preoccupation with marriage? It's not in your line at all.'

'It wasn't. But it is now. I'm thirty-four, Sue, and I haven't had the smell of a job for months. And since I don't intend to earn my living on the streets, the only alternative is a husband.' She got up and began to wander restlessly about the room. Neither of them had thought to switch on the light, and the room was illumined only by a faint glow from the street-lamp outside. 'I can't batten on Mum and Dad for the rest of my life. Donald's not bad-looking, and he's crazy about me. I'll have no trouble with him. But he's such an awful stick, and so horribly suburban. We'll live in this ruddy street until we peg out. Never travel, never own a car, never spend a *bean* extravagantly. He's splashing it about now, of course, but I can see it worries him. He's not used to spending money. He'll clamp down like an oyster after we're married. I know men.'

'You should do, dear,' said Susan. 'Well, it's a grim prospect.'

'You're telling me! And I shan't be allowed even to *look* at another man. He's as jealous as sin.'

'How does he react to your affair with the artist, then? Or doesn't he know about that?'

'Not all the details, I hope. But enough. He looks like the wrath of God whenever Jock's name crops up. But at present he's too damned scared of losing me to make a song about it. Hello! There's the post.'

The postman's cap glistened in the rain and the lamplight as it glided, seemingly unaided, along the top of the high hedge that marked the boundary of No. 13. Dorothy waited expectantly as it reached the end of the hedge and paused, above an equally wet and glistening mackintosh cape, while the postman considered his mail. Then, to her disappointment, he passed the gate and disappeared up the path of No. 14.

'Damn! Nothing for me. And Jock was so certain I would get it yesterday or today.'

'What's he giving you?'

'I don't know. But he ordered it from a

jeweller in Town — and he's the generous type. It ought to be something pretty good.'

'Why not ring him up and tell him it hasn't arrived?' her sister suggested. 'He might ask us out for a drink — which, after all that tea and cake, would go down very nicely, thank you.'

'He's probably still in Town,' said Dorothy. But she went out to the hall, and Susan heard her pick up the receiver and dial a number. Presently she returned, switching on the light viciously as she entered the room.

'No reply,' she said shortly. There was a frown on her pretty face.

'Well, that's what you expected, isn't it? Why the display of temper?'

'I expected him to be out, yes. But he isn't — he's there. I heard him pick up the receiver, and then he replaced it as soon as I spoke.' She threw herself into an armchair. 'He's got another woman there, blast him! And on my birthday, too — the mean skunk!'

★   ★   ★

'What can have happened to the post-man?' asked Mrs Gill. 'He's never as late as this.'

'It'll be the Christmas mail, I expect,' said her friend. 'And he won't know the district, him being a new man. He was already late when I saw him outside No. 5; nearly twenty-five past four, it was.' She laughed. 'Maybe Miss Fratton has murdered him. Mr Gofer was always saying he thought twice about calling at No. 14, she looked that frightening.'

Mrs Gill did not echo the laugh.

'That's something I've never been able to understand,' she admitted. 'Just why has she got her knife into postmen? They always seem such inoffensive men.'

It was evident that lack of this particular piece of information worried her. But Miss Plant could not supply it. 'I did hear a rumour that she'd been crossed in love by a postman,' said Miss Plant. 'Miss Weston would know, I imagine. She and Miss Fratton are thick as thieves. Odd, isn't it? You wouldn't think those two had much in common.'

'Neither they have, Ethel. Miss Fratton

21

is merely a stupid, lonely creature who has been hoodwinked by a designing young woman. She's got no relatives to leave her money to, and Dorothy Weston knows it. There's nothing odd about that. Disgusting, perhaps; but not odd.' Mrs Gill frowned. 'But I do wish I could get to the bottom of her hatred of postmen. It annoys me, not knowing.'

Miss Plant found that easy to believe. 'It'll all come out at the trial,' she said, and giggled.

Mrs Gill stared at her.

'The trial? What on earth are you talking about, Ethel? What trial?'

The giggle stopped. 'It was only a joke,' her friend explained lamely. 'I meant, if Miss Fratton really *had* murdered the postman.'

★   ★   ★

Behind the front door of No. 14 Miss Fratton stood poised, ready to strike as soon as the postman's finger should press the bell or his hand push open the flap of the letter-box. She had seen his cap pass under the street-lamp opposite No. 13, the beam of his torch as he walked up the path; and with a grim chuckle she had moved away from the window to be ready for him.

Tall, gaunt, and balding, she looked like a vulture hovering over its prey. The skin dropped away in deep pouches from under fierce, protruding eyeballs, the hooked nose overshadowed the drooping chin, from which sprouted small tufts of coarse bristle. A sack-like grey dress, high at the neck, enveloped her. In her skinny hands, as she clenched and unclenched them expectantly, the veins ran like ridges.

As she heard his foot on the step and saw the flap lift she flung the front door open. A long arm reached out, clutching the man's shoulder. But even as she felt the wet cape under her fingers she realized he was a stranger. He did not seek to evade her as Gofer would have done, so that she might reach him only with her tongue and not with her hands. In place of Gofer's 'Now, now, lady! None of that! I'm a married man, I am,' the

23

stranger stood staring, paralysed into immobility by the shock of his unusual reception.

Exulting, Miss Fratton looked him up and down. Water trickled from the peak of his cap on to his nose and ran in rivulets from the mackintosh cape. His collar was turned up; but though she could not see his face she sensed the fright she had given him.

Her fingers tightened on his shoulder in delicious anticipation of the unexpected treat. Gofer had become so used to her that he knew all her tricks; she could not startle him. But here was a postman unversed in her ways, a man whose ears were unprepared for the threats, the curses, the vindictive hate that were about to assail them.

'You're late, my man,' she croaked, her voice deep, mannish. 'What's been keeping you, eh? What wickedness have you been up to *this* time? Thieving, no doubt, like the rest of them. Or is it a girl you've got into trouble with your lying, deceitful ways? I know your sort, you see. There's nothing I wouldn't put past a postman.' She peered closer at him. 'Seems to me you're scared about something. What have you done? Is it murder this time? Eh?'

She shook him, her bony fingers biting deeper into his shoulders; until suddenly he wrenched himself free, flung the letters at her feet, and ran down the path to the road.

But he could not escape her so easily. Where workmen had been re-laying the drains a narrow ditch split the garden path. Into this he stumbled; and although he regained his balance without falling, he had dropped his torch and could not find the latch of the gate. As he fumbled for it Miss Fratton, shrieking abuse and heedless of the rain, hobbled purposefully after her victim.

★　★　★

'I hear Thomas Cabell's are not doing too well,' said Miss Plant. 'Standing off quite a number of their employees, they say. And just before Christmas, too. So unfortunate for the poor things.'

'It won't affect the Averys,' said Mrs Gill, sniffing as though the name were an unpleasant odour. 'Not with her father being a director. Donald Heath, though — he works for them. And Mr Harris, at No. 17. It would be a nasty blow for them if he got the sack, with three young children to feed and Mrs Harris so poorly. But he'd be one of the first to go, him being more or less a newcomer.'

'Poor man,' sympathized her friend. 'I always think he looks terribly unhappy. And not at all strong, either. So different from his neighbour, Mr Morris. But then they say fat men are always cheerful.'

'I'm sure I don't know what he's got to be cheerful about, living alone and doing all his own housekeeping,' said Mrs Gill. 'But I suppose he's got money, and he looks healthy enough. I don't think much of some of his friends, though. Very odd-looking men — not at all the type we usually get in Grange Road.'

'I understand he has something to do with horse-racing,' said Miss Plant.

'That I could well believe, Ethel, if I didn't know it to be false. According to

Mrs Archer — and she ought to know, living next door to him — he's a retired merchant. Used to be in the City.'

'Mr Archer works at Cabell's too,' said Miss Plant. 'I don't suppose they would sack him, though. He's been with them for years.'

But Mrs Gill had temporarily lost interest in her neighbours.

'I do wish the postman would come,' she said anxiously. 'I'm expecting a letter from my daughter out at Rawsley. I can't make any plans for Christmas until I hear from her.'

★   ★   ★

As the double rat-rat sounded on the door of No. 17 William Harris rose wearily from his seat at the kitchen table and walked down the hall to pick up the three letters that lay on the floor. In front of the stove his wife was bathing the baby, her tired voice striving vainly to hush its almost incessant screaming. How can I concentrate on accounts, he thought irritably, with all that infernal din?

He looked fearfully at the letters, dreading to open them. Not that it made much difference if they were bills; he couldn't pay them, anyway. Today had been pay-day, and now he had exactly eight shillings and twopence left in his pocket. Eight and twopence with which to buy presents for Marion and the kids, Christmas cards for relatives and friends, all the little extras that the season demanded. Eight and twopence, and God knew how many bills still unpaid! Next Friday he would get another six pounds, less the usual deductions. And maybe, if he were lucky, he would have another princely sum of eight and twopence to add to that already in his pocket.

He scowled at the letters. Six pound a week and commission — only there wasn't any bloody commission. Not now. He'd been transferred to Service because Sales were so bad and they didn't want to give him the sack. Six pounds a week, plus the children's allowances, to keep a family of five and pay the mortgage and the rates. And sixteen shillings and fourpence, if he didn't smoke or drink, to spend on a slap-up Christmas with all the trimmings.

'Bloody hell!' he swore aloud.

'What's the matter, Will? More bills?' his wife asked anxiously.

He shook his head, his attention focused on the letter he had opened. He peered inside the envelope, spreading it wide with his fingers. Then, after a moment's hesitation, he thrust it into his pocket and tore open the others.

'Martin's account,' he said. 'Well, we can't pay it this side of Christmas. They'll have to wait. Oh, Lord! A ruddy solicitor's letter!'

'What about?'

'The money we owe Cheetham's. They're going to sue us.'

'Oh, Will!'

'They pick a nice time to do it, don't they?' he said bitterly. 'Christmas, the season of goodwill! Well, let 'em get on with it.' He paused, fingering the letter in his pocket. 'It's stuffy in here, Marion. I think I'll slip out for a bit.'

'But it's pouring with rain,' she protested.

'Only for a moment,' he said. 'Just down to the gate and back.'

What's come over him? she wondered, as she heard the front door open and shut. There was little warmth in the house; how could he say it was stuffy? And Will never opened a window, anyway. He was all for a good old fug and disliked too much fresh air.

It was the solicitor's letter, she decided, as she turned the baby over on her lap and sprinkled powder on his pink bottom. They had been hard up all their married life, but this was the first time they had been taken to court. And to get a letter like that tonight, when she had wanted to ask him about the pram! He would never agree to it now.

I wish to God something had happened to the postman before he got here, she thought unhappily. Now I'll never have that pram.

★   ★   ★

'You young fool! I've told you a thousand times I won't have you bringing your stuff here,' said Morris, the indignation in his voice contrasting with his cherubic expression. 'I don't want you here at all, come to that.'

Sid Blake scowled. He was young in years, but old in experience. It wounded his vanity to be told off by this old buzzard. 'I had to park it somewhere while I had the car,' he said. 'Where else would I take it?'

'You can take it to hell and back for all I care,' replied the other. 'This is a private house, not a repository. I've built up a good solid reputation in this place, and I'll not have you or any other cracked-brained idiot queering my pitch because you're too scared to hang on to the stuff until the morning. Take it over to the shop tomorrow and — ' He broke off and looked at Blake through narrowed eyes. 'What's this about a car? You haven't got a car.'

'I have — for tonight. You don't think I'd be carting the stuff around on foot, do you? I — er — I borrowed it.'

Morris's anger swelled to bursting-point.

31

'You've left a stolen car outside my house? Good God, man — what do you use for brains? Move it, damn you! Move it quick. Get the hell out of here — you *and* the car!'

'Keep your wool on,' said Blake. 'The car's fifty yards down the road. Nobody's going to connect it with you.'

'I don't care. Get it out of this road. Go on — get weaving.'

'What about the stuff?'

'Leave it,' said Morris impatiently. Anything, he thought, to speed his unwelcome and dangerous guest. He let Blake out of the back door, and watched him vault the fence that separated the garden from the links. Then he went back to the sitting-room, poured himself a large whisky, and swallowed it neat.

Bloody young fool! he thought.

He picked up the case that Blake had left and locked it in a cupboard. Then, lighting a fat cigar, he wandered into the hall to collect the mail.

But the box was empty. He heard a car pass the house, gathering speed as it went, and gave a sigh of relief.

He was smiling as he returned to the whisky. Sid Blake, he told himself cheerfully, would have to pay for the fright he had given him.

★   ★   ★

Sam Archer belched contentedly, apologized, pushed his chair noisily away from the table, and swung his feet on to the arm of the sofa.

'I've eaten too much,' he announced, patting his paunch. 'Dripping-toast always was a weakness with me.'

'That's no excuse for making a pig of yourself,' said his wife. 'Goodness knows how you can expect good manners from the children when you set such a bad example yourself.'

But she smiled as she uttered the reproof, and then turned her attention to the youngest of their three children, who had lost the scramble for the last cake and was now noisily reviling his fate. 'Hush, Johnny,' she said, rumpling his hair fondly. 'I'll get you another. A bigger one.'

'You spoil that child,' said Mr Archer.

'You'll turn him into as big a pig as your husband.' He stood up, stretched himself lazily, and walked over to the window, where he pushed the curtains aside to peer out. 'Still raining, damn it!'

'You're not going out tonight, Sam, are you?' asked his wife.

'Got to. Darts match at the Goat. And I've the van to take back to the garage first. What's the time, Maisie?'

'Nearly five.'

'Is it, though? My word, but the postman's late! He's just gone past. Nothing for us, apparently.'

'Poor man,' said Mrs Archer sympathetically. 'I wouldn't like his job on a day like this. He'll be absolutely soaked.'

'I wouldn't like his job at any time,' retorted her husband. 'Talk about exercise! The very thought of it makes me sweat. Ah, well. I'll just have another cuppa, Maisie, and then I'll be getting.'

⋆   ⋆   ⋆

Ethel Plant, happily replete, leaned back in her chair and gazed out of the window

34

at the pelting rain.

'What a night!' she exclaimed. 'I hope it lets up a bit before I go home. Weather like this makes one sorry for people who have to be out in it. Postmen and policemen, for instance.'

Mrs Gill nodded. 'But they know what they're in for when they take on the job,' she said. 'It's no excuse for shirking. I dare say our postman is sheltering in somebody's porch right now — which he's no right to do, with people waiting for their letters. Some of them may be urgent.'

A car came down the road and turned into the drive of No. 25. Mrs Gill looked at the clock.

'Five to five,' she said. 'Avery's late. Usually home for lunch. But not today.'

'Is she any more friendly these days?' asked Miss Plant. 'Mrs Avery, I mean?'

'Folks like you and me, Ethel, aren't good enough for Mrs Avery,' declared her friend. 'Not in her opinion, anyway. Though goodness knows what she's got to be snoooty about. Her father *may* be Sir Oliver Golding, but he was only knighted because he made a lot of money. He's quite a common old man, really. He bought her a husband, too. A sour-faced, bad-tempered woman like Susan Avery wouldn't have got one any other way. I must say I feel sorry for Avery sometimes, even if he did marry her with his eyes open and one of them — if not both — fixed on her money. Talk about rows! You wouldn't believe the way she goes on at him. I'm not one to be interested in other people's domestic squabbles, but when I'm in the kitchen I can hear them quite plainly if I open the window. They go at it hammer and tongs, though it's usually her as starts it.'

'What do they quarrel about?' asked Miss Plant.

'Everything under the sun, seems like. The poor man can't do a thing right, she's that suspicious. As like as not she's going for him now; she always makes trouble when he's late. But we wouldn't hear it from the kitchen. They'll be in the lounge.'

★   ★   ★

Robert Avery paused to search hastily through a few circulars lying on the hall table. Then, still wearing his raincoat, he pushed open the lounge door. His wife looked up from her knitting and scowled at him. She was not a pretty woman, and the scowl served to increase and highlight the lines on her face.

'You're late,' she said accusingly.

Avery was accustomed to the scowl. But he was relieved to see that it appeared to be no more belligerent than usual. There was nothing in her words or her expression to suggest that the letter had come.

'I was delayed,' he said curtly, too worried to seek to pacify her. 'Has the postman been?'

'No. And don't tell me what delayed you, will you? And take off your raincoat and those wet shoes before you come in here. The woman did the room this morning.'

He hesitated. 'I think I'll go and meet the postman,' he said. 'He's late.'

He hurried from the room, ignoring his wife's astonished and angry protest. Eve might have relented, he thought. But it was safer to assume that she had not, that her letter was already in the post — to be delivered that very afternoon, perhaps. If he could intercept it . . . It was unlikely Eve would write a second time . . .

He turned right towards Tanmouth on leaving the house, putting his head down to protect his face from the stinging rain. It was a relief to know that he was in time. He had thought, when the old man had sent for him just as he was leaving, that he would never make it. Nor would he have done so had not the postman been so late. Praises be, he thought gratefully, to whoever or whatever had delayed the man.

Headlights from an oncoming car illumined him briefly. It was gathering speed, and water sprayed from its wheels as it passed, spattering his trousers. An Austin, he noticed. Probably the Alsters, off on their holiday. A late hour to start, though.

A new doubt assailed him. What if the postman refused to hand over the letter? He would be within his rights, for it would be addressed to Susan. It would be pushed through the letterbox of No. 25, Susan would pounce on it — as she always did — and that would be that!

He stopped, turning his back to the wind and the rain. Should he go home and hope to intercept the letter there? But Susan was already suspicious, no doubt, and would be waiting in the hall or peering from a front window. Better to go on. The postman knew him well; there shouldn't be any difficulty.

His mind made up, Avery turned and plodded on down the road.

★　★　★

'Good gracious me!' exclaimed Mrs Gill. 'Why on earth is Mr Avery going out again on a night like this? He's only just come in.'

Miss Plant could offer no reasonable explanation apart from a suggestion that Mrs Avery's tongue might have been too much for the poor man.

'But why didn't he take the car?' said Mrs Gill. 'Never walks a foot unless he has to. Well, if he meets the postman I hope he gives him a piece of his mind. I certainly will when I see him.'

Had she but known it, her threat was an idle one. Neither she nor anyone else in Grange Road was destined to set eyes again on that particular postman.

2

A Lovely Spot for a Murder

Detective-Inspector Richard Aloysius Pitt ('Loy' to his intimates) leaned back in the armchair and surveyed with satisfaction his slippered feet resting on a log by the side of the fire.

'I had almost forgotten I possessed a pair of slippers,' he said. 'Must be months since I had the leisure to wear them.'

'Make the most of it while you're here, then,' said his sister. 'Tomorrow I might even give you breakfast in bed.'

He chuckled. It was an odd sound to emerge from such a gaunt and forbidding face, and one that his colleagues seldom heard. But Wendy Ponsford experienced no surprise. She knew her brother better than most.

'Don't overdo it,' he warned. 'I might decide to retire and become a parasite, battening on you and Dick for the rest of my life. It's a tempting thought.'

'Not for you it isn't,' she answered. 'Leave is one thing, retirement another. It wouldn't suit you at all. Come to that, it wouldn't suit me and Dick either. You're an uncomfortable person to have around the place for long.'

'Perhaps you're right,' her brother agreed; 'although only a sister would be so uncomplimentary.'

Wendy Ponsford looked at the clock and stood up. 'Seven-fifteen. Time to get the supper; Dick'll be home soon. Help yourself to a drink if you want one, Loy. And don't let the fire out.'

Left to himself Pitt sank farther into the armchair, lifted his feet to the mantelshelf, and closed his eyes. He was too comfortable to bestir himself, even for a glass of beer. But he was not destined to relax for long. The telephone rang in the hall. 'Answer that, Loy, will you?' his sister called from the kitchen. 'My hands are covered with flour.'

He heaved himself up resignedly and padded out to the hall.

'That you, Loy?' came his brother-in-law's loud voice over the wire. Detective-Sergeant Ponsford, slightly deaf, always shouted on the telephone. He meant to make himself heard. 'Good — you're the chap I want. Listen. A ruddy postman has vanished; absconded with the mail, probably. I'm going round now to the G.P.O. to get the details. Thought you might like to come along.'

'Think again,' said the Inspector. 'This is the first evening of the first spot of leave that has been granted to yours truly within living memory, and I don't intend to turn it into a busman's holiday. And I might add that Wendy is now preparing what from here smells like an extremely tasty supper. I'll think of you and your postman while I'm eating it.'

'The Super thought it was a good idea,' said Dick.

'Do you mean to tell me, you — you miserable policeman, you — that you had the nerve to let the Superintendent know I was here?' exploded Inspector Pitt.

'Come off it, Loy,' said his brother-in-law. 'I'm not saying we'll need you; but

43

you know damn' well that if we do no one's going to worry two hoots about your being on leave. Or maybe you haven't heard that there's a shortage of coppers? You're on the spot, Loy — in more senses than one. So I thought (and the Super agrees with me) that you might as well be in on this from the beginning. Just in case, you understand. Nothing definite.'

'Wrong again, my lad,' said Pitt. 'Here's something quite definite: I'm not playing.'

'I'll pick you up in ten minutes,' said Dick. 'Don't keep me waiting. I want my supper, too.'

He rang off before his brother-in-law could reply.

'Was that Dick?' called Wendy from the kitchen. 'Don't say he's going to be late again?'

'There are many adjectives I could apply to your wretched husband,' Inspector Pitt said with feeling. 'I only regret that 'late' is not one of them.'

Mr Templar was a very worried man. Nothing like this, he said, had happened

44

in all his experience as postmaster at Tanmouth.

'He should have returned here by ten past six at the latest,' he explained to Dick. (Inspector Pitt stayed in the background. His was a watching brief — he had insisted on that. He would take no active part in the investigations until officially involved.) 'The men work on a basis of two minutes per house, and we can gauge fairly accurately the time needed to complete a delivery.'

'What's the man's name?' asked Dick.

'Laurie. John Laurie.'

'Address?'

'25 Tilnet Close. Off Hamshott Lane.'

The Sergeant nodded. 'Anyone been to look for him?'

'Yes. I sent a mail-van round the route at 6.30. No sign of him, the driver said; although it would be easy to miss him in weather like this, of course. They went to his house, too. Laurie had no reason to call there — it would have been most irregular had he done so, for Tilnet Close isn't on his round — but I was taking no chances. Then I tried the police-station and the hospital; I thought he might have met with an accident. After that there was nothing I could do but call in the police. And I hope to goodness you find him soon, Sergeant.'

'We'll do our best, Mr Templar. Was he on a bike?'

'Yes.'

'Can you give me a list of the roads he was due to visit?'

'I have it here,' said the postmaster. 'I doubt if you'll need it, though. I've telephoned to selected persons on his round — some of those who were due to receive registered packets — and it seems fairly certain he ceased delivery in Grange Road.'

'Well, that's a help,' said Dick. 'And Grange Road is a nice quiet spot in which to disappear. Any idea how far down the road he got?'

'Yes, roughly. A Miss Weston, at No. 13, said she saw him pass the house and go next door. I tried No. 25 next; 14 to 24 are either not on the telephone or did not reply. Laurie didn't call there, nor at 31 either; yet he had registered packets for both those houses.' He paused, frowning. 'That's odd. Now I come to think of it, he also had a registered packet for No. 13. I wonder why he didn't deliver that, as he actually passed the house?'

'Swelling the loot, perhaps,' the Sergeant suggested.

'But he delivered them correctly as far as the beginning of Grange Road,' the postmaster objected. 'To those I telephoned, anyway.'

'We'll sort that out later,' said Dick. 'The first thing is to circulate Laurie's description (I suppose he is still in uniform, which will help), and then get down to Grange Road and make a few inquiries on the spot.'

'There's one other point,' said Mr Templar. 'Laurie was not on his usual round. Normally he works the Camber-sleigh Park district; did so this morning, in fact. It was only because Gofer was taken ill at lunch-time that I switched Laurie on to it. He'd worked over that way some years back.'

'He'd know the route, then?'

'Most of it. But there's been a lot of new building north of the golf-links, and last year we altered some of the rounds. It so happens that Grange Road would be new to Laurie. But I don't see how that can be important, do you?'

'What sort of chap is this Laurie?' asked Inspector Pitt, unable to resist taking a hand. 'Has he been with the post-office long?'

Mr Templar eyed him with interest. The Inspector's silence had puzzled him. 'He's pretty average,' he said. 'Flies off the handle at times, and inclined to be moody. But he's a steady-living chap; doesn't drink, doesn't smoke. He's been with us nearly six years. Got married the year before last.'

'What are his outside interests?'

'I'm told he's a keen fisherman,' said the postmaster. 'I don't know about any other interests.'

Inspector Pitt, apart from occasional wistful references to the supper he had not eaten, had recovered his good humour by the time he and Sergeant Ponsford had left the post-office. The

48

mystery of the missing postman had begun to intrigue him.

'If Laurie really has pinched what remained of the mail it seems a daft job to pull,' said Sergeant Ponsford. 'Why deliver half of it? Why not take the lot? You'd think he'd have stuck to the registered stuff, anyway. There can't be much profit in Christmas cards and bills.'

'What sort of a district is Cambersleigh Park?' asked Pitt.

'Not as grand or as green as it sounds. Pretty near a slum, I'd say. Why?'

'Just a fancy that occurred to me. We're taking it for granted that the mail has been stolen, but maybe it's only missing. Maybe Laurie just dumped it some-where.'

'Why should he do that?'

'To get rid of it, of course — along with his job. Suddenly became fed up and decided to clear out. Tramping the streets day after day must become monotonous; perhaps the change of locality made him realize what a mug he was to go on with it. So off he went — just like that.'

'And where would he go?'

'Anywhere, so long as it wasn't Cambersleigh Park.'

Sergeant Ponsford stared at him. This was a new Pitt. 'Cut out the James Barrie act,' he said. 'A man doesn't get notions like that in this sort of weather. If he rebelled at all it would be in favour of home and a warm fire.'

The Inspector sighed. 'I know. As I said, it was only a fancy. Blame it on my empty stomach and the leave that looks like being cancelled.'

Grange Road ran parallel to the coast, with only the golf-links between it and the sea. Where the houses petered out it began to climb the Downs, eventually joining the Tanmouth — Durnbourne road. The houses, all on the north side of the road, were varied in size and character — bungalows, villas, chalets, detached and semidetached — and apparently owned no allegiance to town-planning. Because of the uneven lie of the land Nos. 11 to 17 were below the level of the road, and those from No. 22 onward were increasingly high above it. It was, in fact, an untidy-looking road.

Yet it had a charm of its own.

Between Nos. 19 and 20 there was a break in the houses of some two hundred yards, where the golf-links crossed over to the north side of the road. Most of Grange Road was badly lit, but along this stretch there was no lighting at all.

'A lovely spot for a murder,' said Inspector Pitt, peering out of the rain-streaked windows of the car. 'Let's hope the missing postman didn't come to a sticky end on the thirteenth tee.'

'That's the eleventh,' Dick corrected him. 'I think we'd better start at No. 24 and work back from there. We know he didn't get as far as No. 25.'

If Mrs Gill had had the slightest suspicion that anything further of interest might occur that evening she would never have left the parlour window. She hastened back to it at the sound of the car and peered between the curtains. Visitors for the Averys, she decided. But as the headlights were dimmed and she saw the beam of a torch approaching up her own garden path, she almost ran to the front door in her eagerness.

The appearance of two men in raincoats and trilby hats, and behind them a more shadowy but unmistakable police-constable, was one of the major events in Mrs Gill's fifty-eight years. She clutched the door-handle for support as they filed past her into the little hall. Then, remembering her manners, she darted ahead of them into the parlour and began to stoke the dying fire. She did not wish them to escape her too soon.

'We won't bother you for long, ma'am,' said Dick. 'We just want to know if the postman called here this evening.'

Mrs Gill was all attention.

'He certainly did not,' she said. 'And I'd very much like to know what became of him. He never passed this house, that I'll swear. Miss Plant and I — she lives down the road, at No. 3 — we were sitting here, right in the window, having our tea. And I kept a special look-out for the man, seeing as I was expecting a letter.'

Inspector Pitt peered out of the bay-window at the gate, clearly illumined by the street-lamp outside, and nodded to himself.

'You couldn't have missed him, I suppose?' asked the Sergeant. 'I understand he was late this evening.'

Mrs Gill, thus put on her mettle, proceeded to justify herself.

'Miss Plant saw him outside No. 5,' she said. 'Twenty-five past four, that was. She came straight here, and we sat over our tea until half-past five. We hadn't drawn the curtains, either. It wouldn't take him an hour to get here, would it?'

'It shouldn't,' Dick agreed.

'I hope nothing's happened to him,' Mrs Gill continued. 'Such a nice man — always so cheerful and polite. Oh, I'm forgetting. It was a different postman, wasn't it? Not Mr Gofer.'

'How did you know that, ma'am?'

'Miss Plant told me. A rather surly little man, she said he was. Just grunted when she said good-evening to him. Still, weather like this is enough to make anyone bad-tempered, isn't it?'

The Sergeant agreed that it was.

'What can have happened to him, I

wonder? Miss Plant suggested he might have been murdered by Miss Fratton. She was only joking, of course. But it makes one think, doesn't it?'

Interested but bewildered, the Sergeant begged for enlightenment.

'Miss Fratton? She lives at No. 14 — she's supposed to have a 'down' on postmen. Goodness knows why. But then she's half crazy anyway.' She paused thoughtfully. 'Why not call next door at No. 25? Mr Avery ought to have seen the postman when he went out.'

'When was that, Mrs Gill?'

'Just after five o'clock. He had only been home a few minutes, and then out he pops again. On foot, too, which is most unusual for him. He nearly always takes the car. I happened to notice him because a car was passing at the time. And he was going towards the town, so he should have met the postman, shouldn't he?'

'Did you notice what time he returned?' asked Dick.

'Oh, yes. At half-past five.'

This prompt answer did not surprise the detectives. It was obvious that Mrs

54

Gill took a deep interest in the affairs of her neighbours. Outside in the street Pitt said, 'I suppose we look in at No. 25?'

Dick nodded. 'I suppose so. I don't like pandering to the old girl's nosey-parkering, but we can't afford to disregard her remarks about this chap Avery. He seems a better bet than the Fratton woman, despite all that talk of murder.'

Susan Avery was surprised, Robert Avery surprised and uneasy. As Sergeant Ponsford explained the reason for their visit Pitt watched them both. The woman was about forty-five, and looked as though she had been that age for many years; there were no traces left of youth in her hard, unhappy face. It was difficult to realize that she had once been young, and presumably possessed of some attraction. Avery was about the same age as his wife, but had been endowed with more good looks. His dark hair was greying at the temples, his suit was new and well cut, his hands manicured. A bit of a dandy, the Inspector thought him, and no doubt a success with the ladies.

No, said Mrs Avery, she had not seen the postman that afternoon, nor had any letters been delivered at the house. That was what she had told the people at the post-office when they had rung up; why were they making fresh inquiries now? 'My husband went out to look for him when he got home at five o'clock,' she added. 'But you didn't see him, did you, Robert?'

Avery frowned and shook his head. 'He had probably passed here by then,' he said.

'At what time does the afternoon post usually arrive?' asked Dick.

'About half-past four or a little earlier,' said Mrs Avery. 'He's very regular.'

Sergeant Ponsford looked at Avery.

'Weren't you rather optimistic, sir, expecting to meet him half an hour later? What made you think he hadn't got as far as this?'

'Because I didn't pass him down the road, as I sometimes do. I guessed he must be late.'

'It must have been an important letter you were expecting, sir, going out in weather like this to anticipate its delivery,' said Inspector Pitt. 'Bad luck you never got it.'

Both pairs of eyes switched their attention from the Sergeant to the Inspector.

'There was a registered packet addressed to Mrs Avery,' said Dick. 'It wouldn't have been that you were after?'

'To me?' A gleam shone in the woman's eyes. 'How did you know there was a letter for me, Robert?'

'Damn it, woman, I didn't!' said her husband. 'Haven't I just explained that? I went to meet the postman, that's all. No law against it, is there?'

For a moment there was silence in the room. Then Sergeant Ponsford said, 'It sounds rather an odd thing to do, sir, if you'll forgive my saying so. However — you didn't see the postman?'

'No, I didn't. Nor his bicycle.'

'Meet anyone else?'

'No. No pedestrians, anyway. There were one or two cars.'

'In which direction were they going?'

'Well, there was one coming from the

town just as I left the house, and there was another parked near the eleventh tee, pointing the other way. I thought it was empty; but the driver can't have been far away. It overtook me some minutes later, farther down the road.'

'And how far down Grange Road did you go, Mr Avery?'

'To No. 4.' The man was more confident now. His previous unease had vanished. 'I called there, but the people were out.'

'You came straight home after that?'

'Yes.'

'Thank you, sir. Now, about this parked car. You are sure there was no one in it?'

'I've said so, haven't I? Of course, they may have been lying on the floorboards. I can't answer for that.'

'Did you notice the make or registration number?' asked Dick, unperturbed by the other's sarcasm.

'It was an old Vauxhall — same model as mine. The number was 439, I think. But I haven't a clue about the letters. They're not as well lit as the numbers, being away from the rear light. Maybe that's why I don't remember them.'

Dick glanced inquiringly at his brother-in-law, who nodded.

'You are sure it was the same car that overtook you later?' he asked.

'Damn it, man! Don't you chaps ever believe anything you're told at the first time of asking? Of course I'm sure.'

'Thank you, sir. How far down the road did it overtake you?'

'Somewhere around No. 6, I think.'

'I suppose you didn't notice the number of occupants?'

'No, I didn't. I was keeping my head down to shield my face from the rain. Anyway, it was too dark to see.'

Pitt nodded. That seemed reasonable enough.

'There was one of the firm's vans outside No. 19,' Avery volunteered. 'That would be Archer. I dare say he dropped in for his tea before taking the van to the garage. It wasn't there when I returned, anyway.'

As they left the house Pitt glanced at the windows of No. 24. They were in darkness except for a faint, flickering glow behind the parlour curtains. 'Mrs Gill will be glad to see us go,' he said. 'Now she can switch on the light and relax.'

'What did you make of Avery?' asked Dick.

'Not much. He was lying about the letter, of course. But that was for his wife's benefit, I imagine, not ours.'

'But it was addressed to her.'

'The registered letter was. He may have been expecting another. And I bet he's on the receiving end of a rocket now. She didn't look too pleased, did she?'

They reached the break in the houses without obtaining any news of the missing postman. He had not been seen by the occupants of Nos. 23 to 20, nor had any mail been delivered. As they passed the eleventh tee Dick said, 'We'll look there later. That's where Avery said he saw the Vauxhall.'

'It's where I said would be a good place for a murder,' Pitt reminded him. 'Don't give Avery all the credit.'

Maisie Archer was a cheerful little woman with untidy hair and few claims to beauty. When she opened the door of

No. 19 to the police she had a black smudge on her forehead and her hands were grimed with coal-dust.

'I've been cleaning out the kitchen grate,' she excused herself. 'If it's my husband you want, he's down at the Goat. You could get him there if it's important. He doesn't leave till closing-time as a rule.'

Dick explained the object of their visit.

'Oh, the postman. Yes, Sam did say something about seeing him go past around five o'clock,' said Mrs Archer. 'Fancy that, now! Whatever can have happened to the poor man?'

But the Sergeant was not prepared to speculate on an answer to that question. 'When did your husband go out, Mrs Archer?' he asked.

She considered this before replying.

'I wouldn't like to say for certain, but it'd be about quarter past five, I think. He had to take the van back to the garage first, you see.'

Nos. 17 and 18 were a pair of semi-detached villas, poorer in character than most of the houses in Grange Road. But

Mr Morris, of No. 18, had no air of poverty about him. He was short and plump and genial, and a bright yellow waistcoat stretched like a gleaming desert across the vast expanse of his stomach. Smoking a cigar, he ushered them into a cheerful room in which a large television set was the outstanding piece of furniture.

'No. No delivery here this afternoon,' he said decisively, producing a bottle of whisky. 'I was expecting a letter from my bookie, too. Had a good win Wednesday — over seven quid to come. Have a drink, gentlemen?'

They declined with regret. 'Did you see the postman pass the house?' asked Dick. 'We're trying to find out how far down the road he got.'

Mr Morris shook his head, poured himself a generous whisky, added the merest splash of soda, and sipped with relish. Inspector Pitt experienced a slight constriction of the throat, and moistened his dry lips with his tongue.

'I'd like the name and address of your bookie, sir,' said Dick. 'We don't yet know what's happened to the mail; but if the money was actually in the post . . . '

He did not finish the sentence, but the other took his meaning readily.

'Jack Oakie, 37 High Street,' he said. 'And the money would be in postal orders. He don't pay me by cheque because I haven't got a banking account. Don't believe in paying a bank to look after my money. I can do it better myself.'

'He'd send it by registered post, I suppose?'

'No. Nothing under ten quid. He says it's cheaper to insure against loss for small amounts.'

As they were leaving Dick said, 'There was a car parked a short way up the road earlier this evening, Mr Morris. A Vauxhall. Anything to do with you?'

'Nothing. Nothing at all,' said Morris hastily. 'I've had no visitors this evening, officer.'

'A most hospitable gentleman,' said Pitt, as the front door closed behind them. 'Would his dislike of banking-accounts have any connection with income-tax, d'you think?'

'I shouldn't be surprised,' said Dick.

The interior of No. 17 was very different from that of its neighbour. No covering of any sort adorned the bare boards of the hall; the carpet in the living-room was worn almost threadbare. Furniture was sparse and ill-assorted, and no fire burned in the grate. Mrs Harris, who opened the door to them, apologized for the coldness of the room, explaining that she and her husband had been sitting in the kitchen to save fuel.

'Oh, yes,' she said nervously, in answer to Dick's question. 'He certainly called here. Two letters, I think there were. Or was it three? I know my husband put one in his pocket, but . . . well, I'd better get him for you, hadn't I?'

She almost ran from the room.

'Life comes a bit hard for the Harrises, I imagine,' said Pitt. 'It doesn't look as though they're burdened with too much money.'

William Harris was even more nervous than his wife. Yes, he said, the postman had delivered three letters that afternoon. No, he had not seen the man. He had not been out of the house since he returned from work at lunch-time.

'Lunch-time? That's early to knock off, isn't it?' said Dick.

'Most of us are on short time up at Cabell's,' Harris explained. 'I'm one of them.'

'Hard luck,' sympathized the Sergeant. 'But about this postman now. You didn't open the door when he called?'

'No. I heard the knock, and when I went into the hall the letters were on the floor.' He had a nervous trick of running the tips of the fingers of each hand across the ball of the thumb. They were moving now at an ever-increasing speed. 'What's up, Sergeant? With the postman, I mean.'

Dick explained that the man had disappeared.

'Pinched the mail, d'you think? Well, it's a pity he didn't do it a bit earlier. He could have had my letters with pleasure. Bills, all of 'em.'

'So he got as far as this,' said the Sergeant, when the two officers were outside the house. 'And probably as far as No. 19. It looks as though your hunch about the eleventh tee has it, Loy.'

'You can always depend on Aloysius Pitt,' the Inspector said modestly. 'I wonder what put the wind up friend Harris?'

'We did, I imagine.'

'I know that, you ass. But what made him lie to us?'

'Lie? What are you getting at?'

'Notice his slippers?' asked the Inspector. 'No? Well, I did. There was mud all round the soles — and yet he said he hadn't been out since lunch. The rain didn't start till after two o'clock, remember.'

'Neither it did. And it's been fine for the last few days. So he *did* go out this afternoon, eh?'

'Looks like it. Come on, let's investigate that ruddy tee.'

But the eleventh tee yielded nothing. They enlisted the aid of the constable and extended their search, moving in a line parallel to the road. The ground was open but uneven; and they had almost reached the end of the gap when the constable's torch passed over and then came back to rest on something that made him call out to the others.

'Here's his bike, Sergeant,' he said excitedly.

There was no mistaking the post-office red. 'Well, that's that,' said Dick. 'But no mail, and no postman.'

'What now?' asked Pitt. 'Do we play round the course until we find the body?'

'You're getting too old for that sort of lark,' said his brother-in-law. 'I think this is where we report back to the Super. We might call in at the Goat on our way, though.'

The Goat was crowded. As they opened the door of the public bar waves of hot, beer-laden air engulfed them. They made their way to the bar amid a dying clatter of tongues.

The publican was nervous. He was not aware of having transgressed the law, but one never knew . . . He sighed with relief when Dick asked for Archer. 'Sam?' he said. 'Over there, playing darts. The big fair-haired chap.'

If Archer's companions were uneasy at this sudden appearance of the Law, Sam himself was unperturbed.

'We'll finish the game when I come out, lads,' he said, finding the double top with his last dart and grinning broadly as he accepted the Sergeant's invitation to step outside. 'Shouldn't be more than six months, I reckon. Not with my record.'

His testimony established what the police had already presumed: that the postman had certainly got as far as No. 19. 'He was just pushing off on his bike when I looked out of the window. A few minutes to five that was, and raining like stink.'

Dick asked him at what time he had left the house.

'Me? About twenty-past. I took the van back to the garage and collected my bike. Then I came on here. Never miss a game of darts if I can help it.'

* * *

Superintendent Howard greeted the Inspector cordially. 'You're in on this officially now,' he said. 'The Chief Constable got on to your department right away. The old man's worried about this case; mail robberies are priority with him. The last one we had was the very devil. Of course, the post-office people will be sending down one of their own men; which is just as well, as I gather your department is damned shorthanded. Sorry about your leave, of course. But there it is.'

'That's all right, sir,' Pitt assured him. 'As long as I'm allowed to eat occasionally.'

The Superintendent laughed. 'Tummy rumbling, eh? Well, I won't keep you now. Sergeant Ponsford here will also be working on the case; I expect you'd like him with you. We'll send out a party to search the links. Anything else?'

'You may be able to trace that car. The Vauxhall, number 439. And I'd like any available information on Avery and Harris. They may fit in somewhere.'

'Do you think the Vauxhall is connected with Laurie? That he cleared off in it, perhaps?'

'Could be, sir; although the bicycle was dumped some way from where Avery said he saw the car. I think we'll have to know a bit more before we start theorizing.'

It was nearly ten o'clock when they reached the post-office, but Mr Templar was still there. He was distressed to hear that no trace had been found of the missing postman.

'I simply can't understand it,' he exclaimed. 'Why should a man like Laurie suddenly turn into a thief? I suppose the mail must have contained *some* articles of value — though he couldn't even be sure of that — but most of it would be useless to him. Even if he gets away with it, how can he expect to profit sufficiently to compensate him for the loss of his job here? It just doesn't make sense. Oh, I forgot! This is Mr Hennessy. He's investigating on behalf of the Post Office.'

Hennessy, a fair-haired, cheerful man of medium height, shook hands with the two police officers. 'I'd have been here before this,' he said, 'but I had a spot of bother with the car. How's it going, Inspector? Any luck?'

'Well, we've found his bike,' said Pitt. 'That's about the lot to date.'

'The mail is my main concern, of

course,' said the other. 'What has happened to the man may turn out to be more your pigeon. But I dare say one will lead us to the other.'

Pitt nodded. 'What I want now is information about post-office routine. For instance . . . ' He turned to the postmaster. 'Who sorts the mail preparatory to the postman taking it out for delivery?'

'The man himself, as a rule,' said Templar. 'Sometimes the office staff gives him a hand. But Laurie sorted his own mail this afternoon — with a little help from me.'

'Would he be able to memorize most of the addresses?'

'I should think so. It becomes a habit, you know.'

'Any particular system in the sorting?'

'Yes. We divide the mail into bundles, each bundle containing the letters for a street or group of houses. The bundles are tied with string, so that if the postman happens to drop the letters in his hand it only disorganizes the sorting of a small fraction of the mail.'

'A long street like Grange Road would have to be subdivided, I suppose?' said the Sergeant.

'Yes. A side-turning or some other obvious break would be used as the division. Actually, I made up the mail myself for Grange Road, on account of it being new to Laurie. The first bundle went up to No. 19 — there's a break in the houses there — and the second to Wadhams Lane.'

'How about registered mail?' asked Pitt.

'Well, it's signed for at every stage, of course. I give a receipt for it when it arrives here, the postman does the same when he takes it out, and the addressee when he receives it.'

'Is it bundled separately?'

'No. It goes in with the rest of the mail, and on top of each packet is the receipt form.'

'Attached to it?' asked Dick.

'No.'

'What would happen if a postman returned without the receipt?' asked the Inspector. 'Said he'd lost it, perhaps?'

'There would be an inquiry, of course. If the addressee admitted receiving the packet I imagine no further action would be necessary. If not — well, that would depend on the result of the inquiry. But the postman is the responsible person. It's his pigeon.'

Hennessy, when invited by Pitt to accompany them on their proposed visit to Mrs Laurie, declined the invitation. 'I want to work from this end first,' he said. 'Remember I've only just got here. But I'll keep in touch with you fellows.'

As they neared Tilnet Close Dick said, 'I'm not looking forward to this. I hate interviewing the wives. And she will probably be a tearful young woman of unspeakable proportions. They always are.'

But Jane Laurie was more frightened than tearful, and neither Dick Ponsford nor any other man could have found fault with her proportions. In fact, she was a remarkably beautiful young woman. She wore a red dressing-gown with a low-cut neck, and a transparent ninon nightgown showed between the folds of the gown as she walked. Jet-black hair fell in deep curls to her shoulders. Her eyes were grey and set wide apart, her skin almost translucent in its clarity. The Sergeant decided that John Laurie must have had a very strong motive for absenting himself from such a charmer.

The living-room into which she led them was untidy and not over-clean. The fire had died in the grate, but the room was still warm. 'I'm sorry I'm not dressed,' she said. 'I wasn't expecting anyone.' Her voice was disappointing. It had a thin, tinny quality, and an obvious striving after refinement it did not quite achieve. 'Was it about my husband you wanted to see me? You've found him?'

'No, ma'am, not yet,' said Pitt. 'We're here to ask you a few questions. We won't keep you long.'

She sat down on a chair. The neck of her dressing-gown opened as she leaned forward to clasp her knees, and Dick, standing near her, was embarrassed. He stepped back, landing heavily on his brother-in-law's toes. At the Inspector's smothered curse the girl looked up, her

74

eyes watching them uneasily.

'What sort of questions?' she asked.

'Well, for a start — have you any idea what has happened to your husband?' said Pitt.

'No.'

'When did you see him last?'

'This morning, before he went to work.'

'He seemed quite normal then?'

'Yes.'

'Has he been worried lately?' asked the Inspector. 'How about money matters?'

'He's been all right,' she said. 'A postman doesn't get much, but we managed.'

'And, to your knowledge, nothing has occurred to upset him?'

'No.'

Inspector Pitt tugged heavily at his lower lip. 'Not even a slight upset at home, perhaps?'

She did not seem to resent the question. She stood up and rested both hands on the mantelshelf, her eyes staring into the ashes of the fire.

'We had the usual tiffs,' she said. 'He

wasn't always easy to live with. But there was nothing serious.'

'Did you have a tiff this morning? Or last night?'

'No.'

Sergeant Ponsford, annoyed with himself for being affected by the girl's beauty, said brusquely, 'Is your husband a jealous man, Mrs Laurie?'

Her eyes narrowed. 'No more than most,' she said.

'There wasn't any particular man he objected to? That you quarrelled about, perhaps?'

She turned on him angrily. Pitt thought the anger was forced; but it was very effective.

'You've no right to talk like that,' she protested. 'If he's gone it's not because of me.'

'No offence meant, miss — ma'am,' Dick said hastily, realizing he had gone too far. 'But no money troubles, everything fine at home — it doesn't make sense, does it? There must be *some* reason to account for his disappearance.'

'Well, it's no good asking me,' she said,

listless after her sudden outburst. 'I just wouldn't know.'

'Has he any intimate friends?' asked Inspector Pitt. 'Someone in whom he might have confided?'

'He wasn't one for friends,' she said. 'Kept himself to himself, John did. If he was going to tell anyone he'd tell me. But he didn't.'

It was late, and there seemed little to be gained from further questioning. Mrs Laurie was obviously relieved when they bade her goodnight. But before they left she asked — breathlessly, as though the question cost her considerable effort:

'You're quite sure that my husband is . . . that he stole those letters?'

Inspector Pitt shook his head.

'We're not sure of anything,' he said, 'except that both the mail and your husband have disappeared.'

'Seems to me she doesn't care two hoots about her old man,' Dick remarked, on their way back to the station. 'Interested in what happened to him, of course; but only from a selfish point of view.'

The Inspector absently agreed. Was it another of his flights of fancy, he wondered, or had Mrs Laurie unknowingly told them more than she had intended? And if so . . .

He would say nothing to Dick, he decided. It was too far-fetched a theory to subject it to his brother-in-law's sarcastic comment. So far-fetched, indeed, that he was inclined to laugh at it himself.

At the station they were met by Sergeant Roberts, a close friend of Dick's.

'That Vauxhall of yours was stolen,' he said. 'The owner has just rung up. Says he left it on some waste ground near the Orient Cinema at three-thirty this afternoon. He and his missus went to the flicks and then on to supper at a near-by café — which is why they didn't discover earlier that it had gone.'

'But you haven't found the car itself?' asked Pitt.

'No, Inspector. Nor Laurie either.'

3

A Few Queer Types

At 10.30 the next morning Mrs Gill, approaching the end of Grange Road with Mrs Heath on her way to the High Street, was pleasurably surprised and flattered to see a police car turn the corner and pull up, and the two detectives descend from it to await her approach. But her pleasure was mixed with annoyance that they should have found her in the company of Mrs Heath. She had something to tell them, a titbit she had been mentally chewing for the past minute. And it could not be told in Mrs Heath's hearing.

She was therefore relieved when Inspector Pitt drew her away from her companion.

'I'm so glad I've seen you,' she said, her voice low but vibrant. 'I was wondering whether I should telephone when we got to the High Street. But Mrs Heath would have thought it odd, I'm sure. She might have overheard, too, because none of those telephone boxes are sound-proof, are they? And yet I felt you ought to know *at once*, Inspector. Time is often so important in these matters, isn't it?'

'Know what, Mrs Gill?' he asked.

'About Donald Heath. I was passing No. 9 just now when Mrs Heath called to me from a window and asked me to wait for her. That rather surprised me, Inspector, because we're not really very friendly. We pass the time of day when we meet, of course; but actually I doubt whether she could call anyone in Grange Road a *friend*.

'However, I waited, naturally. But when she joined me outside the gate she remembered she had left her purse on the dresser. Donald — her son, you know — was closing the front door, and she called out to him to get it for her. Which he did, Inspector. And when he came to the front gate to give it to her I couldn't help but notice that he'd got the biggest black eye I'd ever seen. Of course, I remarked on this to Mrs Heath after Donald had gone back to the house; and what do you think she said? That he had walked into a wardrobe in the dark! But — well, I ask you, Inspector!'

'How does this affect the police, Mrs Gill?' Pitt asked quietly.

'Eh?' Mrs Gill, somewhat breathless after her spate of words, looked at the detective in astonishment. 'But surely, Inspector! I mean, after what happened last night — the postman disappearing in this very road, and Donald Heath with a black eye this morning that he certainly hadn't got yesterday! It's most suspicious, don't you think?'

'Suspicious of what, ma'am?'

'Well, of . . . of . . . ' Mrs Gill hesitated. She would have liked to expound her hastily formed theory, but remembered in time that she was talking to a policeman. They made notes of what one said, and asked one to sign statements, and things like that. It might be wiser not to be too explicit. She said, slightly truculent, 'I'm not saying what it's suspicious *of*, Inspector. That is for you to decide. But the newspapers and the wireless are always telling us to report anything suspicious to the police, and — well, I've reported it.'

'Thank you, Mrs Gill. I'll bear it in mind,' said Pitt. 'Now, about Miss Fratton. Yesterday you referred to her as having a 'down' on postmen. Can you enlarge on that at all?'

'No, Inspector, I cannot. And surely you did not take my remarks seriously? About murder, I mean? It was just a joke.'

'We cannot afford to overlook any possibilities,' he told her gravely.

Mrs Gill's mind was troubled as she rejoined her companion. Mrs Heath, almost bursting with curiosity, questioned her continuously on their walk to the bus. But Mrs Gill was saying nothing. Maybe she had said too much already, she thought. You never knew where you were with the Law.

'That's given the old dear something to chew on,' said Sergeant Ponsford.

Pitt nodded, not altogether pleased. 'I was a mug to pull her leg,' he reflected aloud. 'Properly handled she might prove valuable, with her knowledge of the locals. But she won't talk if she gets the wind up. I'll have to curb my sense of humour.'

'There's some as say you haven't got one,' his brother-in-law answered.

It was a fine, dull day, with a brisk wind blowing. To the Inspector Grange Road looked attractive in contrast to its appearance the previous night. It was here that the cliffs started to climb gently eastward to Coppins Point. One could not see the beach from the road, but the green of the golf-links, the white boulders that fringed the cliff-top, the bluer green of the sea beyond, enchanted him. He liked colour in wide, unbroken masses, and the varied styles of the houses did not seem to him untidy. He welcomed them after the orderly rows of the big towns.

'Maybe I was right last night, after all,' he declared. 'This view does something to me. It may have done something to Laurie.'

'Something or somebody did,' said the Sergeant. 'But not the view. He couldn't see it.'

Miss Fratton was not on this occasion lurking behind her front door, but her appearance was sufficiently startling, even to a police officer. She wore the sack-like grey dress of the previous day; it merged so perfectly with the grey skin that it might have been a corpse that confronted them.

Until she spoke. There was nothing sepulchral about her voice.

'Apologize and be done with it,' she rasped. 'I want none of your sort hanging around.'

They stared at her, uncomprehending. 'I beg your pardon — ' Pitt began.

'All right. But see it doesn't happen again. There's too much slackness in Government departments.'

The door had almost closed when the Inspector, aware that Miss Fratton was ending the interview before it had begun, swiftly interposed his foot between the door and the jamb.

'There must be some mistake,' he said. 'We are — '

He got no further. Miss Fratton, enraged that any man should dare to set foot over her doorstep without permission, swung the door wide open. Then, with a savage grunt of satisfaction, she slammed it heavily against the intruding foot.

Pitt was wearing a thin pair of shoes. He had a corn on his right foot, and it was against this that the door impinged. With a howl he removed his toe, and the door was swiftly closed.

'Blast the woman! I'll have her up for assault and battery,' he growled, standing on one foot and massaging the other.

Dick laughed. 'It's not only postmen she's got a down on,' he said. 'I wouldn't say she was over-fond of policemen, either.'

They had turned to walk back to the car when the front door opened again. It was not the gaunt Miss Fratton who stood there now, but a smiling young woman with red hair.

'I'm sorry about that,' she said. 'You're detectives, aren't you? Won't you come in?'

They advanced gingerly into the hall, expecting further assault from the grey monster.

'I'm Dorothy Weston,' said the girl. 'I live next door — No. 13. Miss Fratton's rather devastating, isn't she? She mistook you for someone from the post-office. The postman was late yesterday afternoon, and she made a complaint about it. She thought you had been sent to apologize. She doesn't like postmen, you know.'

'So I understand, miss,' said Pitt. 'And it's about this missing postman that we wanted to see Miss Fratton. He may have called here.'

'Yes, he did. I saw him. But — good Lord! Hasn't he turned up yet?'

The girl's surprise reminded the Inspector that Mrs Gill had asked no such question. Mrs Gill had taken it for granted that the man was still missing. Why, he wondered.

'Bring them in here, Dorothy.' Miss Fratton's voice was no longer harsh. 'I don't trust those men. Bring them in here, dear.'

They went into the sitting-room. Miss Fratton, still a menacing figure, stood before the fire; hands clasped behind her, feet planted firmly apart. Both men were tall, but Miss Fratton was taller.

'What do you want?' she demanded.

There was no apology for her previous behaviour. Dick watched the bristly chin, the staring eyeballs, with fascinated revulsion.

Pitt began to explain, but Miss Fratton interrupted him.

'Postman?' She spat the word out at him. 'Disappeared, has he? That's one of them the less, then — the thieving villains.'

'I'm told he delivered letters here yesterday afternoon,' the Inspector persisted. 'Did you see him, ma'am?'

'Yes, I saw him. *And* I spoke to him. *And* I told him what I thought of him.' She chuckled grimly. 'He won't be late with my letters again. Won't be thieving them, either. Not after yesterday.'

'What's this about thieving?' asked Pitt. 'Did he — ?'

'They're all thieves,' Miss Fratton declared, leaning forward to glare at him. 'Thieves and liars and worse. All of them.'

Pitt turned in despair to the girl, who winked.

'Did he seem quite normal, ma'am?' asked Dick, more from habit than in expectation of a lucid answer. The woman was mad, and the whole interview a waste of time.

The eyeballs swivelled in their sockets without any apparent movement of the head. 'Normal? They're none of them normal. This man was new — he didn't know I'd be waiting for him.' Again she laughed to herself. 'He'll be more careful next time,' she said. 'He won't try any of his tricks on *me!*'

'But what *happened?*' persisted Pitt.

'He ran away. He fell into the ditch, and his trousers were soaked. I could see them dripping under his cape. And he dropped his torch, he was in such a hurry. I got hold of him — I wasn't going to have him stealing *my* letters. But he ran away, and I . . . ' She stopped, and turned to the girl. 'Can't we get rid of these men, dear? I was hoping we might have a nice little chat.'

The Inspector mumbled his thanks and turned towards the door. As Dick followed the girl caught his arm. 'Wait for me outside,' she whispered. 'I want to speak to you.'

But Miss Fratton's ears were sharp. She launched into a tirade against the two men, accusing them of conspiring to take her Dorothy away from her. That done, she turned to the girl, her voice changing to a softer note as she pleaded with her to stay. It was a performance that filled the two male spectators with amusement; but Miss Weston seemed quite unmoved. A slight smile on her red lips, she waited until the older woman had finished. Then she said, firmly and without any trace of emotion:

'See you tomorrow, perhaps. But I must go now. Goodbye.'

And she went.

Outside on the pavement Dick took off his hat and mopped his brow. 'Phew!' he exclaimed. 'What a woman!'

The girl laughed. 'Walk down the road with me a little way,' she said. 'She'll be watching us from the window, and it upsets her to see me talking to men.'

'Is she quite mad, miss?' asked Pitt.

'I don't know, really. She's certainly

funny about men, and postmen in particular. And me, of course. But I suspect a lot of it's put on. She likes to be thought of as a character.'

Pitt wondered at the 'of course.'

'She ought to be put away,' said Dick firmly. 'What has she got against postmen, anyway?'

'I'm one of the few who know the answer to that,' said the girl. 'It seems that some years ago she had quite a nice little fortune — before she came to live here, that was. Even so, life wasn't particularly bright for her, chiefly because of her height and her looks. She was so tall and so darned ugly that the men wouldn't look at her, fortune or no fortune.'

'Can't say I blame them,' muttered Dick.

'No. But then this man — the postman — turned up. He wasn't so fussy as the others, and by pretending to be in love with her he swindled her out of most of the money. Even that didn't turn her against him; she was so desperately anxious to be loved, you see. They used to do football pools together, the postman filling in the coupons and Miss Fratton supplying the cash. They betted on quite a large scale, she said. It didn't cost the man a penny, and she was happy in doing something to please him.

'Then they had a really big win. And, the coupon being in the postman's name, he just collected the money and cleared off. She never saw him again.'

'And that broke her heart?' the Sergeant suggested.

'I suppose so.'

Inspector Pitt thought her callous. He hadn't exactly taken to Miss Fratton; but then Miss Fratton hadn't shown any great liking for him. With the girl it was different.

Miss Weston guessed something of his thoughts.

'She had to have some love in her life,' she said. 'That's the way she's made, poor thing. She took a fancy to me when we came to live next door, and now I'm the apple of her eye. I don't know whether I'm supposed to be daughter or sister — or just a friend. Or perhaps she doesn't want a definite relationship — she just wants someone to love.' She laughed self-consciously. 'It isn't easy for me — I'm not good at pretending. Of course, I can't help feeling sorry for the poor old thing. She's quite harmless, you know. I dare say she's rather terrifying to strangers, but I think most of it's put on. She isn't like that inside.'

'We'll have to take your word for that, miss,' said Dick. 'She scared the living daylights out of me. Er — you don't think she might have something to do with the disappearance of this postman, do you?'

'I shouldn't think so. Not unless she scared him so much that he's still running.'

The Inspector smiled. 'You didn't see him yourself, miss?'

'I saw his cap, mostly. It looked just as though it were gliding along the top of the hedge, without any body underneath. I was disappointed when he passed the house and went next door because I was expecting a present from a particular friend of mine — it was my birthday yesterday. And the postman must have had it, because they rang up later to ask if it had been delivered. At least, I suppose it was that. They said it was a registered packet.'

'Do you know what was in the packet, miss?'

'No. I must find out.'

They watched her walk back up the road. Dorothy knew they were watching. And because they were men she walked with a studied, swinging gait that caused her skirts to sway caressingly round her shapely thighs and legs.

'Nice bit of homework,' said Dick. 'I wouldn't have thought she'd need to rely on that old harridan for a friend.'

'She's probably got others,' said Pitt. 'And perhaps the philandering postman didn't get *all* the money.'

'You're a cynic, Loy. Come on, let's tackle No. 9.'

There was no doubt about Donald Heath's black eye. The flesh was swollen and discoloured, the eye nearly closed. He fidgeted uneasily under their stares, fearful as to the reason for their visit. Had he known they were policemen he would not have answered their knock. But now it was done he would have to bluff it out.

'We are police officers, Mr Heath,' said Pitt. 'Yesterday afternoon a postman disappeared while delivering letters in this road. Can you help us in the matter?'

He shook his head. 'I don't know as I can.'

'Did you get any letters by that post?'

'Yes, two.'

'Either of them registered?'

'No.' If only one had been!

'So you didn't speak to the postman, sir? Didn't even see him, I suppose?'

'No,' he said again. And then, unable to restrain the sudden surge of hope that had arisen with their questions: '*Should* there have been a registered letter for me, officer?'

'Yes, sir. Were you expecting one?'

So Aunt Ellen had sent the money! If the letter had contained a refusal she would not have registered it. True, he was no better off; he still hadn't got the cheque. But he could write again and explain what had happened. It would take a few days before he could expect a reply, and in the meantime anything might happen. There was no alternative, however; and at least he knew now that the money would come.

Inspector Pitt said, 'Maybe you didn't hear me, sir. I asked if you had been expecting a registered letter. If so, perhaps you can tell me what it contained?'

Heath said hurriedly, 'I'm sorry, officer. I was wool-gathering. No, I wasn't expecting it. It may have been a small cheque. For Christmas, you know.'

'That's a nasty eye you've got, sir,' said Dick. 'Must have been quite a scrap. I hope the other fellow's got something to show for it.'

The young man tried to laugh, but there was little mirth in the sound. 'It wasn't a fight,' he said. 'I slipped on a rug and knocked my eye against the mantelpiece.'

'The Heath family want to get together on their stories,' said the Inspector later. 'And what's the matter with the people in this road, anyway? Are they all mixed up with Laurie? Or is it just a coincidence that practically everyone of them seems to have a skeleton in the cupboard?'

'Search me,' said Dick. 'Why should they want to get rid of the postman, anyway? They can't all be like Miss Fratton.'

'We'll try this chap Carrington at No. 5,' said Pitt. 'He's the last of those who should have received a registered packet.'

No. 5 was a small bungalow with a wide frontage and a garage at the side. It lay some way back from the road, from which it was screened by a tall hedge. A similar screen separated it from its neighbours, and there were several tall conifers in the front garden. It looked a gloomy and neglected place.

But there was nothing gloomy or neglected about the interior. The lounge was a long, narrow room stretching the width of the bungalow, with windows overlooking the back garden and the golf-links beyond. It was gaily and tastefully furnished, with a log-fire burning brightly at one end. The walls were covered with pictures, both prints and originals. At sight of the latter the

Inspector whistled softly. He knew something about pictures. These were good.

Jock Carrington evinced none of the uneasiness which had characterized most of the inhabitants of Grange Road when confronted with the police.

'I've just been hearing about this missing postman,' he said. He was an alert-looking man in the middle forties, squarely built and prematurely grey, and spoke with a Scots accent. 'A pal of mine — he's here now — came round to verify the rumour. But I couldn't help him, any more than I can help you fellows. I was in Town yesterday — got back about 7.30. I gather the chap disappeared long before that, eh?'

'Yes,' said Pitt. 'Were any letters delivered in your absence, Mr Carrington?'

'No. What's he done, officer? Did he really clear off with the mail, as rumour has it?'

'We don't know, sir. We haven't found him yet. There was a registered letter for you, by the way.'

'Probably my fountain-pen, back from

the makers,' said Carrington. 'Damn! I've had that pen for years.'

'Where did your friend pick up this rumour, sir?' asked Dick.

Carrington went to the door of the lounge. 'Hey, Mike!' he shouted.

Pitt wandered off to look at the pictures.

A tall, good-looking man of about thirty-five came into the room. He grinned when he saw Dick, and held out his hand.

'If it isn't my old friend Sergeant Ponsford!' he exclaimed. 'Just the chap I wanted to see. What's all this about a missing postman?'

The Sergeant did not share the other's pleasure at the encounter. 'I was hoping you'd be able to tell me that, Mr Bullett,' he said. 'Where did you get hold of the news?'

Mike Bullett winked. 'I get around,' he said. His voice dropped to a whisper. 'Who's the gent with an eye for art?'

Dick told him. At the sound of his name Pitt rejoined them. 'You're a lucky man, Mr Carringon,' he said. 'That little lot must be worth quite a tidy sum.'

'They are, Inspector,' said Carrington. 'Being an artist myself — though not in that class, of course — I like something to aspire to.'

Pitt nodded. 'Now I can place you, sir. I went to your exhibition in Goldney Street last year. And very good it was, too — if you'll accept praise from a complete amateur.'

'I'll accept praise from anyone, Inspector. I simply lap it up.'

'I shared this bungalow with Jock for a couple of weeks,' said Bullett. 'He thinks I packed it in because the exchequer wouldn't run to it. Well, it wouldn't. But it was those damned pictures that really got me down. I prefer pin-ups. And I still have to come in and keep an eye on the ruddy things when he's away. Here, Sarge! Tell me about this postman. A reporter has to live, same as policemen.'

Reluctantly Dick told him the bare facts. At mention of the missing man's name Bullet interrupted.

'Laurie? John Laurie? Damn it, I know the blighter! We've sat fishing together for hours. What's more, he even saved my life. Well, well!'

'Tell me more, Mr Bullett,' said Dick.

'Oh, there wasn't much to it. No heroics. I slipped on the steps at the end of the breakwater and Laurie fished me out.' He showed the Sergeant a deep scar that crossed the ball of his right thumb. 'That's where I collected that little lot. Caught it on a nail.'

'Do you know Laurie well, then?' asked Pitt.

'Not intimately, if that's what you mean. I doubt if anyone does. He wasn't a sociable chap — his conversation never got much farther than fish or the weather. I would never have known he was a postman if he hadn't turned up one day in an old uniform.'

'When did you last see him, Mr Bullett?'

'Oh, ages ago. Over a year, anyway. I believe he got married, and I — well, I don't seem to have so much time for fishing nowadays. Crime is looking up in these parts, Inspector.'

With the people of Grange Road fresh

in his mind, Pitt did not doubt this last assertion. 'Have you met his wife, sir?' he asked.

'No. But maybe I ought to. Just because her old man pinched Her Majesty's mail, it doesn't alter the fact that he fished me out of the water. It may not have been a particularly heroic deed, but it meant a lot to yours truly. I can't swim, you see. I'd better rally round — she may be in a bit of a stew, poor thing. What's the address, Sergeant?'

Dick told him. 'If you're covering this for the *Chronicle*, Mr Bullett, I suppose you will be interviewing some of the folks in this road?' he asked.

The reporter shook his head. 'I don't think so,' he said. 'I'm told Laurie was new to this district. I'll get more information from his previous round. Well, cheerio. I'll keep in touch. If anything breaks give me a ring, will you?'

'So you know Mike Bullett, do you?' said Carrington, after his friend had left. 'He's an amusing cove, taken in small doses. Good at his job, I imagine. He's not easily shaken off once he gets his

101

teeth into something.'

'The people at No. 4, sir,' said Pitt. 'Alster, I believe the name is. Have you met them?'

Jock Carrington grinned. 'Once,' he said. 'But it wasn't a friendly meeting. I'd just pinched their car.'

The Inspector looked his astonishment.

'I didn't intend to pinch the ruddy thing,' Carrington explained. 'It happened when Mike was staying with me. I came home late one evening and left the car in the road. Some time afterwards I went out again, got into the car, and drove off to pick up a girl friend. It wasn't until she remarked on the absence of a floor mat that I realized I was in the wrong car!'

'That must have been rather unnerving,' said Pitt.

'I'll say it was! Of course, I realized what had happened. Mike had gone off in mine without telling me — he used it as he liked — and the Alsters had parked theirs in the identical spot. Their Austin is the same model as mine, and I didn't notice the difference. Anyway, I called and apologized. They weren't very pleasant about it, however.'

When they left the bungalow Pitt said to Dick, 'You didn't look too pleased at meeting your reporter friend. I wouldn't have called your greeting effusive, anyway.'

'The man's a menace, Loy. As Carrington said, you can't shake him off.'

'That's characteristic of the breed,' said the Inspector. 'But they have their uses. They're a confounded nuisance at times, I admit; but throw 'em a few crumbs and they do sometimes reward you with a whole loaf.' He smiled. 'I bet it wasn't pure philanthropy that made Bullet ask for Mrs Laurie's address. Notice how keen he was to get away? He smells a story. The human interest, they call it.'

'Maybe he'll develop another interest when he sees her,' said the Sergeant. 'She's got what it takes.'

'Don't be coarse, Dick.'

On their return to the station they learned that the stolen Vauxhall had been found at Elftwick, a small hamlet five miles from Lexeter on the Tanmouth road. It had been abandoned in a side-turning within a hundred yards of the main road. Avery, who at the Inspector's request accompanied them to Elftwick, was positive the Vauxhall was the same car he had seen in Grange Road the previous evening.

After the fingerprint men had finished the two police officers and Hennessy searched the car thoroughly. It yielded little information. There was no blood, no sign of a struggle. The soft cushions on the rear seat gave no indication that someone had sat there recently. 'If Laurie left Grange Road in this, ten to one he did so willingly,' said Pitt.

'You think so?' commented the Sergeant. 'Personally, I think it stinks. Laurie couldn't have stolen the car himself, and he hadn't time to fix it with a pal to meet him. Why, he didn't even know, until just before leaving the post-office, that he was going to be in Grange Road at all. And if you are suggesting that a friend happened to be there in a stolen car on the very day that Laurie decides to do his stuff — well, it stinks even higher.'

Hennessy laughed, but Pitt looked slightly ruffled. 'All right, all right!' he said. 'No need to be offensive. We'll sort that one out later. The point now is — where would they go from here? And how?'

'Bus — unless they cadged a lift. The nearest railway station is Lexeter. They may have gone that way.'

'We'll try the bus depot at Lexeter, then.'

'Not me,' said Hennessy. 'I've got other fish to fry. But good hunting.'

If Laurie had left Grange Road in the Vauxhall he must have done so shortly after five o'clock, Pitt decided. It was ten miles to Elftwick, and the journey could not have taken less than twenty minutes in the bad weather conditions prevailing the previous evening. If he went on from there by bus it could not have been much before 5.30 when he left Elftwick.

'It shouldn't be difficult to trace him,' said Dick. 'Not if he's still in uniform and carrying a mailbag.'

'I'm not so sure. Remember Chesterton's postman? Besides, if Laurie was picked up by arrangement there'd be a civvy suit for him in the car. And a suitcase for the mail. But the point that puzzles me is this: where was Laurie when Avery passed the Vauxhall? There was no one in the car, he said. And even if Laurie was delivering letters at No. 17, Avery would have seen the bicycle.'

The Sergeant considered this.

'Maybe Laurie and his pal were dumping the bike,' he suggested.

'All right. And that's another puzzler. Why dump it so far from the car? There was no attempt at concealment — it was just dumped.'

'The whole set-up's crazy,' said Dick. 'None of it makes sense when you think it over.'

At the bus depot they learned that there was an hourly service from Tan-mouth to Lexeter, passing the Elftwick turning at fourteen minutes to the hour. Laurie, therefore, would have caught the 5.15 bus from Tanmouth.

The conductor on that bus was not at work, but they found him in his garden. Yes, he said, two men had boarded the bus at Elftwick the previous afternoon. He remembered them well; the bus had been full and they had had to stand. One of them had a large suitcase, and had insisted on standing near the entrance to keep an eye on it. Both men had got off at Lexeter.

'Ever seen either of them before?' asked Pitt.

'No.'

'Okay. Let's have their descriptions.'

'Well, the older one (it was him as had the suitcase) was a short, thick-set chap,' said the conductor. 'About thirty, I suppose he'd be. Dark, he was, and sullen-looking. A bit shifty, I thought him, though he was dressed quiet enough — dark suit, with a fawn raincoat and a dirty trilby. The other was taller, about my height. He'd be around twenty — real spiv type. Long overcoat, padded shoulders, pointed light brown shoes. He didn't look so hot under the coat, though. His trousers was pretty rough. He'd got red hair and plenty of it — didn't wear a hat. All over the place, his hair was.'

'Both of them clean-shaven?'

'Yes.'

'Did you catch any of their conversation?'

'They didn't talk. I didn't know they was together until they got off the bus.'

As they drove back to Tanmouth Pitt said, 'The dark chap could have been Laurie. Pity we haven't a photo of him. It's a description that could fit a good many men.'

The Sergeant grunted. 'I wish I could feel more certain that Laurie was ever in the ruddy Vauxhall,' he said gloomily.

'To be honest, so do I. Well, we'll circulate a description of these two birds. That red hair may help.'

On their return to the station they were greeted by Sergeant Roberts. 'Another dramatic development in the Great Mailbag Mystery,' he said. 'A Mrs Gill, of 24 Grange Road, rang up this afternoon to say that a dark, sinister-looking man was prowling up and down in front of her house. We sent a car right away, but the bird had flown. If bird there ever wert,' he added, 'which, after listening to the good lady on the telephone, I take leave to doubt.'

'It could have been Laurie, I suppose,' said Pitt. 'Mrs Gill wouldn't know him. But why the hell would he be watching her house?'

'No reason at all,' said Dick. 'Which is good enough for assuming it was him. Nothing that fellow does makes sense. He runs out on a regular job and a smashing wife to pinch a bundle of mail that may contain nothing of value; he delivers half of it and then pinches the rest — keeps some of the letters for Grange Road and delivers others; he gets picked up by a pal he couldn't have arranged to meet at a place he didn't know he was going to be, and walks half-way across the links to dump his bicycle. Don't tell me you're jibbing at the thought of his spending Saturday afternoon admiring Mrs Gill's curtains.'

The Inspector laughed. 'Snap out of it, Dick,' he said. 'Let's call on this chap Gofer. There is just a chance he was in on this — that Laurie bribed him to sham an illness, knowing he was the obvious man to take over Gofer's round.'

But Gofer had not been shamming. That doubt was removed as soon as they saw the man. They found him in bed, and he was obviously far from well.

The news of Laurie's disappearance shocked him.

'Somebody must have bashed him one,' he declared. 'John Laurie's not the chap to do a thing like that. Why the hell should he? If you asks me, I reckon I'm the lucky one. If I hadn't gone sick it's me you'd be looking for now, Inspector, not Laurie.'

'How much notice did he get before going out in the afternoon?' asked Pitt.

'Hour, hour and a half, maybe. But he had the sorting to do as well.' A sudden thought struck him. 'Blimey, he had my cape and leggings! Borrowed 'em before I left. They was a bit big for him — Laurie's only five foot six, five inches shorter'n me — but it come on to rain hard after lunch, and he'd left his at home, so he weren't worrying about the fit.' He sighed. 'Well, it's goodbye to that little lot.'

'There are a few queer types in Grange

Road, aren't there?' Pitt suggested.

But Gofer didn't think they were queer. Only Miss Fratton. When he mentioned her he laughed. 'Cripes! I bet she give Laurie a turn. I forgot to warn him about the old girl. Talk about language! I don't know how she come to learn such words.'

Their next call was on Mr Jack Oakie. The bookmaker's office was closed, but they found him at his home. He was a tall, lugubrious man. Yes, he said, he had sent Mr Morris his winnings — seven pounds five shillings — in postal orders, and they should have been delivered on Friday. No, the letter had not been registered; it was cheaper to insure the smaller amounts against loss. No, the payee's name had not been filled in, but the orders had been crossed.

'I thought Mr Morris had no banking-account,' said Pitt.

'That's right,' the bookmaker agreed. 'The crossing was done in error. But Morris won't have no difficulty in getting them cashed.'

If he ever receives them, thought Pitt,

as he made a note of the numbers on the counterfoils.

Mrs Gill, when questioned, could tell them little more about the mysterious watcher.

'Quite light, it was. About three. He kept walking up and down on the other side of the road, and sometimes he wandered off on to the golf-links. I didn't know what to do, Inspector. I haven't a telephone, you see, and I didn't like to go next door on account of their not being very friendly. But I thought, maybe he's planning something — I *must* tell the police. So I put on my hat and coat and went down the road to phone. And when I got back he had gone.'

'What sort of a man was he, Mrs Gill? What did he look like?'

'Well, really, Inspector, I didn't notice. I was so upset, wondering what to do. He wasn't very tall, anyway. His coat-collar was turned up, and he had a hat on — a trilby, I think it was. I didn't see his face at all, not even when I went out. And — well, that's all.'

'And he was watching just this

particular house?'

'Well, I *thought* he was,' Mrs Gill said cautiously. 'I suppose he might have been watching the others as well. It's difficult to say, isn't it?'

He led her on to talk of her neighbours, hoping to pick up some piece of information that might prove useful. Mrs Gill, lulled into a sense of security by his friendly manner, let herself go. But it was not until she reached the Heath family that the Inspector's interest was aroused.

'The father was no good,' she said. 'In and out of prison, I'm told. Women, that was his trouble. The son's got an eye for them, too. He's gone on that Miss Weston, you know. And he isn't the only one, either. There's Mr Carrington, at No. 5; he's sweet on her. And if you ask me, Inspector, he has put Donald Heath's nose right out of joint. He's got money, you see, and Dorothy Weston isn't the type to let money escape her. She's round at his bungalow all hours of the night. Well, you can't carry on like that without people getting to know about it, can you? And Donald Heath's a quick-tempered young man. Very excitable. As I said to Miss Plant only last night, I wouldn't put anything past him, not even murder.'

At the sound of that last word she paused, remembering her uneasiness in the presence of the Inspector that morning. She must not say things like that, she told herself. One never knew.

'Of course, that's just an expression, Inspector,' she said, with what was meant to be a gay little laugh. 'You mustn't take me literally. People don't murder other people for things like that, do they? In books, perhaps — but not in real life.'

Remembering his resolution of the morning, Pitt refrained from comment. 'What's Heath's job?' he asked.

'I don't know what he actually *does*, but he works up at Cabell's. So do quite a lot of other people in Grange Road: Mr Avery, Mr Harris — oh, and Mr Archer, too.'

'The Alsters, Mrs Gill. The people at No. 4. Do you know them?'

'Not very well, Inspector. But they seem quite nice. They have two dear little children, and they're beautifully behaved.

So unusual these days, don't you think?'

Presuming that she was referring to the children's behaviour, and not that of their parents, Pitt agreed that it was unusual. He said, 'I've called there twice, but they seem to have been out each time.'

'They've gone away,' said Mrs Gill. 'At least, Miss Plant — she lives next door to them, you know — she hasn't seen them since yesterday midday. I expect they are visiting relations for Christmas. And that reminds me — I still haven't heard from my daughter out at Rawsley. Most annoying. I suppose her letter was lost with the rest of the mail.'

Inspector Pitt was not interested in Mrs Gill's domestic worries. But he had one more query to put.

'When you spoke to me this morning, ma'am, you took it for granted that the postman was still missing. Why?'

'Why, Inspector?' Mrs Gill was flustered. 'Well, I — really, what a question to ask! I'm sure I don't know *why*. One just feels these things, I suppose. After all, he hadn't just popped off for an hour or so, or he wouldn't have left his bicycle there, would he?'

'Left his bicycle where, Mrs Gill?' The Inspector's voice was no longer friendly.

Her fluster deepened. 'Well, wherever you found it. I'm sure I don't know where that was.'

'I think you do, ma'am. I'd advise you to tell me the truth, or the consequences may be unpleasant.'

Mrs Gill shuddered at the implication contained in his words.

'I didn't mean to spy on you,' she said weakly. 'But I was so upset, what with the postman not calling and then your visit, I thought perhaps a little walk before going to bed might calm my nerves. And then when I got to the corner of No. 20 and saw a light on the golf-links I felt I just *had* to know what was going on.' Inspiration came to her, and she brightened. 'I considered it my duty, Inspector; it might be something the police ought to know about, I thought, and I never was one to put self first. And I couldn't know it was you, could I?'

Inspector Pitt looked at her in grudging admiration.

'No,' he said gravely. 'You couldn't, could you?'

4

Footsteps Behind Us

As Dorothy Weston had told her sister, she was not in love with Jock Carrington. But she was in love with his money, and with the good times and security that his money promised, and she did not mean to abandon these without a struggle. Besides, she liked Jock, even felt a certain amount of affection for him — which was more than could be said about her feelings for Donald Heath.

But could Jock ever be inveigled into matrimony? He was such a solid, down-to-earth character, with none of the irresponsibility one expected from an artist. He would not lose his head over her, not even in the wildest moments of passion. In the months she had known him he had never hinted at the possibility of marriage, had said nothing that promised permanence to their

118

relationship. Was that because he felt so sure of her that a more binding tie seemed unnecessary? Or was it because, as she feared, he regarded her as just another incident in his amatory life?

It was to force his hand — to make him realize that she was no longer willing to continue as before — that she had gone for a walk with him that Sunday afternoon.

Jock Carrington was not fond of walking. Neither, he knew, was Dorothy. But since it was she was had proposed the outing, presenting herself at his front door shortly after lunch — and since his car had gone to the garage for servicing — he could not easily refuse her.

Jock too had his troubles. He was undecided about Dorothy. She was an ideal companion for a night out, and a most satisfactory lover. They had had some good times together, and he saw no reason why the good times should not continue. But he had an uneasy feeling that Dorothy was beginning to take too deep an interest in him; an almost possessive interest, it seemed. If she were considering him as a possible husband, might it not be wiser to drop her? Gradually, of course; he had no wish to hurt her. Or should he tell her bluntly that he was not the marrying kind? Let her know where she stood? If she wanted marriage, there was always young Heath. Dorothy had told him more than once — to arouse his jealousy, no doubt — that Donald Heath would marry her whenever she cared to name the day. Well, let him.

So preoccupied were they with their thoughts that they reached Coppins Point without either of them broaching the matter uppermost in their minds. They talked little. The wind was fresh, and they needed all their breath to fight against it. The going was easier on the return journey, however, and Dorothy tried desperately to head the conversation into the required channel. But Jock, although equally desirous of making his position clear, had not yet found words in which to frame it, and ignored the leads she gave him.

It was as the girl jumped down from a high tee into the surrounding rough that she felt her right ankle bend sharply over.

'Ouch!' A hand on his shoulder, she stood one-legged, rubbing the injured ankle. 'It hurts like the devil. I must have sprained it.'

He was all solicitude. 'I'll carry you, shall I? It's not far.'

She laughed. 'I'm no light weight, Jock,' she said. 'I'll make it if we take it slowly.'

He made her sit down on his raincoat, took off her shoe, and massaged the ankle. It had already begun to swell. 'Lucky you're not working,' he said. 'You couldn't dance with that little lot.'

Arms round each other's waists, they moved slowly homeward, taking a circuitous route to avoid the more uneven going. We must look like a courting couple, thought Carrington; and was thankful for the approaching darkness.

The same thought had occurred to Dorothy. And because she was in pain and feeling somewhat sorry for herself, and rather desperate, she echoed it aloud.

'And I almost wish we were,' she added. 'It must be rather fun.'

This is it, he thought. 'Of course it's

fun,' he agreed. 'It's what comes after that isn't.'

'Marriage? That could be fun, too.'

'Oh, I dare say it's all right for some. But you and I — we're not the marrying kind. It wouldn't do for us.'

'It might,' she said. Ahead of them were the lights of Grange Road, coming nearer with every painful step. There was little time left, and now that the topic had been raised she wanted to pursue it, no matter what the end might be. 'I used to think that way once. Now I'm not so sure. Maybe I'm getting old, Jock, but dancing in the chorus doesn't appeal to me any more. I want something permanent, something more secure.'

'Marriage isn't always permanent,' he answered her. 'Not always secure, either. But if that's what you want, then good luck to you, darling. I'll give you a bang-up reference when you find the right chap.' He squeezed her waist and laughed.

'We're getting morbid; let's go back to my place for a drink.'

Dorothy did not laugh. It was as she

had feared; she would just have to marry Donald.

They had walked some distance in silence when she stopped and turned.

'What's the matter?' asked Jock. 'Ankle hurting you?'

'Sh!' For a moment she listened. 'I thought I heard someone following us,' she whispered. 'It's too dark to see, but I could have sworn there were footsteps behind us.'

'You're imagining things,' he said. 'Spraining your ankle, and then all that tripe about marriage. It's enough to give anyone the jitters.'

Reluctantly she obeyed the pressure of his arm. To capture her attention he said, 'About your birthday present. It's a damned shame it should be pinched, after all the trouble I took to choose it.'

'What was it?' she asked.

'A brooch. Emeralds, and in a most unusual setting. I must see if the shop has another like it.'

'Thanks, Jock.'

She smiled up at him in the darkness, feeling behind her to squeeze the hand at her waist. He was a good sort. It wasn't his fault if he didn't want to marry her, and she certainly couldn't accuse him of making love to her under false pretences. She had thought of reproaching him for having cut her on the phone when she had rung him up on her birthday. Now she decided not to. It was none of her business if he had another girl.

As they walked her ears were strained to catch the sound of a soft footfall behind them. It was a creepy feeling, out there on the deserted golf-links with the swish of the waves breaking on the beach coming faintly to her ears. She wished it were not so dark. Why should anyone want to follow them, what could . . .

Carrington heard it first and wheeled swiftly, disengaging his arm from the girl's waist so that she had to put her swollen foot to the ground to steady herself. The pain of it made her wince.

Behind them a tall figure moved and then was merged in the dark background. 'By God, you're right! There *is* someone,' said Jock.

Crouching low, he began to move back

along the way they had come.

He was almost out of sight when the girl screamed. She could not help it. The thought of being alone, unable to run, with the unknown watcher near her . . . waiting, perhaps to strike . . .

Her scream brought Carrington racing back. 'What was it? What happened?' he demanded.

At the feel of his arm about her she regained some control. 'Nothing happened,' she said weakly. 'I got scared, that's all. Jock! Who was it, do you think?'

'God knows! I might have caught the blighter if you hadn't screamed.' He could feel her shivering, and his annoyance left him. 'Here! Let's get to hell out of this.'

He picked her up and began to carry her towards the road. Dorothy, her arms round his neck, would have enjoyed the experience had not fear possessed her. But it was for Jock she was afraid, not for herself.

A light danced towards them across the grass, and two tall figures materialized out of the night.

'Trouble, Mr Carrington?' asked a voice.

'Oh, it's you, Inspector. Yes, Miss Weston has sprained her ankle.'

'I'm sorry. But is that all, sir? A few moments ago we heard a scream. We were coming to investigate.'

'There was someone behind us,' Carrington said shortly. He did not wish to discuss the incident with the police. 'Miss Weston got a bit scared, not knowing who it might be.'

'And would you know, sir?'

'No, I wouldn't. Nor why, either. And if you don't mind, Inspector, I'd like to get Miss Weston indoors. She's upset, and I've no doubt her ankle is painful. Added to that, she isn't exactly a light weight. So if you'll excuse us . . .'

'He looked a bit shaken himself,' said Sergeant Ponsford, as they watched Carrington cross the road with his burden and disappear into the grounds of No. 5.

'Miss Weston's no sylph, as he said. If he had carried her any distance he had a right to be shaken,' answered the Inspector. 'All the same, I wonder

. . . Perhaps a call at No. 9 might not be out of order.'

As they crossed the road a burly figure bore down on them, a torch flickered on their faces. 'Evening, Sergeant — evening, Inspector,' said Sam Archer. 'How's crime?'

'The same as usual,' Pitt answered. 'Unpleasant.'

The man laughed. 'Well, you can't grumble,' he said. 'You chose it.'

'That's true,' the Inspector agreed. 'I must certainly remember not to grumble in future. Have you been for a walk? Too early for darts, isn't it?'

'Yes. They're not open yet.'

'Keeping the muscles in trim, eh? I'm told it's a strenuous game,' said the Sergeant.

'All right, you can laugh,' said Archer, laughing himself. 'But if everyone stuck to darts of an evening there wouldn't be any crime. No time for it. And where would you chaps be then, eh?'

'Playing darts, presumably,' answered Pitt.

Heath himself opened the door to

them. He showed no surprise at their visit. 'What is it this time, Inspector?' he asked.

There were carpet slippers on his feet, his breathing was regular. 'Have you been at home all this evening, sir?' asked Pitt.

'I have.'

'You didn't by any chance hear a noise out on the links about ten minutes ago? As though someone were screaming?'

'Good Lord, no! But then I had the radio on. There's not more trouble down this way, is there?'

'I hope not, Mr Heath. Could I have a word with your mother? She might be able to help us.'

'Mother's at the pictures. She's been out since half-past three.'

It largely depended, thought Pitt, on where Miss Weston had been when she screamed. But she must have been nearer to Heath's house than to the bungalow; which meant that Heath should have had ample time to get home without undue haste, change his shoes, and be ready to present an innocent front to any callers.

'There's no proof either way,' he said to

the Sergeant. 'But if I were Carrington I'd watch my step. Mrs Gill may have been right when she said Heath would stop at nothing to keep his girl.'

Dorothy Weston had the same thought; but she dare not voice it to Jock. If Jock even suspected it was Donald who had followed them he would go right along and demand an apology. And anything might happen then.

She stilled her fears with the reflection that in the future Donald would have little cause to complain. Since Jock would never marry her, the sooner their liaison ended the better. She would have this last evening with him, and then it would be over. But she would not spoil it for them both by telling him that now.

I hope to goodness, thought Dorothy, that I'm not getting soft on him now it's too late!

It was past midnight when she left the bungalow. As she passed No. 9 she noticed that a light still shone from the downstairs front window, and wondered what could be keeping Donald up so late. *Had* it been he who had followed them on the golflinks? Was he watching for her return? She hurried on as fast as her still swollen ankle allowed, not wishing to be involved in a scene so late at night.

It was as she was letting herself in at her own front door that she heard the noise. If it was a scream it was a strangled scream, cut off before it reached its full volume. It came from No. 14, and was followed by a heavy thud. Then there was silence again.

Terrified, the girl stood listening. Had Miss Fratton met with an accident, or had the sound been indicative of something more sinister? A door closed softly at the back of the house. Or was it a window? Then, after a pause, came a scrabbling sound, as though someone were climbing over the wooden fence that separated Miss Fratton's garden from the golf-links.

It was no accident, then. Someone had attacked Miss Fratton; murdered her, perhaps. Unless she acted promptly . . .

The need for action calmed her. She went into the house and telephoned the police, giving them a brief account of what she had heard. Then, unable to bear a period of waiting, she limped down the road to No. 9.

The light was still on, but she had to wait a full minute before he answered. When he did so she looked at him in surprise. Donald was usually so immaculate, but now he wore a brown leather jerkin, zip-fastened to the neck, and a pair of worn and dirty corduroy trousers. His hair was tousled, and there were streaks of dirt on his cheek. With his black eye, he presented a most unkempt appearance.

But there was no time to ponder on that now. Quickly she told him what had happened.

Donald Heath hesitated. 'It's a matter for the police,' he said. 'We ought not to interfere.'

'But she may be dying!' the girl protested. 'We must do *something*.'

As they stood arguing a car turned into Grange Road, accelerated swiftly, and then pulled up outside No. 14. 'That's the police,' said Dorothy, and limped off. Donald Heath, after a moment's hesitation, followed her.

There were three of them. Dorothy explained their presence to the sergeant in charge, and followed them round to the back of the house. The kitchen window was open, and one of the police climbed through to open the back door to the others. Since nobody stopped them, Dorothy and Donald went in too.

Miss Fratton, clad in a faded purple dressing-gown, lay in the hall; her feet at the entrance to the parlour, her head against the stairs. Dorothy clapped her hands to her mouth. 'She's dead!' she whispered.

Behind her Donald said nothing. His hands were clammy and he felt a little sick. He was glad no blood was visible.

More policemen kept arriving. Inspector Pitt was there now, and a doctor. The latter lifted the woman's head, undid her dressing-gown, and felt for her heart. Then he arranged her more comfortably and stood up.

'She'll be all right,' he said. 'Someone knocked her out with a blow on the head, but there's no real damage done. She'll come round soon.'

Miss Fratton did come round. She half opened her eyes, gazed at the assembled company, and closed them again. Then, holding her head, she groaned loudly.

They got her into an armchair, and Dorothy, accompanied by Donald, went out to the kitchen to make tea. For a reason they could not explain, they talked in whispers.

'Whatever can have happened?' she said, as they waited for the kettle to boil.

'A burglar, I suppose. Miss Fratton must have heard him and come downstairs, and he dotted her one to get away.'

'But why here? Nobody would expect to find anything of value in a place like this.'

Donald said nothing.

As she poured the hot water on to the tea-leaves Dorothy remembered something else. 'You were up pretty late, weren't you?' she asked. 'What were you doing?'

'Nothing in particular. Just messing around. I couldn't sleep.'

'Well, there's no need to get yourself up like a tramp,' she said severely. 'I never saw such a sight.'

'You're a nice one to talk!' he retorted. 'You had only just got home yourself. And I don't have to ask what *you* had been up to.'

She flushed. But she was glad — and surprised — that he did not mention Jock.

They took the tray into the parlour. Inspector Pitt, notebook in hand, was talking to Miss Fratton.

'There isn't much to go on,' he said. 'You heard a noise, came downstairs, saw a shadowy figure that immediately pounced on you and knocked you out. And that's all?'

'Isn't it enough? It is for me.'

'Do you know what he hit you with?'

'No, I don't. I forgot to ask him.'

A constable tittered. The Inspector frowned, and the titter ceased.

'You can give me no description of your assailant, Miss Fratton?'

'He was tall, I think. If it *was* a he. I don't know.'

'Do you usually leave your kitchen window unlatched at night? There's no sign of forcible entry.'

'Of course I don't. I must have forgotten.'

The routine questions went on. Dorothy marvelled at Miss Fratton's equable temper. Had that bang on the head knocked the spirit out of her? Or was she actually enjoying this brief excitement in a dull life?

But Miss Fratton did not remain equable for long. She caught sight of Dorothy, smiled tenderly, scowled at Donald Heath lurking behind the girl, and then launched an attack on the Inspector.

'How can I tell if anything's been stolen? I haven't had a chance to look, have I? You get all these men out of my house right away. Have them look for the thief, instead of nattering here. It's high time that young girl was in bed.'

Completely disregarding the others, she raised herself out of the chair, took the younger woman gently by the arm, and led her from the room.

Inspector Pitt shrugged. 'We'll get no more out of her tonight,' he said. 'May as well pack up, Dick. In any case, I doubt whether this has any connection with Laurie.'

'Tough, isn't she?' said the Sergeant. 'Seems to have recovered completely. Do you think she'll bother to let us know if anything's been stolen?'

'I'll have a word with Miss Weston,' said the Inspector. 'She's got her head screwed on properly. Which is more than can be said for your station sergeant, dragging us out of bed on a job that doesn't concern us.'

5

A Tricky Business, Blackmail

It may have been the large, unformed lettering that gave Avery a premonition of disaster and prompted him to slide the letter into his jacket-pocket as he sat down to breakfast. But unobtrusive as was the action it did not escape his wife's notice. She was watching him as she always watched him when he opened his mail. Susan Avery had her suspicions of her husband's private affairs.

'What's that letter you're putting in your pocket?' she asked sharply. 'Why don't you open it first?'

'Just a bill,' he retorted. He bolted down his breakfast, swallowed a last mouthful of tea, wiped his mouth on his napkin, and went out to the kitchen. But he knew Susan too well to risk opening the letter at home. It must wait until he got to the office.

He began to clean his shoes.

She stood in the doorway, watching him, annoyed that she had not caught him reading the letter. 'Who's it from?' she asked.

'What?'

'That letter. The one you said was a bill. Who's it from, Robert?'

'How should I know? I haven't opened it yet.'

He put the brushes and polish away in the cupboard and bent to kiss her. 'Goodbye,' he said. 'Home at the usual time, I expect.'

But she was not so easily defeated. She pushed him back into the kitchen as he sought to pass her, upbraiding him, her voice shrill in its jealous anger. 'I know damn' well it wasn't a bill, Robert, or you wouldn't have pushed it into your pocket like that — secretly, hoping I wouldn't see what you were up to. It's from a woman, isn't it?'

'Don't be a fool, Susan.' Through the open window he could see Mrs Gill in her kitchen. 'And don't shout. Do you want that woman to know everything that goes on in this house? If you *must* make a scene for God's sake do it quietly! Anyway, I can't stop to argue with you now. I'm late.'

Harris and Heath were waiting for him outside. It had become customary for him to give them a lift to the works, but now Avery regretted the custom. He did not want to listen to their chatter, their grouses and grumbles. The unopened letter was still in his pocket, waiting to be read.

But that morning there was no chatter, no grousing. Heath and Harris sat silent throughout the short journey. Avery remembered they had been equally silent on the Saturday, and wondered what ailed them. It was no business of his, however. Whatever the cause of their silence, he was grateful for it.

At the office there were letters to be dictated, people to see, orders to be given. An hour passed before he had the opportunity to open the letter in private. He read:

DEAR SIR,

I have some letters you wrote to a certain lady. They was addressed to your wife, but I expect you would prefer she didn't read them. Nor she needn't if you do as this letter says. But it will cost you two hundred quid. The money is to be in one-pound notes and wrapped in two parcels and addressed to John Laking, 18 Duke Street, Lexeter. And see as they are properly stamped. They are not to be posted in Tanmouth, neither. Catch the two-thirty bus Wednesday for Rawsley and get off at the Red Lion. Walk up the lane opposite, right to the top, then turn right and post the money in the first letter-box. It's on the left, on a telegraph-pole. Then walk back to Rawsley the way you came, and catch the next bus to Tanmouth.

Do as above and you'll get the letters. If you go to the cops or try any funny business I'll send them to your wife.

P.S. In case you think this is a try-on, there are six letters and the lady's name is Eve.

Avery read the letter through again. It was unsigned, and written on cheap white notepaper in a queer jumble of script and block capitals. And as the writer claimed, it was no hoax. They would be the letters Eve had said she would send to Susan — on moral principles, she had explained, and not through any wish to embarrass him.

Two hundred pounds! Even if he wished he could not lay his hands on that sum by Wednesday. Susan could; Susan had plenty of ready cash. But he could hardly appeal to her. Yet if the writer were in earnest . . . If Susan were to read those damned letters!

There was only one alternative. Despite the threat in the letter, he must go to the police.

★   ★   ★

Inspector Pitt read the letter carefully, examined the envelope, and then read the letter again.

'Any idea where this came from, Mr Avery?' he asked.

'Not really. But I imagine the six letters referred to were in the mail stolen on Friday evening. It's probably that damned postman who is responsible.'

'H'm! Well, I don't want to pry into your personal affairs, sir — but I suppose it's the usual story?'

Avery shrugged his shoulders. 'More or less, Inspector. My marriage has not been a happy one.'

Pitt nodded. 'And the usual result, eh? The lady blackmailed you, and you refused to stump up?'

'No,' said Avery. 'It wasn't quite like that. She was a queer girl, with a moral code very much her own. I had known her about a year; in my job I'm away from home a lot, and it was easy for us to meet. And then, without the least warning, she told me she wasn't going to see me any more.

'Well, I thought, that's that. But unfortunately it wasn't. Last Wednesday I got a letter from her, saying she was going abroad the next day and had decided to send my letters to my wife. She explained that she was doing this not out of animosity but because her conscience told her it was the right thing to do. If my wife and I were to build a new life together, she said, it must not be based on deception. She hoped Susan would forgive me, and that we would live happily ever after. Or words to that effect.'

'A bit of an optimist, eh, sir?' said Pitt. 'I'm not a married man, of course; but wives aren't usually that magnanimous, are they?'

'Mine isn't, anyway,' the other answered shortly.

So I imagined, thought Pitt. 'Did you get in touch with the lady again?' he asked.

'I tried to. But her flat was empty and she had left no address. My only hope was to get hold of the letter before my wife saw it. Unfortunately, it didn't arrive on Friday morning, as I had expected.' He paused. 'I'm afraid I wasn't alto-gether truthful at our first interview, Inspector. You see, it was to intercept that letter that I went out on Friday afternoon.'

Pitt smiled. 'I imagined it was something like that, sir. If you'll forgive my saying so, you didn't spin a very convincing lie. But to get back to this letter, Mr Avery. Would you be prepared to pay two hundred pounds for the return of those letters?'

'If I had it, yes. But I haven't — which is why I've come to you.'

'You would have paid the money and kept quiet about it?'

'Frankly, yes. Unethical, I know. But I suppose most married men would do the same.'

Pitt looked at him curiously.

'This is none of my business, Mr Avery. But may I ask why, if your marriage is not a success, you are so anxious to preserve it?'

'There's a very simple answer to that, Inspector. Money. My wife's father is Sir Oliver Golding, who virtually controls Thomas Cabell's. I owe my job to him. But I'm not likely to get very far with the firm if my wife and I fall out, am I? So, being an ambitious man with an eye to the future, I prefer to keep my marriage off the rocks. And if you want a further reason I might add that Sir Oliver is an old man and my wife his only offspring. Good enough?'

'Yes, thank you. But even if we get these letters back, isn't it likely that the lady may write to Mrs Avery again? To check up, so to speak?'

'It's possible,' Avery agreed. 'But unlikely, I think, now that she has left the country — as I presume she has. Anyway, it is a risk I have to take.'

'Well, we'll do what we can, sir. It's a tricky business, blackmail, but — well, we'll do what we can.' Pitt spoke briskly. 'But before you go, Mr Avery, there's one other little matter I'd like to clear up. I believe that as you left your house on Friday afternoon a car passed you coming from the direction of Tanmouth. Now, we're anxious to trace that car. For one thing, it must have passed the Vauxhall; the driver may even have seen the postman. So if you can help us there . . . '

'It was a black Austin saloon,' said Avery. 'I thought it might have been the Alsters' — as I told you, they were out when I called at No. 4. But it's a popular make. Difficult to trace, eh?'

'How many people in the car, sir?'

'I'm afraid I didn't notice. I only gave it a brief glance.'

'We have been trying to locate the Alsters, Mr Avery. You wouldn't know where we could find them, I suppose?'

'Afraid not, Inspector. I know they were going up North for Christmas, but I haven't the faintest idea what day they were leaving. And I doubt whether it was their car I saw. They have two kids, and I'm sure they wouldn't leave it as late as that before starting on a long journey.'

After Avery had gone Sergeant Pons- ford was inclined to be critical. 'I suppose it's genuine?' he said. 'If he had a hand in Laurie's disappearance he might have written this himself to throw us off the scent.'

'I think it's genuine,' said the Inspector. 'And it was posted in Lexeter. That might be our car-stealing friends, eh?'

'Perhaps. But I happen to know this address in Duke Street. It's a small tobacconist's. And I know John Laking. A most respectable old gentleman.'

'All right. An accommodation address, then.'

'No. Laking is an ex-police-sergeant. He wouldn't be very accommodating to a couple of blackmailers. Besides, how can they hope to collect? Avery can tip us off and then follow the instructions to the letter, and we nab them when they call at the shop. It would be dead easy. And why the details about time and place of posting? If the idea is to make certain that Avery doesn't double-cross them, and they intend to watch the pillarbox — how can they be sure the parcels don't contain bundles of newspaper instead of money?'

'They can't,' Pitt said slowly. 'But I've been thinking. I don't believe that address has any significance whatever — because the parcels are not intended to reach it.'

'Eh? How do you make that out?'

'Suppose Laurie wrote that letter? He still has his uniform. What is to prevent him from emptying that particular letter-box a few minutes before the authorized postman does so? All he needs is a skeleton key, and I've no doubt his pal

147

could fix him up with that.'

Sergeant Ponsford whistled. 'You've got something there, Loy. Looks like we had better do a recce out Rawsley way.'

'Rawsley,' said Pitt. 'Now, where have I heard the name of that place before?'

The telephone rang. Sergeant Ponsford picked up the receiver and, after listening for a moment, handed it to the Inspector.

'For you, Loy. The manager of the Southern Bank. Something to do with those missing postal orders.'

Pitt's eyes glistened. 'This may be a break,' he said. 'Well, we can do with one. Hello! Yes, this is Inspector Pitt speaking.'

'My name is Crouch, Inspector,' came the voice over the wire. 'I'm the manager of the Southern Bank here. Those postal orders we were asked to look out for — they have just been handed in by a client of ours, a Mr Toogood. He is in my office now. Do you wish to speak to him?'

'I certainly do,' said Pitt. 'But not over the phone. Keep him there — I'll be right round.'

Mr Toogood was a mild little man, greatly embarrassed by the predicament in which he now found himself. It was his first brush with the police, and he did not relish it.

'I had no idea there was anything wrong with the postal orders, Inspector,' he said earnestly. 'No idea at all.'

'How did they come into your possession, sir?' asked Pitt.

'From a colleague. He has no banking-account, and asked me to cash them for him. They are crossed, you see. He told me they were the proceeds of a betting transaction.'

'What's the name of this colleague of yours, Mr Toogood?'

'Harris, Inspector. William Harris. We're in the same department at Thomas Cabell's. But I can assure you that he is perfectly honest — there must be an explanation, although I don't know what it can be.'

They got rid of him, signed a receipt for the orders, and headed east out of the town.

'First Avery, then Harris,' said Pitt. 'And Donald Heath is not entirely free from suspicion. We'll have the whole of

Grange Road involved before we're through.'

Despite Mr Toogood's assurance, William Harris did not look like an innocent man when he was shown into the room which the firm had placed at the officers' disposal. He glanced at the postal orders in the Inspector's hand and nodded, his fingers beating a rapid tattoo on his thumbs.

'How did you come by these, Mr Harris?' asked Pitt, after cautioning him. He took the nod as an acknowledgement that Mr Toogood had spoken the truth.

The man did not answer. Pitt repeated the question.

'I — a neighbour gave them to me,' mumbled Harris.

'Mr Morris?'

He nodded. 'He asked me to cash them for him.'

He looked the epitome of guilt. Pitt turned to the Sergeant. 'Get Morris,' he said curtly. 'We'll clear this up here and now.'

Sergeant Ponsford was at the door when Harris spoke again.

'All right,' he said. 'Morris didn't give them to me. They were in a letter addressed to him which the postman delivered at my place by mistake. Friday afternoon, that was. I opened it, thinking it was for me. And when I saw the money — ' He paused. The words had come jerkily before, as though each one caused him a separate and acute pain as he uttered it. Now they poured forth in spate. 'I didn't mean to keep it, Inspector. But it's Christmas, and I'm broke. There's nothing in the house, no presents for the wife and kids. I thought I'd borrow it until after Christmas so that I could buy them a few things. Morris wouldn't miss it; he's always got plenty of money. I could give it back to him later, spin him some sort of a yarn. And being pushed through my letter-box like that, it seemed I was meant to have it. But I never thought of it as stealing, Inspector, honest I didn't. I was only going to borrow the money.'

'The law regards it as stealing,' said Pitt.

'But I haven't spent the money!' Harris

cried eagerly. 'It's all there, isn't it?'

'That makes no difference, Mr Harris.'

Inspector Pitt eyed the man thoughtfully. Was he speaking the truth? Or was his confession a blind, an attempt to conceal a more serious crime? No. 17 was the last house at which Laurie was known to have called on Friday afternoon. The significance of that fact, however, was lessened by Archer's assertion that he had seen the postman pass No. 19.

'Mr Harris — when we spoke to you on Friday evening you told us you had not been out of the house that afternoon.'

'That's right.' The man seemed genuinely surprised.

'And you didn't see the postman?'

'Oh! Sorry, I'd forgotten. Yes, I did see him. At first I thought I'd better call next door and give Morris his letter. There was some idea in my mind he might lend me the money — that's why I didn't mention it to my wife. I got as far as the gate and then — well, I changed my mind.'

'Where did you see the postman?'

'When I got to the gate. He was just

152

riding off on his bike.'

'You saw him quite plainly?'

'His back, yes. There was a car coming down the road at the time.'

That car again. 'What make of car?' asked Pitt.

'I don't know. I didn't pay much attention to it.'

'I see. Were you in Lexeter on Saturday?'

'In the morning, yes. I was out with the service van. Why?'

Pitt did not enlighten him. They took him to the police-station, where he was formally charged with the theft. Pitt felt rather sorry for the man. He had seen the poverty apparent at his home, and if Harris was speaking the truth the sight of the money must have been a great temptation.

'I fancy he's more a fool than a knave,' he said to Dick. 'I don't like him, but I think he's innocent as far as Laurie is concerned.'

Later he had another talk with Harris. He wanted further information about Morris, and argued that Harris must have known the man fairly intimately to have contemplated borrowing money from him.

But Harris was disappointing.

'We're just neighbours, Inspector. We have a chat when we meet, which isn't often. But I've never been inside his house or met any of his friends.'

'What's his job?'

'I don't know. I think he's retired. He never talks about himself.'

'H'm! A bit of a mystery, eh? Does he have many visitors?'

'Not many, to my knowledge.'

'What sort of people are they?'

'Young chaps, mostly. They — ' He stopped. 'It's not right to question me about him, Inspector. Morris's affairs are none of my business. I'll not say any more.'

Pitt did not press him. He decided to have a chat with Mrs Gill. If she had any information on Morris or his friends she would not be as reticent as Harris.

★ ★ ★

154

Mr Templar was distressed at the continued disappearance of Laurie. 'Where the devil can he have got to?' he asked the Inspector. 'You wouldn't think a fellow in postman's uniform could go unnoticed for more than two whole days.'

'He could hide out with friends,' said Pitt. 'And if his disappearance was planned I've no doubt he'd arrange for a change of clothing.'

The main purpose of his visit had been to inquire about the Alsters, and here the postmaster was able to help him. From December 12 (the day on which Laurie had disappeared) until the end of the month all their mail was to be redirected to a Scarborough hotel.

'It looks as though that Austin may have been theirs,' Pitt said hopefully to Dick. 'It couldn't have been Carrington's if he was in Town. I'll get the Scarborough police to check.'

That afternoon they visited Rawsley. It was a small village, and the Red Lion was on the outskirts. The letter-box described by the blackmailer was in a country lane; a few yards past it, on the opposite side of the road, was a large country house named Goshawks. This was an isolated building with fields and woodland on either side of it. Farther still the lane ran steeply downhill and then up again, through thick woodland, for some five hundred yards; after which it veered right towards Rawsley village through flat fields in which a new housing estate was already well under way.

The box was due to be cleared at 3.45 in the afternoons, about half an hour after Avery, if he carried out the blackmailer's instructions, would post the money on Wednesday. Inquiries at Lexeter (Pitt deemed it unwise to question the village postmistress) elicited the information that the box was cleared by the postman making the afternoon delivery. Goshawks was the last house on his round, and after leaving it he cycled back to the village through the new estate.

Back at Tanmouth they discussed the possibilities.

'If it's Laurie I still think he may clear the box himself,' said Pitt. 'But Laurie or no Laurie there's an alternative. Why shouldn't the men, whoever they are, waylay the postman as they may have waylayed Laurie? Either before he clears the box — in which case they take his keys and clear it themselves — or after. It's just another mail-robbery; only this time they have ensured the tidy sum of two hundred quid as part of their haul. Or think they have.'

Dick nodded. 'Could be. But it would have to be after the box is cleared, not before. Too many houses that side. A likely spot would be on the uphill stretch through the woods. The postman would have to dismount there.'

A constable came in with a message. 'A man named Bullett to see you, sir,' he said.

Dick Ponsford groaned. 'I wondered how long it would be before he turned up again. Get rid of him, Willett. Say we're out, or sick of the palsy. Anything you like as long as you get rid of him.'

'No,' said Pitt. 'Sorry, Dick. I know you think he's a menace, but this time we may be able to use him.'

Michael Bullett was all smiles and

affability. The Sergeant wondered whether he had got wind of the blackmail. Or was it Harris?

But Bullett had a surprise for them.

'Why so glum, Sergeant?' he bantered. 'Not pleased to see me?'

'We're busy, Mr Bullett,' said Dick.

'Well, that's something, anyway. I was beginning to think that the affair of the missing postman had dried up on you. What's new?'

'Nothing,' said the Inspector. 'Nothing for the papers, anyway.'

'The same old secrecy,' complained the reporter. 'No co-operation. Well, never let it be said that a Bullett failed in his duty. Let me heap coals of fire on your head, Inspector, and tell you that I have news for you.'

'What news, Mr Bullett?'

He grinned at them impishly. 'I've had a letter from John Laurie,' he announced. 'Yes, I thought that would make you both sit up.'

'Let me see it, please,' said Pitt.

The note was typed. Amateurishly typed, with uneven spacing and several erasures and cancellations. And it was short. It reminded Michael Bullett that the writer had once done him a service by pulling him out of the water. Since the writer was forced to be absent from home, would Mr Bullett now repay that service by keeping an eye on his wife?

The signature was also typed. John Laurie.

'I'll be frank with you, Inspector,' said Bullett. 'If I could see any way of using that letter myself I wouldn't have brought it to you. But I can't, and — well, there it is.'

'When did this come?' asked Pitt.

'By this afternoon's post. I found it in my room when I returned from the office.'

'And the envelope? Where's that?'

'Burnt,' said Bullett. 'All right, don't say it. But how was I to know that the bloody thing would be important? How many envelopes are? I chucked it into the fire before I read the letter. If I'd known it was from Laurie . . . But I didn't, and you can't take it out of me for that.'

'Did you notice the postmark?'

'No. That's all there is, Inspector, so make the most of it.'

There was no address, no introduction of any sort. The paper was flimsy, the kind used for carbon copies. It would be impossible to trace.

'I'm sorry,' said Bullett. 'I know how you feel. Sore, eh?'

'I'll keep this, Mr Bullett,' said Pitt, too annoyed at the other's carelessness to respond to his apology. He knew he was being unreasonable; Bullett's action had been perfectly natural. But that postmark might have given them a lead to Laurie.

'That was the general idea,' the reporter answered carelessly.

Behind the cheerful, brash exterior of the man Dick detected a note of nervousness.

'Are you publishing Laurie's letter in your paper, Mr Bullett?' he asked.

'To tell the truth, Sergeant, our readers aren't greatly interested in John Laurie,' said Bullett. 'He was news when he disappeared and he'll be news when you find him. But until then ... ' He shrugged. 'Apart from the people who didn't get their letters on Friday, the general public couldn't care less.'

'You knew him well, didn't you?' asked Pitt.

'I suppose so. As well as most people.'

'We may be seeing him on Wednesday,' the Inspector told him. 'Care to come along?'

The reporter gazed incredulously from one to the other of the two policemen. His eyes narrowed.

'You're pulling my leg,' he declared eventually. 'What's the big idea? You wouldn't be wearing out your backsides in this office if you knew where to lay your hands on Laurie.'

'And you're jumping to conclusions,' answered Pitt. 'We don't know where he is now. But we know where he may be on Wednesday afternoon.'

Incredulity gave way to amusement. 'You do, eh?'

'We do. Our trouble is that we wouldn't know him if we saw him. That is why I'm inviting you to come along.'

Bullett hesitated. Then: 'Okay,' he said. 'Count me in, Inspector. I always was a sucker for fairy-tales.'

Harris came up before the magistrates on the Tuesday morning. He pleaded guilty. Morris was in court, and caused a ripple of surprise by offering to pay his neighbour's fine if one was imposed. The chairman talked at length about turning the other cheek, complimented Morris on his offer, and bound Harris over on payment of costs.

The two neighbours left the court together.

'Thank goodness that's over,' said Pitt. 'And no awkward reference to Laurie, praise the Lord!'

'I wouldn't have cast Morris in the rôle of Good Samaritan, despite his geniality,' said Dick. 'It just shows how one can be mistaken.'

That afternoon, with Hennessy's assistance, they completed their plans for the arrest of the blackmailer. Avery was uneasy when told that he would have to carry out the instructions given in the letter. 'I hope to goodness nothing goes wrong,' he said fervently. 'What about the money? Have I actually got to find

162

two hundred quid?'

'That's up to you, sir. Personally, I would suggest newspaper.'

'Newspaper it is, then. Anything else?'

'No. But catch that bus tomorrow, Mr Avery, and don't hang around after you've posted the parcels. Leave that to us. It is your job to get back to the Red Lion and catch the next bus home. If my guess is right you've no need to worry.'

Avery stood up and held out his hand.

'I shall, of course. So would you in my place. But I'll be there, Inspector — and good luck to you.'

He departed cheerfully enough, but he was not so happy on Wednesday, when he boarded the Rawsley bus at twenty minutes past two in the afternoon. The confidence Inspector Pitt had inspired in him had begun to evaporate soon after leaving the police-station on Tuesday. By the morning, following a sleepless night, he was nervy and despondent. He had been foolish, he thought, to consult the police. Better to have scraped around and raised the money rather than jeopardize his whole future. The police were gambling on a hunch; but what were they staking? Absolutely nothing. It was he would would have to pay if their hunch was wrong.

By lunch-time he had convinced himself that the plan must fail. Susan would get Eve's letters, and he would lose his job. Only the realization that it was now too late to raise the money made him go through with it.

He carried the two packages conspicuously in his hand as he mounted to the top deck of the bus and took a seat at the back. The arrival of each fresh passenger caused him momentary alarm. He could not know if he was being watched, if the blackmailer perhaps intended to travel on the same bus. He even experienced an odd feeling of guilt towards the unknown man. He was deceiving him, luring him into a trap. Not for the first time he wondered if the phoney packages looked what they were. Just how thick was a wad of one hundred one-pound notes?

Since he had subconsciously assumed that the blackmailer would be a man, he gave no heed to the women passengers.

He did not look at the woman on the seat in front until she turned and spoke. Only then did he recognize his neighbour, Mrs Gill.

'Fancy meeting you on a bus, Mr Avery! I thought you went everywhere by car.'

He was annoyed that she should be there. Apart from his dislike of the woman, he did not want a witness to whatever might happen that afternoon. And certainly not such a busybody as Mrs Gill.

'The car's in dock,' he answered shortly, his eyes on a tall, shabby-looking man who had just boarded the bus.

'How trying,' said Mrs Gill. 'But it always happens, doesn't it? They let you down when you need them most. Are you going to Rawsley?'

He nodded. The shabby man had sat down on the other side, a few seats ahead. Avery was sure that he had glanced back at him before doing so.

His hands began to sweat.

'So am I,' said Mrs Gill. She found considerable satisfaction in having her neighbour at her mercy, unprotected for once by that supercilious wife of his. 'I'm going to visit my daughter. Her husband has a fruit-farm there, you know. Doing very nicely, too. One child, they've got — a boy. And a real imp of mischief if ever there was one. Business or pleasure, Mr Avery?'

The question was so out of context that Avery, whose attention was still focused on the shabby man, looked at her in bewilderment. But Mrs Gill, who normally never deserted a topic until she had pursued it to the bitter end, had already forgotten this one. She was on her feet and with bulging, excited eyes was gazing down over his shoulder into the street.

'Heavens!' she exclaimed. 'There's that man again!'

To Avery at that moment there could be only one man. Forgetful that his neighbour was ignorant of his secret, he jumped to his feet and looked fearfully in the direction in which the woman pointed.

'Where?' he asked quickly. And then, realizing his mistake: 'What man?'

'The one who was watching my house Saturday afternoon,' said Mrs Gill. 'Look! There he goes! Outside Lewis's.'

Avery looked. But the pavement was crowded with shoppers, and he could not tell which was the man Mrs Gill had indicated.

'I'm sure it was him,' she said. 'I didn't see his face, but it was the way he walked. I ought to have told the Inspector about that, didn't I? Pity I never thought of it.'

Her glance left the street and came to rest on Avery's white, strained face. For a moment she looked at him speculatively.

'Maybe the Inspector was right,' she said, as the bus started jerkily. 'Perhaps it wasn't my house he was watching. It could have been yours — couldn't it, Mr Avery?'

6

Maybe Murder to Follow

Mike Bullett glanced at his watch, at the silent constable behind him, and then once more fixed his gaze on the letter-box. From his viewpoint in the attic at Goshawks he could see it clearly — could see also a hundred yards or so up the lane. It was that way the postman would come; that Laurie might come, the Inspector had said. Beneath the box the lane was obscured from his vision by the high stone wall of the house and the tall trees that fringed it. But what happened below the box did not matter. Not to him, unless it were to provide him with copy; although he was sceptical of that also. It was the box itself he must watch; it was the box and the lane above it that would hold all his interest in the affair.

If he had any interest. But then, why should the police try to fool him? There must be a cogent reason behind their preparations.

He felt his eyes water. The red box danced blurrily on the other side of the window, and he blinked. There was no need to focus his attention so rigidly. There would be ample warning of the postman's approach.

'He's late,' he said, rubbing his eyes with the back of his hand. 'It's after a quarter to. If he doesn't come soon it will be too dark to recognize him.'

'They're often late in these country districts,' said the constable. 'Anything up to half an hour or more. As long as he isn't early it doesn't signify.'

Another half-hour! And already he had been gazing at that blasted letter-box for nearly an hour. He shifted uneasily, and wondered why he had always prided himself on the strength of his nerves. But then this was different. There had been nothing to break the monotony of just looking. His companion had not encouraged conversation. Not that Bullett felt like talking; he was too keyed up. If only he could relax, could take his eyes off that ruddy box for a moment!

About half an hour previously a man had walked down the lane, posted something in the letter-box, and then walked back again. Although Bullett knew nothing of the police arrangements, he guessed that somehow this man's action was important, for the constable had immediately announced it over the radio. But after that there had been nothing. Did nobody ever take a walk in that blasted village? he wondered.

'Here he comes, sir,' said the constable.

Bullett wondered momentarily at the stolid calm of the man, and then forgot him. His eyes were fixed on the peak-capped figure free-wheeling leisurely down the lane. He watched him cock a leg over the saddle and ride with one foot on the pedal, the other poised. He watched him jump off the machine and then run with it for a few hurried steps until he leant it against the telegraph-pole on which the letter-box was mounted.

'Is that Laurie, sir?' asked the constable.

Michael Bullett shook his head

absently. The postman had his back to him, had unlocked the box, and was emptying the scanty mail into his bag. So intent was Bullett on the man's actions that he fancied he heard the clang as the door of the box closed, the faint noise of the key turning in the lock. The postman vanished, to reappear a moment later inside the gates of Goshawks. The reporter had a clear view of him as he cycled slowly up the drive and round to the front door of the house. Then the jutting eaves hid him from sight.

'No,' said Bullett. 'No, that isn't Laurie.'

The constable was busy once more with his radio transmitter. Bullett did not turn round, hardly listened to what the man was saying. He continued to gaze out of the window, although there was now no need for him to look and nothing to look at. Presently the postman reappeared. The reporter watched him idly as the man rounded the bend in the drive.

Suddenly his interest quickened.

'Hey!' he exclaimed. 'That isn't the

same man, constable. That's not the postman I saw a moment ago.'

'No, sir. One of our chaps has taken his place,' said the other, and began to pack up his set. 'We'll be moving now, Mr Bullett. Nothing more to be done here.'

Farther down the lane, on the far side of the wood, a large blue van was parked in front of one of the houses under construction on the new estate. Behind it was a builder's lorry loaded with materials of the trade. The drivers of both vehicles lounged at the wheel, the only other persons in sight being the men working on the estate.

Inside the van Inspector Pitt and Sergeants Ponsford and Roberts sat with Hennessy and two young constables. None of them had much to say. At the news that the postman had cleared the box, that he wasn't Laurie, they sat a little more erect. There was a grim look on their faces. If trouble was coming it would come soon.

'I hope to God Hewitt'll be all right,' Dick said anxiously. 'We don't know what sort of men we're up against.'

'Hewitt knows how to look after himself,' said Roberts. 'He's tough.'

But he too looked anxious.

The Inspector said nothing. He was as concerned as the others that no harm should come to Constable Hewitt, but he could not feel about the man as he knew his companions felt about him. To Pitt Hewitt was just a constable who had volunteered for a dangerous job. To them he was also a friend.

'Any moment now, sir,' said Roberts.

A police whistle shrilled from the direction of the woods.

At the sound the engines of van and lorry came to life, the van leaping forward as the driver of the lorry swung his vehicle squarely across the road to block it. Round the bend ahead came a black saloon car, its horn blaring as the driver saw the lorry, engine screaming in second gear, tyres shrieking as the brakes were jammed hard on. Then, with a dull thud, the car smashed into the side of the lorry, its bonnet disappearing from view underneath.

As the police poured from the van and

raced back down the road two men scrambled out of the wrecked car and ran towards the houses, leaping over ditches and piles of rubble as they made for the fields beyond.

'After 'em!' shouted Dick.

With Hennessy and one of the constables close behind him, he gave chase, calling to the builder's men to head the fugitives off. But if the men heard they took no notice, although they had stopped work and were watching the chase with interest. Cursing them under his breath, the Sergeant pounded on. He was a big man, but he moved fast over the ground. He was gaining on the two in front when one of them stopped and turned. Dick saw the glint of metal in the man's hand and with a yell to the others he flung himself to the ground, almost knocking the wind out of his body. With his face pressed close to the wet soil, he heard the report of a gun. A bullet sang its way over his head and thudded into the ground behind.

'Damn and blast it!' he swore, straining his body against the earth, trying to sink into it. There was little fear in him, but a deep anger that the man ahead should hold the whip-hand, could make him grovel for his life. It was the first time he had ever faced a gunman.

Twice more the gun barked and the bullets sang past him. One hit a stone and went ricocheting off into the distance. He heard a faint cry behind him, but did not dare to look round.

Then there was silence.

Cautiously the Sergeant raised his head. The men in front were on the run again, now fifty yards away; sprinting past the houses, making for the fields and the woods beyond. He scrambled to his feet. Hennessy had been quicker than he, was already some distance ahead. Dick looked behind him quickly. A young constable was at his heels, panting. There was a hint of fear in his eyes, but he ran doggedly on.

What has happened to Loy? wondered Dick. He remembered the ricocheting bullet and his heart sank.

As the fugitives ran under a scaffolding one of the workmen acted. A shower of bricks came clattering down, some landing squarely on the target. The leading man dropped, and his companion, unable to avoid him, tripped and fell. With a shout of triumph the police hurled themselves at the prostrate men.

But their triumph was short-lived. The second man was too quick for them, was up on his feet and away before they could reach him. With dismay Dick saw that he still held the gun.

Leaving the constable to deal with the apparently unconscious man on the ground, Dick and Hennessy, with Roberts close behind, went after the gunman. They had left the houses and were stumbling across rutted, boulder-strewn land. It was hard going, and they could hear the man, now only a few yards ahead of them, wheezing noisily. We'll get him before he reaches the wood, thought Dick — if he doesn't use his gun.

The gunman must have had the same thought. He turned, backing away from them, the gun poised in an unsteady hand. Resisting a wild desire to rush him, Dick dropped quickly. But Hennessy was either slower or less cautious. As the gun cracked Dick saw him clap both hands to his stomach, stumble forward a few steps, and then collapse on the ground.

A wild rage seized the Sergeant. As the man fired again he was on his feet and running, his only thought to get his hands round the other's neck and squeeze the life out of him. The gun clicked harmlessly, and he saw the terror in the man's eyes. Then he leapt forward, his fingers closed on the fugitive's throat, and they fell together, the Sergeant uppermost.

'You bastard! You murderous bastard!' He spat the words softly between half-clenched teeth, and each word was punctuated by a vicious blow of the gunman's head against the stony ground. By the time they had prised his fingers loose and pulled him clear of his victim the latter was unconscious.

'Leave him to the law, Dick,' said Pitt's quiet voice. 'You're a policeman, not an executioner.'

Dick nodded. He felt suddenly cold and empty and very, very tired. As anger left him he remembered the cause of it and walked unsteadily across to where a constable knelt by the side of the unconscious Hennessy.

Pitt followed him.

'There's an ambulance and a doctor on the way,' he said. 'He'll still have a chance if we can get him to hospital quickly.'

Dick stood for a moment looking down at the man's pale face. He liked Hennessy; Hennessy had guts. Then he turned away. He wanted something to do, something to make him forget. He began to walk quickly back towards the road, the Inspector at his side.

The sound of the shooting had brought people from their houses. There was a crowd on the road. Michael Bullett detached himself from it and came to meet the two officers.

'Quite a battle, eh?' he remarked. 'Anyone hurt?'

'Hennessy,' said Pitt. 'You wouldn't know him.' Now that the reporter had served his turn he wanted to be rid of him. But in fairness to the man he had to give him a brief account of the arrests.

'So the postman wasn't Laurie?' he said.

'No,' said Bullett. He was gazing at the battered features of the gunman, as the latter was assisted, none too gently, towards captivity. 'What happened to him? Someone beat him up?'

'He was injured resisting arrest,' answered Pitt. 'He wouldn't be Laurie, I suppose?'

'No. Nor's the red-haired chap they've just shoved in the van. Never set eyes on them before. Is this man Hennessy bad, Inspector?'

'Pretty bad,' said Pitt, with a quick look at Dick. 'Hit in the stomach.'

Constable Hewitt, still dressed as a postman, was standing by the van. The Inspector went over to him.

'Good work, Hewitt. You all right?'

'Yes, thank you, sir. They held me up just where you said. No rough stuff, and I didn't ask for any.'

'Did they pull a gun on you?'

'No, sir.'

At Tanmouth police-station the two men were formally charged and put in the only available cells. 'I imagine the dark chap's the boss of that outfit,' said Pitt. 'We'll tackle him first.'

But the gunman showed no great willingness to talk. The station sergeant recognized him as a small-time crook who had not previously been known to carry a gun. His name was Sid Blake.

'Want to make a statement?' asked Pitt.

The man scowled but said nothing.

'You're in a spot, Blake,' Pitt said. 'You've heard the charges against you. They're bad enough — but if Hennessy dies . . . '

He shrugged his shoulders.

'I'm not talking,' said Blake. He glared across the room at Dick. 'I'm sorry it wasn't you as bought it, copper. But I'll get you later.'

The Sergeant took a quick step forward, his fists clenched.

'Why, you slug — ' he began; and then stopped, feeling Pitt's restraining hand on his arm.

'Slug, is it?' The gunman grinned evilly 'Slug, eh? Well, I've drilled holes through bigger cabbages than you, copper.'

'Take him away,' said Pitt, disgusted.

'Just a minute, sir.' Dick had seen the terror in the man's eyes when he had threatened him, and knew Blake had not forgotten the beating he had already received at his hands. His present insolence was born of the knowledge that the Inspector would allow no physical persuasion to be used.

But if no Inspector was present . . .

He took his brother-in-law aside. The gunman watched warily as they talked in low tones. Then:

'All right,' said Pitt. 'But no force, mind.'

'There won't be a mark on him, sir,' said Dick, and winked.

Blake saw the wink. Before Pitt could reach the door he had changed his mind. 'I'll talk,' he said sullenly. 'But don't leave me alone with that bastard. I don't trust him.'

'Cut out the pleasantries,' Pitt said sternly. 'What happened to Laurie?'

Blake looked at him in astonishment. 'Who's Laurie?' he asked.

'The postman. The man whose mail

you pinched Friday afternoon.'

'Oh, him. We didn't have nothink to do with him. All we done was to pick up the bag when he threw it away.'

Pitt stared at him.

'Start at the beginning and let's have it in detail,' he said.

It was not a very lucid statement. He had been visiting a friend in Grange Road, said Blake, leaving his mate Willie Sullivan to mind the car. He had just rejoined Sullivan when the postman passed them on his bicycle, followed by a car. The latter pulled up ahead of the postman, who dumped his bicycle on the grass, jumped into the car, and was driven off.

'Some chap come along just after, but soon as he had gone we had a dekko and found the mail-bag. We left the bike — it weren't no use to us.'

'The car,' said Pitt. 'What make was it? Did you see the number?'

'A black Austin it was. The driver was a little chap; or maybe it was a woman. I dunno. Nor I don't know the number, either.'

'All right. This friend of yours in Grange Road — where does he live?'

'That's his business,' said Blake. 'He don't want nothink to do with the police. He's very partic'lar.'

'Any friend of yours, Blake, is likely to have quite a lot to do with the police,' said Dick. 'Including Mr Morris.'

The man looked at him innocently. 'Morris? Who's he?' he asked.

'Never mind,' said Pitt, frowning. 'What have you done with the mail?'

'Knocked off some of it and burnt the rest.'

'And your attempt to blackmail Mr Avery? How about that?'

The man shrugged. 'Now you're talking riddles,' he declared. 'I don't know nothink about blackmailing this Mr What's-is-name.'

Willie Sullivan might have red hair, but there was nothing else fiery about him now. He was no longer the dandified spiv as described by the bus conductor, but a very frightened young man. Pitt sensed his fear and played on it, repeating the warning he had given Blake.

'But I didn't have a gun, sir,' pleaded Sullivan. 'It was Blake done the shooting, not me.'

'That makes no difference,' said Pitt. 'You knew he had a gun and you knew he intended to use it. You're as guilty as he is, Sullivan.'

'But I didn't know, Inspector! He never told me. It was only when we was on the run . . . I couldn't do nothink about it then.'

Pitt shook his head. 'You're in a spot, Sullivan. If I were you I'd pray damned hard that the wounded man pulls through.'

The youth's statement agreed with Blake's as far as it went. He didn't know the name of Blake's friend, he said, nor in which house he lived; it was his first visit to Grange Road. He had got out of the car while waiting for Blake, not wishing to be caught by the police in a stolen car.

He denied all knowledge of the letter to Avery.

'I can't read nor write,' he confessed. 'If there was a letter Blake must have wrote it.'

'But you were in on it? You knew the purpose behind this afternoon's hold-up?'

'He just said it'd be a good haul. He said it would be easy.' Reminded once more of his peril, he added earnestly, 'Blake didn't have a gun Friday, Inspector. How was I to know he'd pull one today?'

Pitt ignored this. When Sullivan had been taken back to his cell he said, 'Looks like we've been chasing the wrong bloody car, Dick. It's the Austin we want, not the Vauxhall. These two thugs are incidentals — a couple of red herrings.'

The Sergeant swore blasphemously.

'Robbery with violence, blackmail, being in unlawful possession of firearms, resisting arrest, shooting at and wounding an officer — and maybe murder to follow. And that's only a few of the charges against them. Damned big incidentals, aren't they?'

'Yes. But they are getting us no nearer to Laurie, and it's Laurie I'm after. We've got to trace that Austin, Dick. Blake, Sullivan, Harris, Avery, Mrs Gill — they all all saw it. That's why I think those two birds were telling the truth. About Laurie, anyway.'

'A small man or a woman,' said Dick. 'That's how Blake described the driver. We haven't got much to go on, have we?'

'I'm not taking too much notice of that,' said the Inspector. 'It is very easy to misjudge the height of a person sitting down. Particularly under the circumstances we have in mind.'

Superintendent Howard joined them. 'I've just heard from the hospital,' he said. 'They think Hennessy has a fighting chance.'

Pitt gave him an account of the afternoon's arrests, and explained the impasse to which it had brought them. 'I had begun to think Laurie might be dead if he didn't show up at Rawsley. Gofer's belief in the man rather impressed me. But that note to Bullett indicates he's alive all right. Or was, when the note was written. And it looks like he got into the Austin of his own free will. He must be hiding out with friends.'

'There isn't even a motive now,' said Dick. 'If he really did abandon the mail, then it wasn't robbery. What the devil is the fellow up to?'

'We've heard from the Scarborough police,' said the Superintendent. 'The Alsters have booked rooms at the hotel all right, but they are not due to arrive there until the twenty-third. We can't wait that long; we'll have to broadcast for them.'

'Ten to one it wasn't their car,' Pitt said gloomily. 'And if we have to check on every Austin in the country ... We'd better make a start on Carrington's, although there's absolutely nothing to connect him with Laurie. And I think another call on Mrs L. is indicated. Damn it, the woman must know *something*!'

There was a light showing through the curtained windows of the living-room at No. 25 Tilnet Close. But the long pause that elapsed between their knock and Mrs Laurie's response suggested that their visit was either unwelcome or inopportune.

Yet she did not seem surprised to see them. As she stood in the doorway Dick was again impressed by her unusual beauty.

'What is it this time?' she asked. 'I've got company.'

'I'm sorry,' said Pitt. 'We won't keep you long.'

The living-room door opened and Michael Bullett walked out. He grinned at them.

'Let them in, Jane,' he said. 'It doesn't pay to obstruct the police. But I'd have you know, Inspector, that you've spoilt a very pleasant tête-à-tête.'

Despite Bullett's cheerful exuberance, the Inspector fancied that the reporter was not altogether pleased to see them. His gaiety had a false ring. Mrs Laurie was sullen and embarrassed. Was that because she had been found in Bullett's company? She had certainly frowned at his reference to a tête-à-tête.

He wondered too at the reporter's use of her first name. Their acquaintanceship had seemingly progressed rapidly in the few days they had known each other. Bullett must have taken full advantage of Laurie's written request to keep an eye on his wife, and was obviously finding the task to his liking. And, eyeing the girl's vivid beauty, the Inspector could appreciate the reason.

She wore a wine-red jumper, high-necked and close-fitting, that emphasized the curves of her figure. Her slim legs were encased in nylon, her dark hair had recently been waved and set. She looks more like a minor film star, thought Pitt, than a country postman's wife. How does she do it on the pay?

Or perhaps she doesn't?

It was an idle thought which was to assume greater prominence in his mind during the course of the interview. Noting the attraction which the girl had for Bullett — and even for Dick Ponsford — he wondered whether she might not be, as Dick had previously suggested, the cause of her husband's flight. Had he become so sickened of her affairs with other men — or with one man in particular — that, disillusioned after two years of such a marriage, he had decided, perhaps on the spur of the moment, to clear out?

A little delving into the girl's past might prove profitable, Pitt decided; and he remembered the fancy that had come to him on his previous visit to Tilnet Close.

She seemed unaffected by the news that her husband appeared to be innocent of the charge of which he had been suspected.

'It's a twice-told tale, Inspector,' Bullett explained. 'I've just been putting her wise to what happened out at Rawsley this afternoon.'

Pitt frowned. He had stressed that Bullett's report for the *Chronicle* should not connect the arrests with Laurie's disappearance. He hoped the man had been more discreet professionally than he had been with his girl friend.

'It is an offence in itself to abandon the mail,' he said. 'Your husband isn't out of the wood yet, Mrs Laurie. But unless he acted out of sheer lunacy he must have had a reason. And if it wasn't robbery — well, what was it?'

'I'm sure I don't know,' she said.

'It was connected either with his job or

with his private affairs,' the Inspector persisted. 'More likely the latter. That is why we are here, Mrs Laurie.'

She gave Bullett a fleeting glance. Pitt interpreted this as meaning that she objected to being questioned in front of the reporter. But when he suggested that the latter should leave — a suggestion which Bullett immediately seconded — she vetoed it firmly.

'Mr Bullett was a friend of my husband,' she said. 'I would rather he stayed. Anyway, there's nothing more I can tell you.'

'Perhaps there is, Mrs Laurie. For instance, had you known your husband long before you married him?'

'Yes. Several years.'

'Was yours a long engagement?'

She hesitated, and again glanced at the reporter before replying. Has she taken him into her confidence? wondered Pitt. If so, whose side is he on now? Better deal warily with Mr Michael Bullett, he decided.

'No,' said Mrs Laurie.

'How long? A month?'

'We weren't engaged at all. We just got married.'

Pitt considered this. If she and Laurie had known each other for some years, why the hasty marriage? Not the usual reason for haste, anyway; and a girl with her looks could not have lacked suitors. Why discard them all and rush into marriage with Laurie? The missing postman was no dashing hero, by all accounts. A sober, taciturn man given to irrational moods and a penchant for fish.

'Were you engaged to someone else previously, Mrs Laurie?' he asked.

The grey eyes narrowed, a frown wrinkled the smooth forehead. She turned once more to Bullett, obviously seeking his counsel.

'You're putting me in a tough spot, Inspector,' the reporter said awkwardly, more serious than usual. 'I'm all for law and order, of course, and out to give you what help I can. But Laurie asked me to look after his wife — you know that. So I'm pulled both ways, you see. Naturally I'd advise her to tell you everything she

192

can which may bear on her husband's disappearance, but — well, what the devil can a previous engagement have to do with it? Seems a bit unnecessary to pry into that, doesn't it?'

'You're a reporter, Mr Bullett. You should know that the police do not ask questions out of idle curiosity,' Pitt answered brusquely. He turned to the girl. 'There is always the possibility that your husband has met with foul play, Mrs Laurie. It may be that these two men we arrested this afternoon know more about that than they have admitted. On the other hand, we cannot ignore the fact that love and jealousy are two of the strongest motives for murder. A previous suitor who resented your marriage to another man — '

'Steady on,' Bullett protested. 'What about the note Laurie wrote me? Doesn't that prove he is alive and kicking? You don't want to go putting the wind up her to no purpose.'

'Someone else could have written that note, Mr Bullett. There was no signature.'

They both stared at him.

'You mean you think he didn't write it?' asked Bullett.

'I didn't say that. I said it was possible. And even if he did write it, a lot may have happened since then. It was posted on Monday, presumably — and today is Wednesday.' It annoyed Pitt that the reporter should monopolize the conversation. It was the girl he wanted to get at. He said, facing her, 'It is now five days since your husband disappeared, Mrs Laurie. If, as you say, there was no quarrel between you — well, isn't that a long while for a man to leave his wife in ignorance of what has happened to him? Wouldn't he have written? Sent you money, perhaps — if he had it?'

She made no answer, but sat with eyes cast down, her fingers plucking at her skirt. Once more it was Bullett who spoke.

'Exactly, Inspector. And Laurie *has* sent her money. Does that satisfy you?'

The two police officers stared at him. It was a startling announcement. 'May I see the letter, please?' said Pitt.

She got up and walked over to a small

bureau. 'It came this morning,' she said, handing the Inspector an envelope.

The address was typewritten, with a Tanmouth postmark. Inside the envelope were four one-pound notes. There was no accompanying letter.

'I only knew about this when I called here, of course,' said Bullett. 'I was going to ring you later.'

'Mrs Laurie should have done that this morning,' Pitt said curtly. 'It's from your husband, ma'am?'

She shrugged her shoulders. 'I suppose so. That's just how it was when I opened it, anyway. And who else would be sending me money?'

Who, indeed, wondered Dick.

'You have no relatives living locally?' asked Pitt.

'No.'

He pocketed the envelope. 'I'll keep this, if I may,' he said. 'Now, about that previous engagement, Mrs Laurie. Was there one?'

She did not protest that the reason for asking the question no longer existed. 'Yes, there was,' she said, a defiant ring to

195

her voice. 'And now I suppose you want to know all about it?'

'If you please.'

'He was a schoolmaster,' said the girl. 'He didn't approve of my doing the things I like doing. He was furious when I went to the palais on my own, for instance. Well, I wasn't going to have him laying down the law like that — and before we were married, too. So I just told him we were through, and that was that.'

It was a long speech for her.

'And where is this gentleman now?'

'Goodness knows. He left Tanmouth just before I was married. Somebody told me he'd got a job in Hampshire, but I don't know.'

'And his name?'

'That's my business. And his. I'm not having him dragged into this — he didn't even know my husband.'

They gave Michael Bullett a lift when they left. He was apologetic for his championship of Mrs Laurie. 'But if a chap has saved your life you can't turn him down when he asks for help, can you?' he said.

'You must find it rather trying,' Dick said innocently. 'No doubt she takes up quite a lot of your time.'

The reporter grinned at him. 'I'm not complaining,' he said. 'I never was one to neglect my homework.'

'This schoolmaster,' said Pitt, when they had dropped Bullett. 'I'll get our fellows to trace him. It shouldn't be too difficult. Someone in the town must have known Mrs L. when she was engaged to him.'

'I suppose so. But I'm with Bullett in this, Loy. I think you're off on a false trail.'

'Maybe I am,' agreed the Inspector; 'but I want to be certain of that before I abandon it.'

At the police-station there was a message from Dorothy Weston asking them to ring her.

'It's about Miss Fratton, Inspector,' she said over the phone. 'You asked me to let you know what her burglar had taken.'

Pitt had forgotten about Miss Fratton's burglary, if burglary it was. He could not see any likely connection with Laurie, and so had little interest in the affair. It was really a matter for the local police.

'Anything missing?' he asked.

'It's most mysterious,' said the girl. 'The only thing he seems to have taken is a torch.'

Inspector Pitt laughed. 'I dare say he didn't take even that,' he said. 'Miss Fratton has probably mislaid it.'

'I don't think so, Inspector. It wasn't her own torch, you see. She put it on the hall-stand Friday evening, and now it isn't there. And she swears she hasn't touched it herself.'

Pitt pricked up his ears. 'Whose torch was it?' he asked.

'It belonged to the postman,' said Miss Weston. 'He dropped it in his hurry to get away from her Friday afternoon. Don't you remember her telling you about that?'

Thoughtfully the Inspector replaced the telephone-receiver. He could think of only one reason why someone should go to such lengths to recover a torch.

Fingerprints.

And why should John Laurie be so anxious that his finger prints should go undetected?

7

Deader'n a Doornail

Mrs Gill, on being requested the next morning to identify the man she had seen watching the house on Saturday afternoon, twittered and protested and was secretly delighted.

'She'll bungle it for certain,' said Dick, as they went ahead of her into the yard, where a line of men was already in position. 'She's so thrilled at the police asking for her help that she'll identify the first man she sees rather than admit failure. To a nosey-parker like Mrs Gill this is absolute bliss. And I bet she hasn't a clue, really. Her previous description of the man was just about as vague as it could be.'

But if the Sergeant was right in thinking that Mrs Gill would enjoy the identification parade, he failed to appreciate that she would therefore prolong her enjoyment to the uttermost. There was to be no snap decision. Up and down the line she went, scrutinizing each man with great thoroughness. Then she requested that they should be made to walk across the yard and back; and it was only after this manœuvre had been repeated several times that she eventually — and somewhat reluctantly — identified Blake as the man they were seeking.

'That's him,' she said confidently. 'There were several looked the same, but it was the way he walked. Sort of jerky. I noticed it particularly when I pointed him out to Mr Avery on the bus yesterday.'

This was news to the police. Avery had neglected to mention his encounter with Mrs Gill.

'Probably making sure that Avery was on the bus,' said Pitt. 'He had bags of time to get to Rawsley by car after the bus left.'

'What do you think he was doing in Grange Road Saturday afternoon?' asked Dick. 'It might have gummed the works if he'd been caught.'

'Getting a line on his victim, I dare say.

He would want to know something about Avery's style of living before deciding how much he could hope to milk him for. Only Morris knew his identity — always supposing it *was* Morris he visited Friday evening. And that's a point we might try to clear up right now.'

But there was no answer to their knock at No. 18. An inquiry next door elicited the information from Mrs Harris that her neighbour had left the house shortly after nine o'clock that morning. He had told her husband he would be away for a few days.

'And very wise of him, too,' commented Pitt. 'He must have guessed he was due to answer some awkward questions. Well, he can't help us with Laurie; Morris can wait. You know, Dick, I'd been hoping it was Laurie Mrs Gill saw outside her house on Saturday. At least we would have been certain then that no harm had come to the fellow. As it is, no one seems to have seen him since he passed the Archers' house on Friday evening.'

'But two people have heard from him,'

said Dick. 'Personally, I'm not losing any sleep on Laurie's account. As for Morris, I suppose he read about Blake and Sullivan in this morning's papers. That would put the wind up him.'

'Either that or Harris tipped him off that we had been asking questions.'

'Why not ask Harris?'

William Harris was nervous but defiant. Yes, he said, he had certainly mentioned to Morris that the police had been inquisitive about him. And why shouldn't he? They hadn't told him not to.

The broadcast appeal for the Alsters was answered that day. Mr Alster had reported to the police at Peterborough, where he and his family were staying with relatives. They had left Tanmouth, he said, at 2.30 on the Friday afternoon and were in Peterborough by 6.30. This latter time had been confirmed by the relatives.

'That lets him out, then,' said Pitt. 'Blast!'

A letter addressed to him was lying on his desk. He picked it up idly and slit the envelope.

'So now we check on all the black Austin saloons in the country.' The Sergeant's voice was lugubrious. 'If we live that long, of course.'

Pitt passed the letter to him. 'What do you make of that?' he asked.

It was typewritten and brief. It said that the police might be interested to learn that on the previous Friday afternoon, at about five o'clock, Donald Heath, living at No. 9 Grange Road, had been seen by the writer to rush from his house and attack the postman. The writer was unable to say what the outcome of the attack had been.

The letter was unsigned. There was no address.

'Someone with a grudge against Heath,' observed Dick. 'It's probably true, though — hence that black eye of his. How about Miss Fratton? Heath is one of her rivals for Miss Weston's affections, and I wouldn't put anything past that old harridan.'

'Perhaps. But Heath would have had to chase the postman quite a distance for Miss Fratton to witness the incident from her window. And I don't suppose she was actually in the street. Besides, would she split on someone who had assaulted a postman? You know how she feels about them.'

'That's true,' Dick agreed. 'She would be more likely to fall on his neck and kiss him. Ugh! The very thought of it makes me shudder. Talk about a fate worse than death!'

Pitt laughed. 'It isn't likely to happen to you,' he said.

'No. I'll take good care of that. But if Miss Fratton didn't write it who did?'

'Carrington, probably. I admit he doesn't seem the type — but his house is not far from Heath's, and both of them are running after Miss Weston. It's a mean way of disposing of a rival; but then love, I'm told, does funny things to a man. And if Carrington's Austin is the car we are looking for he could well have witnessed the assault on his way to pick up Laurie. Did you notice if he had a typewriter?'

'Yes. A portable. It was on that table by the fireplace. But isn't all this — the car, the note — rather flimsy evidence on which to suspect a chap like Carrington? And don't forget he had an alibi for Friday.'

'He had one, yes. That doesn't mean he's going to keep it. I agree there's little against him — come to that, there's precious little against anyone except Blake and Sullivan — but it won't do any harm to investigate him more closely. Until Laurie is picked up, or someone finds his body, we've nothing to go on except the Austin. And we may as well start with Carrington's.'

'What about Heath? You're not going to ignore this letter, are you?'

'Of course not. But Heath hasn't a car — it couldn't have been Heath who picked up Laurie. I admit to some curiosity, however, as to what prompted him to hit the postman.'

'From the look of his eye it was the postman who hit him,' said the Sergeant. 'And that doesn't say much for his knowledge of self-defence. Heath is quite a lamp-post, and Laurie's only a little chap.'

'Yes, that's true.' Pitt's voice was thoughtful. 'You know, Dick, there may be something there. Why is it — ?'

He paused, frowning.

'Why is what?' asked the Sergeant.

'Oh, nothing. I was day-dreaming again.' The Inspector picked up his trilby and jammed it on his head. 'Come on, let's pay friend Heath another visit.'

He was still frowning as they left the building.

The dominant fear in Donald Heath's mind had been dispelled. Aunt Ellen had coughed up; had coughed up handsomely. The cheque had arrived on Wednesday morning; the borrowed money had been replaced. But he had other worries to brood over, and was no more pleased at receiving a visit from the police now than he had been on Saturday morning.

'Tell them I'm out,' he said to his mother. 'Get rid of them somehow.'

'Don't be a fool, Donald.' Mrs Heath's voice was sharp. 'You can't treat the police like that. If they want to see you, then see you they will. If not now, then later. And don't look so guilty. Try smiling for a change; it might suit you.'

But his smile was a sickly effort. It faded altogether at the Inspector's first question.

'Who says I attacked the postman?' asked Heath.

'That's neither here nor there, sir. The point is — did you?'

'Yes.' If there had been a witness to the incident there was no point in denying it. 'At least, not the way you mean. I didn't hit him; it was he who hit me. That's how I got this black eye.'

'But you must have threatened him? He wouldn't have hit you for no reason at all.'

'Well, he may have thought I was going to attack him. But all I did was to run after him. I can't think why he should have lammed out the way he did.'

'What made you run after him?'

'I was expecting a letter.' The young man chose his words carefully. He did not want them to probe too deeply into that aspect of the affair. 'A most important letter. I was all keyed up, waiting for it to arrive. And when it didn't I . . . well, I thought the man might have mislaid it. I knew it ought to have come by that post.'

'And what happened then?'

'I called to him from the door, but he said that was all. And then — well, I lost my head, I suppose. Silly of me, I know — but I just chased up the road after him. I'm not sure what I meant to do. Ask him to look in his bag, perhaps — something like that. But before I could say a word he turned and hit me smack in the eye.'

'And then?'

'Well, I hadn't been prepared for anything like that. The blow sent me flying, and by the time I'd picked myself up and collected my wits he was some way down the road. I thought of going after him. But I'd cooled off a bit by then, and I realized I'd made a fool of myself. So I came home.'

'You are a tall man,' the Inspector said thoughtfully. 'The postman, by all accounts, was on the short side. How did he manage to knock you down so easily?'

'Well, he did.' Heath's tone was defiant. 'I ought to know, didn't I? As I said, he caught me unawares. And come to think of it, he didn't strike me as being particularly short, either. I never got a good look at him, of course — it was dark, and raining like hell — but I'd have said he was tall. Still, you know best. I'm not arguing about it.'

When they had left the house Pitt said, 'Hear that, Dick? Why did Heath get the impression that the postman was tall?'

The Sergeant laughed.

'If someone knocked *you* down would *you* admit that he was only half your size? Of course you wouldn't. It's true that neither of us has seen Laurie, but everyone — Templar, Gofer, Mrs Laurie — they all say he's on the short side. So did Bullett. Heath was merely supplying himself with an excuse, that's all.'

'Perhaps,' said Pitt. 'But, tall or short, it's an odd way for a postman to behave.'

Workmen were busy replacing the soil where the ditch had been dug across the U-shaped path of No. 14. As they walked up the other arm of the U Dick said, 'That would be where Laurie tripped and lost his torch. He would have entered from this side, and wouldn't know the ditch was there.'

Miss Fratton was out. The Sergeant danced a *pas seul* on her front porch, to the amusement of the workmen.

'That's the first lucky break we've had,' he said. 'Let's hope she's always out, the old so-and-so.'

'We'll try Miss Weston,' said Pitt.

'It'll be a pleasure,' said the Sergeant.

It was certainly a change, thought Pitt, to be greeted with a smile. Dorothy Weston seemed almost pleased to see them.

'I suppose you've come about Miss Fratton,' she said. 'It's odd about the torch, isn't it? Why should the burglar have taken that and nothing else?'

'I don't know, miss. What sort of torch was it?'

But Miss Weston had no information on that point, and the subject was dropped. Pitt asked after her missing birthday present.

'Oh, didn't I tell you? I'm sorry. Yes, it was a brooch. It never turned up, of course, but my friend got me another.

Absolutely identical, he said it was. Wait! I'll show you.'

They examined the brooch, which was of unusual design. When Pitt said so she seemed pleased.

'Yes, isn't it? But then, being an artist, you would expect Mr Carrington to choose something out of the ordinary, wouldn't you?'

So it was Carrington who had given it to her. An idea was forming in the Inspector's mind. 'Did he have the first brooch copied?' he asked.

'Oh, no. He had bought it from a firm in London — look, there's the name on the box — and they happened to have another the same. I think it's perfectly heavenly. I'm terribly thrilled with it.'

She did not add that her pleasure was intensified by the fact that Jock had given her the brooch only the previous evening. If he was prepared to go to such trouble over a birthday present did it mean that he was regretting his previous remarks on marriage? Perhaps not — but it was nice to dwell on the possibility.

'I hope you won't think this an

impertinent question, miss, but is there some sort of an understanding between you and Mr Carrington?' asked Pitt.

'Oh, no, Inspector. At least, he hasn't asked me to marry him, if that's what you mean.'

But you wish he had, thought Pitt.

She's got nice legs, Dick reflected — and asked after her ankle.

'It's much better, thank you. It still hurts if I put my full weight on it, but I can hobble around.' Dorothy smiled at him. She liked big men. 'How about the postman? Have you found him yet?'

'No, miss, we haven't.' It was the Inspector who answered. 'Tell me, did you see Mr Carrington on Friday?'

'No.' Dorothy remembered how she had hoped he would call. 'That was my birthday, you know. He telephoned me in the morning, of course, just to greet me. And I rang him up later, after the postman had been. Or hadn't been, rather. I wanted to tell him his present hadn't arrived, but he was out. At least . . . ' She frowned. 'I *think* he was out.'

'What makes you say that, miss?'

She smiled ruefully.

'I was a bit peeved at the time. You see, I heard the telephone ring in the bungalow, and I could have sworn someone picked up the receiver and then replaced it without answering. And as he'd told me he was going up to Town that day — for lunch, he said, and to see a film — I began to suspect he had been fooling me. I thought he had another girl there, and I'm not used to being given the brush-off by my boy friends.'

The Inspector replied gallantly that he could well believe that. 'What time did you phone him, miss?' he asked.

'About ten to five. You know, I've seen him twice since then, but I haven't liked to ask him straight out if he *was* at home that afternoon. I told myself I was being sensible; but I rather suspect it was because I didn't want to risk a possible blow to my self-esteem. Are you married, Inspector?'

Slightly taken aback by the question, Pitt replied that he was not.

'Ah! Then I can't expect you to

understand women. They're odd creatures, though I say it myself.'

'I thought she was going to propose to you,' said Dick, as they left the house. 'It looks as though she's got you taped as a possible if Carrington lets her down. I hope you like red hair.'

But his brother-in-law was in no mood for frivolity.

'Looks like we're on to something, Dick,' he said. 'I know they are an unreliable bunch of witnesses, but everyone from Nos. 9 to 19 says that the postman called shortly before five o'clock. Yet Miss Plant saw him going into Carrington's bungalow at four-twenty-five, didn't she? Doesn't that look as though he spent some time there?'

'There or thereabouts. But doing what?'

'Ah! There you have me. Carrington is supposed to be well off. I can't see him going into partnership with the postman in order to pinch half a sackful of mail. Yet if it wasn't that — well, what was it that detained Laurie? Carrington was at home, if Miss Weston's evidence means anything at all. And why should he bother to establish an alibi if he wasn't up to some mischief?'

'But what is he supposed to have an alibi *for?*' asked the Sergeant. 'As far as we know, the only person to have committed a crime is Laurie.'

'That may be so. But it's our job to investigate Laurie's disappearance, and the driver of that Austin must know something. And if the driver was Carrington I want to know why he chooses to keep quiet about it.'

'Okay. Do we tackle him now?'

'Yes. But I don't want to alarm him. Just a routine check — he can't take fright at that. It should have been done before, but perhaps it's as well that it wasn't. He will have been lulled into a false sense of security. And if his alibi was at all shaky in places, it will be even shakier by now.'

But Jock Carrington appeared in no way disturbed by another visit from the police, and readily supplied them with an itinerary of his movements on the Friday.

If it was an alibi, it was not a very

original one. He had gone up to Town by the 10.33, he said, in company with Michael Bullett. They had lunched together with a friend — 'Alan Scott-Waterton, the critic. I'll give you his telephone number' — and had then gone to a cinema. He had caught the 5.47 train home, and was back at the bungalow about 7.15.

'Did Mr Bullett stay in Town with you, sir?' asked Pitt.

'No. I offered to stand him a dinner after the show, but he had to get back.'

'You didn't have dinner in Town yourself?'

'No. I'm not keen on eating out on my own.'

They had lunched at the Grosvenor, he said. He had parted from Scott-Waterton at Victoria after they had seen Bullett off on the 2.21. After that he could not remember meeting anyone he knew.

'Not even on the train coming home, Mr Carrington?'

'Not even on the train, Inspector. I know few people in Tanmouth, and I don't travel to Town regularly. Why?

Don't you believe me?'

'It's not that, sir,' said Pitt. 'But you can see for yourself how impossible it is to check a statement like that.'

'Why bother to try, then? What crime am I supposed to have committed, anyway? Abducted your postman? Why, as far as I know I've never even seen the wretched fellow.'

Inspector Pitt evaded the questions. 'We have reason to believe that the postman was picked up farther down the road by someone in a black Austin saloon,' he said slowly.

Carrington stared at him.

'And my car is an Austin saloon. So that's it, eh?'

'That's it, sir,' Pitt said laconically. 'May we have a look at the car now we're here?'

The artist picked up a key from the hall table and led the way out to the garage. 'There you are, Inspector,' he said. 'She hasn't been used since Thursday of last week.'

There was little they could hope to learn from the car itself, but they inspected the interior meticulously.

'She looks very clean, Mr Carrington,' commented the Sergeant. 'Been polished recently, hasn't she?'

The man flushed. 'I beg your pardon — I should have mentioned that. Yes, she went into Atkins' garage on Saturday for her monthly wash and brush up.'

The manager of the garage confirmed this statement. Mr Carrington, he said, always brought the car in about the middle of the month for servicing and cleaning; but on this occasion they had collected it from his house. Nor had the mechanics who had worked on the car noticed anything unusual. It was, perhaps, a little dirtier than usual. Mr Carrington did not use the car much in winter, they thought.

Pitt wasted no time. Early on Friday morning he was in Town. He did not doubt that Carrington's account of the luncheon party was correct, but he telephoned Scott-Waterton for an appointment and met him at his club.

The critic was a fussy, supercilious little man. He obviously considered it outrageous that the police should doubt any statement made by a friend of his, but he confirmed all that Carrington had said concerning the luncheon.

'After seeing Mr Bullett off at Victoria, sir, did you and Mr Carrington leave the station together?' asked Pitt.

'As far as the taxi-rank, yes. I walked across the road to the Underground, leaving him to look for a taxi.'

'And you understood he was going to a cinema?'

'I did. I heard him say so to Mr Bullett, and I had no reason to doubt his word.' His tone plainly indicated that the Inspector had no reason to doubt it either.

Pitt's next visit was to the jeweller from whom Carrington had bought the brooch for Miss Weston. The artist was apparently well-known at the shop, and the Inspector wondered how many other young ladies had been softened by similar gifts from him. He could not believe that a bachelor would otherwise have much occasion to frequent the shop.

At Pitt's description the manager

produced from beneath the counter a brooch similar to the one Miss Weston had shown him.

'That's it,' said the Inspector. 'I believe Mr Carrington ordered one to be sent to a young lady in Tanmouth. A Miss Dorothy Weston.'

'Yes, I believe he did.' The manager began to thumb through a ledger. 'Yes, here is the entry. We dispatched it on the tenth of this month. I have a note here to the effect that the brooch should be posted in time to arrive on or before the twelfth. A birthday present, I think Mr Carrington said it was.'

The Inspector nodded. 'Did he purchase a similar brooch a few days later?' he asked.

'No, Inspector.' The manager's tone was decisive. 'We had six of those brooches in all, and I still have four left. Look — you can see for yourself. And the second one was ordered by a customer for a friend in Ireland. We dispatched it yesterday.'

It's working out, thought Pitt. Carrington didn't buy a second brooch — he didn't have to, he had the original. Either he got it from Laurie when the postman called at his house (which accounted for its non-delivery to Miss Weston that afternoon), or he took it from the man after he picked him up in his car. But obviously he couldn't explain this to the girl. For her benefit he had to invent the purchase of a second brooch.

There was an I-told-you-so air about the Inspector when he confronted his brother-in-law. But Dick Ponsford did not notice it. He had news of his own.

'We've found Laurie,' he said grimly, 'and he's deader'n a doornail.'

8

It's Murder All Right

It was as a result of that broadcast for the Austin that we found him,' said the Sergeant. 'Fellow named Brown called in here this morning. He lives in Tanmouth but works in Eastbourne, and comes home for week-ends on his motor-bike. Last Friday he was late. As he was coming over the cliff road at about five-twenty he saw a black Austin parked on the grass near Coppins Point. At the time he thought it probably contained a courting couple; but after hearing the broadcast he decided to report it.

'Even with that lead it took us quite a time to find the body. It was jammed half under the rocks at the foot of the cliffs. It would have been covered by the sea at high tide, and it must have been sucked into this sort of pocket in the rocks each time the sea receded. You couldn't see it from the top of the cliffs. That's why it wasn't discovered before, I suppose; and anyway, there's precious few people get up that way during the winter. We might not have looked there ourselves if the edge of the cliff had not been broken away as though something had been lugged over it.'

'Was he drowned?' asked Pitt.

'No — strangled. It's murder all right. His face is a mess, and most of the bones in his body are broken. Some of the damage was caused by the fall — I'm quoting the doctors, of course — and the rest by the sea pounding him against the rocks. We've had some pretty rough seas lately, remember. But despite the disfiguration, there's no doubt that it's Laurie.'

'Who identified him?'

'His wife and the postmaster. I couldn't get hold of Bullett.'

'How did Mrs Laurie take it?'

'Badly. At first she refused even to look at the body. When we finally persuaded her she took one peek, screamed, and passed out. And I don't blame her, either. He was a proper mess. I haven't

223

got over it myself yet.'

'You don't think they were persuaded into identifying the body as Laurie because of the uniform? He was wearing uniform, I suppose?'

'Yes. All complete except for the cap. The sea's got that, I expect. But I don't think there's been any mistake, Loy. Templar was shaken but firm — if that makes sense. And although nothing on earth could have persuaded Mrs L. to take a second look, she seemed in no doubt at all that it was her husband.'

'I wonder when they did him in,' Pitt said. 'I suppose it is too early to have an opinion on that?'

The Sergeant looked grim.

'This is going to shake you, my lad. They say he has been in the water for at least a week.'

The Inspector was certainly shaken. 'But what about the note he sent Bullett?' he asked. 'I know I suggested someone else could have written it, but that was only a shot in the dark to stampede Mrs Laurie. And there's the money he sent her. How are we to account for that?'

'I know. I said it would shake you, but there it is. I dare say they could be a day or two out; I wouldn't know about that. And Laurie could have written the note to Bullett on Saturday and have been killed later the same day. That would take care of that. But the money — well, your guess is as good as mine. And I just haven't got one.'

Pitt shook his head.

'The Austin being seen up at Coppins Point on Friday bears out the doctors. Whether it suits us or not, he must have died that evening. Which means that someone else sent the note to Bullett; someone who wanted to foster the belief that Laurie was still alive. It was reasonable to assume that Bullett would pass the information on to us, or make it public through his paper. But why the money?'

'Maybe the murderer was seized with remorse,' Dick suggested. 'Thought he ought to provide for his victim's wife. There may be more to come, in that case. Care to take a look at the corpse?'

As the Sergeant had said, the body was

an unpleasant sight. Pitt did not linger in its presence.

'That disposes of any doubt about Laurie's height,' said Dick. 'Gofer was right. Five foot six — and no fractions.'

'Poor chap,' Pitt said softly. 'I don't suppose he had a chance. I've seen a lot of murder, Dick, and I like it less every time. But if it was Carrington . . . ' He shrugged his shoulders. 'Well, we know now why he wanted that alibi.'

* * *

Since Sunday night a change had come over Miss Fratton, Dorothy noticed. A marked change. She was as affectionate as ever towards the girl, but more docile, less belligerent, towards others. Dorothy wondered whether the blow on the head had had something to do with it. Even Mrs Gill, whom Miss Fratton detested, had been received at No. 14 with something approaching courtesy. Drawn by curiosity, Mrs Gill had overcome her fear of Miss Fratton to call on the Monday and inquire after her neighbour's health. She had expected to be shown the door and told to mind her own business. Instead she had been ushered into the parlour and allowed to inspect the bump on Miss Fratton's head.

Mrs Gill could not understand it. Never before had she set foot in No. 14. Emboldened by success, she decided to try again. In time, she hoped, Miss Fratton might come to confide in her, might even disclose the cause of her antipathy towards postmen. Through her, too, she might learn more of the Weston girl; for although Mrs Gill disapproved of Dorothy's appearance and behaviour, there was no denying she was the most promising inhabitant of Grange Road when it came to scandal.

She chose Friday afternoon for her second call. But it was Dorothy, not Miss Fratton, who opened the door to her. Slightly taken aback, Mrs Gill explained the reason for her visit.

'You'd better come in, then,' said Miss Weston. She disliked Mrs Gill. 'Miss Fratton's lying down, but I expect she'll see you.'

Miss Fratton was perfectly prepared to see anyone. The bump on her head had not yet subsided, and was still painful enough to remind her of Sunday evening. But she did not regret that little incident. It had changed her almost overnight from an outcast into an object of sympathy and admiration. Amazed and confused by the kindness exhibited by neighbours who had hitherto shunned her, Miss Fratton had begun to realize how much she had missed in the past. She could have felt almost kindly towards the intruder who had been instrumental in effecting this change in her life — had he been anyone else.

For he was not unknown to *her*, Miss Fratton had decided after due reflection. She had committed a crime, and now she had been punished for it. It had been punishment in rather a drastic form, perhaps, and not one which she would have expected a man of his type to adopt. Not towards a woman, anyway. But no common burglar would have broken into her house solely to steal a torch. No, Miss Fratton decided, the assault on herself had been the purpose of his visit. As for the torch — well, it had been lying handy on the hall-stand. He could have picked it up to use as a weapon, and then kept it to light his way across the links.

Her worry now was over Dorothy. Dorothy, she felt, ought to know. It was unfair to leave her in ignorance. And if her conscience hinted that this desire to confide in her friend was not entirely unselfish, that it was also prompted by the hope that Dorothy would turn even more to her in the future, Miss Fratton paid her conscience little heed.

But it would not do to confide in Dorothy alone. Dorothy would keep it a secret between themselves. If she was to achieve her end others had to know. If it were public knowledge Dorothy could not sit on the fence. She would have to side either one way or the other. And public opinion, hoped Miss Fratton, would force her in the right direction. *Her* direction.

If there was any one person in Grange Road who could be trusted to spread the news it was Mrs Gill. And when Dorothy ushered her into the parlour Miss Fratton decided that the time was ripe for her revelation.

She had rehearsed her part many times in the days that had elapsed since Sunday night. She had even elaborated a little, to lend colour to her story — although, to do her justice, she was perhaps unaware of the extent of this elaboration. But since in her own mind she was *fairly* certain of the man and why he had come, and since she had no intention of invoking the aid of the law, she saw no harm in inventing facts to impress the truth on Dorothy.

'It's a disgrace,' said Mrs Gill, after she had inquired into Miss Fratton's condition, 'that a man can do a thing like that and get away with it. I'm sure I've hardly slept a wink since, wondering who would be next. I don't know what the police are up to, really I don't. There's that postman — a whole week gone by, and still they haven't found him. He might even have been murdered, for all we know.'

She looked keenly at Miss Fratton, hoping that her lead would be followed. But Miss Fratton, although she rose to the bait, was not prepared to swallow it.

'Good riddance to him if he has,' she declared. 'They're a thieving lot.'

She led the conversation back to her own injury. But Mrs Gill, equally determined, was not so easily sidetracked.

'It could have been the postman who attacked you,' she said. 'After all, it's common knowledge that you don't think much of them. Though I'm sure I don't know why. I always think uniforms are so attractive. Even a postman's.'

'I don't,' retorted Miss Fratton. 'They're a cloak to hide the wickedness beneath. As for that postman — slovenly, that's what he was. Looked as though he'd grown out of his oilskins years ago.' She raised herself on her thin elbows to watch the effect on Dorothy as she added, 'It wasn't the postman Sunday night, anyway. I know quite well who it was.'

Both members of her audience stared at her in surprise.

'You do?' said Dorothy. 'But you told the police that you didn't even see the man! You didn't even know if it was a man or a woman.'

'I know, dear.' Miss Fratton tried to

smile sweetly, but it only made more prominent her tufted chin and hooked nose. 'You must remember that I was only half-conscious at the time. I didn't want them hanging around asking a lot more questions; I just wanted to be rid of them. It was only later, when I had had time to think, that the details came back to me.'

Mrs Gill and Dorothy spoke at once.

'Who was it?' asked Mrs Gill; and 'Why didn't you tell the police later, then?' asked Dorothy.

Miss Fratton ignored Mrs Gill.

'I didn't tell them, dear, because I thought it might distress you,' she told the girl.

'Distress me? What on earth are you talking about, Miss Fratton? How do I come into it?'

'Because . . . ' Miss Fratton paused, her eyeballs swivelling from one to the other of her astonished listeners. 'Because it was Mr Carrington,' she said weightily.

'Jock!' exclaimed Dorothy. '*Jock!* Oh, no, that's too absurd.'

'Are you sure?' Mrs Gill had hoped that her visit might prove fruitful, but she had anticipated nothing like this. 'Are you quite, quite sure it was him, Miss Fratton? Why on earth should he do a thing like that?'

'Exactly,' echoed Dorothy. 'Why should he?'

But Miss Fratton was not prepared as yet to answer that question. That would come later. It was not for Mrs Gill's ears.

'I saw him,' she said. 'As he lifted the torch to strike me I saw his face.' This was not true, she knew. But her audience must be convinced.

'I don't believe it,' said the girl. 'I just don't believe it. For one thing, you told the police that you didn't know *what* the man hit you with. And you said he was tall. That wouldn't fit Jock.'

'I was confused, dear.' Miss Fratton was a little alarmed at the vehemence with which Dorothy defended her friend. 'And he *seemed* tall. I was crouching away from him, you see, to avoid his hitting me.'

Mrs Gill stood up. 'The police must be told at once,' she said. 'Shall I ring the Inspector?'

'No,' said Miss Fratton, firmly. 'I don't want the police brought into this. I'm none the worse for it now, and it'll be best to forget the whole thing.' She turned to Dorothy. 'Don't you agree, dear?'

Miss Weston was not deceived. She guessed that there was more to come. Although she sensed something of the motive behind Miss Fratton's revelation, she did not believe that the woman would publicly incriminate Carrington without some justification. That would be libel — or was it slander? Yet it was impossible to believe that Jock . . .

She turned away without answering.

Mrs Gill, still on her feet, was impatient to be gone. The police did not really matter; there were other ears more receptive. And the longer she stayed the greater the danger that Miss Fratton might demand complete secrecy on the matter. That, Mrs Gill knew, would be more than she could manage.

'I'll be running along now,' she said, edging towards the door. 'I can't help thinking you are wrong about not telling the police, but if that's the way you feel, dear, there's no more to be said. And as for Mr Carrington — well, I've no idea why he should do such a dreadful thing.' (Which was untrue. In her own mind she was quite certain that the assault was due to Miss Fratton's interference between Carrington and the girl.) 'But he doesn't deserve to be let off, that I do know.'

With Mrs Gill's departure, Miss Fratton got up from the couch and walked over to the girl, putting a gnarled and skinny hand on her shoulder.

'I'm sorry, dear,' she said. 'I didn't want to hurt you. But I couldn't leave you in ignorance of the type of man he is, could I? It has taken me days to bring myself to the point of telling you.'

Dorothy shook herself free. She never could bear to be touched by Miss Fratton.

'I'm not in love with Jock, if that's what you think,' she said. 'But he and I are friends, and I'm not prepared to hear him slandered without a chance to defend himself. Besides, the whole thing is preposterous. And why on earth did you wait until that old gasbag was here before

235

telling me? You know damned well she'll spread it all down the road. If it gets to Jock's ears — as it will — I expect he will sue you. You ought to be more careful what you say about people.'

Miss Fratton was not worried about the Law. Nor was she prepared to give her reason for wanting a third party present when she revealed her secret. But if she was a little relieved at Dorothy's assertion that she was not in love with Carrington, she was also apprehensive as to how the girl would take the confession she was about to make.

'It isn't preposterous,' she said. 'He had reason to be angry, you know. One shouldn't blame him too much.'

The girl stared at her. Was Miss Fratton actually defending a man? And a man she had always hated at that?

'What reason?' she demanded.

A red flush tinged the grey gauntness of the older woman's cheeks.

'It was me followed you and him Sunday afternoon,' she said, simply but ungrammatically.

'You? But I thought — ' Dorothy

stopped. There was no need to tell Miss Fratton what she had thought. 'What on earth made you do it?'

'I had to.' Miss Fratton's voice was heavy with emotion. 'I just couldn't bear it any longer, seeing you and him together. Or if it wasn't him it was that other one. And when I saw you going up towards the Point with him I thought . . . maybe he was going to propose to you — perhaps take you away from Tanmouth, so that I'd never see you again. I waited for you to come back . . . and he had his arm round you, and . . . Well, I felt I *had* to follow you, dear.'

Miss Weston was used to these outbursts of emotion. This was the old Miss Fratton. 'And what good would that do you?' she asked, unmoved.

'I wanted to *know* — about you and him, I mean. You never tell me anything — I had to find out for myself. But I didn't mean any harm, Dorothy. And when you screamed . . . '

A few drops of water squeezed themselves from behind the protruding eyeballs and chased each other down

237

Miss Fratton's cheeks as she recalled the pain of that Sunday afternoon — far, far worse, she thought, than the pain she had suffered later in the day. She had been so sure that Dorothy was lost to her as she had watched them stroll ahead of her in the dusk with their arms round each others' waists. And remembering that, how could she believe the girl when she said she was not in love with the man?

Dorothy was not impressed. She had suffered Miss Fratton's affection in the past because she had felt sorry for the old girl's loneliness; and also because, as Mrs Gill suspected, she knew Miss Fratton had no one to leave her money to when she died. But this was going too far. She was not prepared to suffer so much interference.

'You had no right to spy on us like that,' she said angrily. 'You frightened the life out of me. And anyway Jock didn't know who it was — any more than I did. As for his having attacked you Sunday night — I just don't believe it. And I don't believe you saw his face, either.

I think you've made it all up so as I wouldn't have anything more to do with him. It was a mean trick, and I'm going down there now to tell him about it.'

Miss Fratton made no effort to detain her. But the slight grimace that twitched her lips added nothing of beauty to her expression.

* * *

Repeated knocking on the front door of the bungalow in Grange Road produced no response. As the police passed the side-door on their way round to the back they noticed that the milk had not been taken in and that the kitchen curtains were drawn across the window. So too were the curtains in the lounge. It was only when they reached the other side of the building, where the two bedrooms were situated, that they were able to peer in through the windows.

'That's odd,' said Dick. 'Why should the lounge curtains still be drawn at three o'clock in the afternoon? He can't be sick; the bedrooms are empty.'

'He's gone, you idiot,' Pitt answered curtly, annoyed with himself. 'That damned woman tipped him off.'

'What woman?'

'Miss Weston. She must have realized that our interest in the brooch was significant of something or other. She probably phoned him later and reported the whole conversation. If she told him that we'd seen the brooch — *and* the box — he would guess that we'd check with the jeweller, and so discover that there never was a second brooch. And that telephone call she made on Friday afternoon; if he knew she had let on about that — how she thought he was at home with another woman . . . ' The Inspector shrugged his shoulders. 'He didn't need a much broader hint, did he? Not after we had told him about the Austin.'

'Do you think she knows he killed Laurie?'

'Not necessarily. She's just a fool girl who happens to be stuck on him.'

'And that explains everything, of course,' said Dick.

'It should do. I don't have to give you a lecture on women, do I?' The Inspector turned to a constable. 'See if you can climb through that lavatory window, Canning. And don't waste time snooping once you're in. Leave that to us. Your job is to open the front door.'

The constable was young and agile. When he had disappeared inside the building the two police officers walked round to the front, ignoring the stares of the curious few who had already gathered in the road outside the bungalow.

The hall was dark. The detectives walked down the passage, opening doors and peering into the empty rooms. As Dick Ponsford reached the lounge he switched on the electric light, for the heavy curtains barred the daylight from the room.

Then he drew in his breath sharply and stood aside for the Inspector.

Jock Carrington was there. He lay face downward on the floor, a shotgun by his side. A red stain round his head marked the green carpet, and his face was a pulpy mess.

241

Pitt gulped and made for the telephone.

'Well, he's gone,' he said, as he picked up the receiver. 'But not the way I thought he'd go.'

9

A Very Serious Admission

The man was so obviously dead that there was no need to feel pulse or heart, but Dick knelt beside the body and went mechanically through the motions. The blood on the face had congealed; the body was quite cold. Carrington had been dead for some hours.

'We'll wait until the others arrive,' said the Inspector, replacing the receiver. He walked over to the fireplace and bent to feel the grate. That too was cold.

As he straightened up he saw the typewriter. It stood on a table between the fireplace and the window. A piece of foolscap paper, almost covered with typescript, was inserted in the machine.

A sentence caught the Inspector's eye. 'Come over here, Dick,' he called softly.

They stood and read it together, not touching the typewriter or the paper in it, leaning awkwardly to read where the manuscript had spilled over the back of the machine on to the table.

It was headed 'For Inspector Pitt,' and continued:

As I gather you have already guessed, I killed John Laurie; and as I have no wish to go through the ordeal of arrest, trial, and subsequent hanging, I prefer to take this way out. If you feel you have been cheated you have only yourself to blame. You should not have shown your hand so clearly in talking to me about the car and to Miss Weston about the brooch. For Miss Weston, as you should have known she would, confided in me that evening.

I did not go to the cinema last Friday. After leaving Scott-Waterton at Victoria I changed my mind and caught the 2.48 train home, and was here when the postman called.

I told you I was not acquainted with Laurie. That was true — but it so happened that Laurie knew me. Furthermore, he had good reason to hate me; although I do not intend to make public the reason, since it would involve a third person who is entirely innocent. When I opened the door to his knock on Friday afternoon he recognized me and forced his way past me into the hall. I objected, and he then told me who he was. A bitter quarrel ensued, which got us nowhere; and eventually he left to continue his round, voicing lurid threats of what he would do to me now that he had found out where I lived.

After he had gone I was worried and uneasy, though not on my own account. I wanted to get the matter settled; I didn't fancy the idea of just awaiting developments. So I got the car out and went after him. Just before I left the house the telephone rang. I picked up the receiver; but hearing Miss Weston's voice, and not wishing to become involved in one of her long conversations, I replaced it without answering.

I caught Laurie up farther down the road, explained the way I felt, and persuaded him to get into the car. We drove out to Coppins Point and walked up and down on the grass, arguing like mad. Both of us lost our tempers. I didn't mind what he said about me, but when he started calling this third person the foulest of names I caught him by the throat to silence him. He was kicking and hitting me, but I was the stronger of the two, and I just held on to his throat. Then suddenly he went limp, and I realized he was dead.

It is pointless to protest that I did not intend to kill him; but having done so I felt a strong desire to escape the consequences. Laurie had been an obstacle to my achieving something I greatly desired. Now the obstacle was removed it would be nice to go on living. So I dragged him to the edge of the cliff, bundled him over, and came home.

During the struggle a small parcel had fallen from Laurie's pocket. I picked this up before leaving the Point, and found later that it contained the brooch I had ordered for Miss Weston.

As I could not hand it over to her as the original — she was expecting it to arrive by post — I made what I imagine was my one mistake. I gave it to her on Wednesday evening, pretending I had bought her another. It was a silly thing to do; but then I never imagined you would even begin to suspect me.

I had not anticipated that the body would remain undiscovered for so long, but I was naturally delighted with the accepted theory that Laurie had absconded with the mail. I thought that made me absolutely safe.

However, I was wrong; so I have taken this way out. But may I point out that I need not have satisfied your natural curiosity? I could have left you in complete ignorance of what really happened. In return for this confession, therefore, I would request that no inquiry be made into the cause of Laurie's quarrel with me. It was a private matter which, if pursued, might bring sorrow and harm to an innocent person.

No signature was appended, but the words 'Jock Carrington' were typed at the bottom of the manuscript.

'I'm sorry,' said Pitt. 'I liked the fellow.'

'So did I,' Dick agreed.

'Maybe I liked him because he was such a damned fine artist,' Pitt continued. 'He was, you know. One of the best. I wonder why he typed his signature at the bottom of his confession? So unbusiness-like. Makes it completely valueless, really.'

'Come to that, I wonder why he is wearing gloves,' said Dick. 'Ever known a man put on gloves before shooting himself?'

'No.' Pitt frowned. 'I wondered about that too.'

They were brown kid gloves, fur-lined. The Inspector bent to examine them more closely. The kid outside was free from bloodstains, but there were dark smears on the fur around the wrists.

'The usual reason is to avoid leaving fingerprints,' said Dick. 'But Carrington wouldn't have to worry about that.'

He stared hard at the body. He was

about to speak again when the arrival of further police interrupted him. Pitt gave instructions to the photographers, and then watched as the doctor examined the body.

'Made a nasty mess of himself, hasn't he?' commented the doctor. 'I'd go for poison myself. *Mais chacun à son goût.*'

'When did he die?' asked Pitt, ignoring this pleasantry.

'Some time last night,' answered the other, glancing at his watch. 'Put it around eleven o'clock and you won't be far wrong. Does that make sense?'

'I'm not sure,' said the Inspector, and meant it.

It was the absence of light that puzzled him. If Carrington shot himself at eleven o'clock the previous night, why were all the lights in the house switched off? Would a man do that before committing suicide? Would he prefer to shoot himself in the dark?

'He might,' said Dick, when Pitt put the question to him. 'It might help to bolster up his nerve. Easier to pull the trigger if you are not actually looking down the spout. But the other lights — those in the passage, for instance — I don't see why he should bother to switch those off.'

Pitt walked over to the table by the fire and once more perused the manuscript in the typewriter. Something green, protruding from under the paper, caught his eye. He picked it up.

It was a local railway timetable for December.

He flicked over the pages. Yes, there was a 2.48 all right. *And* a 5.47, the train by which Carrington had previously said he had returned. Nothing wrong there. And yet . . .

'They've checked the gun for prints,' said Dick. 'Clean as a whistle. Of course, if he hadn't used it for some time and was wearing gloves when he picked it up last night . . . But all the same . . . '

Pitt looked at him. 'You don't like it, eh?'

'No, I don't. Those gloves, and no lights . . . no prints, either. It couldn't be a plant, could it?'

'It could, Dick.' The Inspector's voice

was gloomy. 'It nearly always could. But I don't know.'

He knelt beside the body again, lifting one arm to examine the glove more closely. Turning back the gauntlet, he exposed a smear of blood, about two inches long, on the fur inside. There was a similar smear inside the other glove.

'That's what I don't understand,' he said, as he stood up. 'There's no blood on the outside of the gloves, none on the carpet except round his head. So how the devil did it get on the inside?'

'Looks like he had some blood on his thumb when he pulled the glove on,' said Dick. 'That would account for it, wouldn't it? The blood would come off on the fur.'

'Yes, that's true. But how the — ' The Inspector stopped. For a moment he stared wide-eyed at his brother-in-law. Then he snapped his finger and thumb briskly. 'By God, Dick! So it *was* murder!'

Sergeant Ponsford gazed at him doubtfully.

'Why would he have blood on his hands *before* he shot himself?' demanded

251

Pitt. He bent down and removed the gloves, exposing the white, tapering fingers. There was no cut, no stain. 'See? And even supposing he had, it would come off on the first glove but not on the second — because he would be putting on the second glove, no matter which one it was, with a hand that was already gloved!'

'By golly, so he would!' It was a childish expression which escaped the Sergeant only in moments of deep excitement, and one of which he was absurdly ashamed. But now he did not even realize that he had used it.

'And why isn't there blood on the outside of the glove?' Pitt continued. 'One hand would be on the trigger, but the other would be well up the barrel to steady it. With his face the mess it is there ought to be blood on *one* of them.'

Dick nodded. 'Yes. But even so — murder or suicide — I still don't see why he should be wearing gloves.'

'Whoever shot him *wasn't* wearing gloves,' said Pitt. 'After the murder he rubbed the gun clear of prints. Then he realized that, if Carrington was supposed to have shot himself, his fingerprints ought to be on the gun. So he put gloves on the corpse — and the lack of prints is explained. Ingenious, eh?'

'It would have been all right if he had taken care to clean the blood off his own hands first,' Dick agreed.

'He probably didn't notice it until too late. It was only on his thumb — not on the fingers, I imagine. Maybe he cut himself, or maybe it's Carrington's blood. We can have the blood-groups checked.'

'The lights,' said Dick. 'They must have been switched off by the murderer before he left the bungalow. Lights left on all night would have attracted attention. And now we know why the signature on Carrington's supposed confession was typed.'

'Ah!' said Pitt. 'The confession. We had better have the typewriter keys checked for prints. Is it possible to type properly with gloves on, I wonder?'

'They would have to be damned thin, I imagine,' said the Sergeant. 'More likely he just cleaned the keys and left it at that, hoping we'd make nothing of it.'

The Inspector nodded thoughtfully.

'It's odd, isn't it, that the confession fits so neatly with the theory we have built up? Almost as though the writer had read our thoughts. Miss Weston's repetition of her conversation with us; no second brooch because he got the original from Laurie. It accounts for the time Laurie spent here, the Austin seen in Grange Road and at Coppins Point. It accounts for practically everything, in fact. And yet, if Carrington was murdered — and he damned well must have been — about all we can take for granted is that Laurie was strangled and thrown over the cliffs. And we already knew that.' He sighed. 'I almost wish we hadn't been so inquisitive, Dick. Suicide would have been simpler.'

'Much simpler,' Dick agreed. 'But as it is . . . What about the correspondence that's been going on, Loy? The note to Bullett, the money sent to Mrs L.? And then there's that anonymous *billet-doux* incriminating Heath. Who wrote those? If it was the same person as typed that confession, why didn't he attribute them to Carrington? That would have tied it up nicely. No loose ends at all.'

'He couldn't think of everything,' said Pitt. 'After all, it must have taken a lot of nerve to sit down at that typewriter, with his victim's body still in the room, and concoct even the shortest of confessions. Under the circumstances I think he did damned well. It was careless of him to leave that timetable there, though. It didn't look right. He had to make sure that there was a train Carrington could have caught to get back in time. But had the confession been genuine, Carrington wouldn't have bothered about such a detail.'

One of the fingerprint men came over to report that they could get nothing from the typewriter. 'Looks as though it has been cleaned up, sir. One or two smeared prints, but they're not worth taking.'

'All right,' said Pitt. 'But keep at it. This room, the hall — that's where they ought to be.' He turned to Dick. 'The only prints we *ought* to find are Carrington's and Miss Weston's. Any others — well, they'll need explaining. That's one advantage of Carrington's desire to keep aloof from his neighbours.'

'There's Bullett,' Dick reminded him. 'He was a fairly frequent visitor.'

'Yes. I had forgotten him. Tell me, Dick — when you read that blasted confession, what did you suppose was the reason for the quarrel between Laurie and Carrington?'

'Mrs L.,' the Sergeant answered promptly.

'Yes. So did I. And that fits, too. I always thought she had a boy friend. Of course, it's possible that Carrington murdered Laurie and then got done in by someone else. But I don't like it. It's untidy, somehow.' Pitt paused to watch the removal of the body. 'Who else, besides Laurie, would resent Carrington paying attention to Mrs Laurie?'

'Well, there's Miss Weston. She was keen on the chap. She wouldn't like another woman muscling in. Made that pretty plain, didn't she?'

'Yes. And it was Miss Weston who supplied us with the two most damning pieces of evidence against Carrington. The second brooch — and the telephone call. What's more, she volunteered them. She could have kept quiet about both, and no one the wiser. But she didn't. She trotted them out without so much as a tiny dig from either of us. Either she hadn't the faintest idea what harm she was doing her boy friend or — '

'Or what?' asked Dick.

'Or she did it deliberately, meaning to shop him. She could, in fact, have invented them both. It was her word against Carrington's. And now, with Carrington dead, it's all hers.'

'You mean she fed us that fake evidence just to get us interested, and then killed him before he could deny it? Staged the suicide, wrote the confession? Good Lord!'

'It's a possibility,' said Pitt. 'Didn't she hint Carrington was cooling off? She knew he was going to the cinema, too. A cinema is a poor place to establish an alibi. It was a good bet we couldn't trace him there, even if we tried.'

'Bullett and Scott-Waterton also knew

he was going to the cinema,' Dick reminded him.

'True. But only Dorothy Weston had *all* the information necessary to write that confession. And what motive would either of those men have? Scott-Waterton's an art critic. He might slay Carrington in print, but not in person. And anyway, Carrington was a fine artist. As for Bullett — well, it's true he is now showing considerable interest in Mrs Laurie, but I wouldn't say it's his heart that's involved. I've no doubt he'd have little compunction in seducing his friend's girl if he got the chance, but he wouldn't want her bad enough to commit murder. And anyway, he had never met the girl prior to Laurie's death.'

'You don't rate him high morally, I gather,' said Dick. 'But I'd hate to think the girl did it. I rather like our Dorothy. And although they don't come into these theories of yours, don't forget that both Heath and Miss Fratton had reason to want Carrington out of the way.'

'I haven't forgotten,' Pitt assured him.

There was quite a crowd in the road.

258

As the police officers appeared they pressed closer to the gate, despite the protests of the constables on duty. As Pitt and the Sergeant fought their way through to the waiting car a woman caught the Inspector's arm. Pitt was about to shake her off when he saw it was Mrs Gill.

'I must speak to you, Inspector,' she said urgently. 'I know I promised to say nothing, but I didn't know then that Mr Carrington was dead. That makes all the difference, doesn't it?'

The crowd was all about them. At the back of it Pitt saw the red hair of Miss Weston, and wondered at the pain in her eyes. He recalled the scathing tones in which Mrs Gill had referred to her, his own disgust at the girl's casual attitude towards the fawning Miss Fratton. Even so, was she the kind of girl deliberately to plan and execute the scheme he had just discussed with Dick?

Well, that must wait. He would deal with Miss Weston later. At present there was Mrs Gill. He pushed the woman ahead of him into the car. When they had left Grange Road he turned to her.

'Now, Mrs Gill,' he said. 'What is it you
want to tell me?'

★ ★ ★

Jane Laurie denied all knowledge of
Carrington. She had never met him, she
said, never even heard his name before.
And she made it quite clear to the police
officers that she resented their continued
attempts to connect her with other men.

'My husband's dead now, so I can do
as I please,' she said. 'But while he was
alive I was a good wife to him, and I
won't have you or anyone else saying I
wasn't.'

Pitt saw no reason to apologize, and
told her so.

'Well, you insinuated it, anyway,' she
retorted. 'First Eric — first my previous
fiancé, and then this — this other man.
And I don't like it.'

Her indignation, real or assumed,
became her. But the Inspector was not a
susceptible man. He drew a photograph
of Carrington from his pocket and

showed it to her.

'Have you ever seen that man before?' he asked.

She stared at it for a moment. 'Why, yes,' she said slowly. 'Yes, I think I have. Who is he?'

'Jock Carrington.'

'Oh.' But she did not seem surprised. 'Well, I still haven't met him. Not really. But once or twice I've seen him in the Close, and he's followed me when I've been out. My husband was furious when I told him. But the man never spoke to me, never tried to get off. And as I said to my husband, you couldn't object to his walking on the same pavement, could you? There's nothing wrong in that, I said. But he still didn't like it much.'

'Did your husband ever see him?'

'Oh, yes. Only a few days before he disappeared, when the man was walking up and down outside the house. He wanted to go out and tell him off.'

'And did he?'

'No. I wouldn't let him. I didn't want a scene.'

'And neither you nor your husband

knew who the man was?'

'No.'

'You never mentioned this before, Mrs Laurie.' Pitt's voice was stern. 'Why not?'

She had spoken of the man calmly, with little or no inflexion in her voice. Now her attitude changed. She was nervous, uncertain.

'I don't know,' she said. 'I expect I forgot. Or perhaps I didn't think it was important. It isn't, is it?'

'Does Mr Bullett know about Carrington?' asked the Inspector, ignoring her question.

'I — I may have told him. I can't remember.'

'I can't make that woman out,' said Pitt, as he and the Sergeant drove back to the station, 'but I'm damned sure I wouldn't trust her an inch. A bloody little hypocrite, if you ask me. I only wish I knew exactly how she fits into these murders. Anyway, she gave something away. Her ex-boy-friend was named Eric. That may help to speed up the search for him.'

'We'd better get hold of Bullett,' said

Dick. 'He knew Carrington well. Maybe he can help.'

They did not have to send for the reporter. He was waiting for them at the station. 'What a dreadful business!' he said. 'I simply cannot believe it. Why on earth should Jock commit suicide? So far as I know, he hadn't a care in the world.'

'How did you hear of it, sir?' asked Pitt.

'Some woman phoned the paper. A Mrs Gill, I think it was. I went round there at once, but your constable wasn't forthcoming. There were plenty of the locals hanging around, each with a different version of what had happened. I preferred to get the facts from you — if I can.'

'When did you see him last, Mr Bullett?'

'Some days ago. Tuesday evening, I think. Yes, that's right; the day before that business out at Rawsley. But see here, Inspector — you might let me have the gen on this. Forget I'm a newshound, and remember that Carrington and I were friends.'

'I know, sir. That's why I'm hoping you

may be able to help us. For instance, there's the gun. Did you know he had one?'

'No, I didn't. I've never seen it there.'

'Was Mr Carrington a lady's man?'

'In a way,' said the reporter. 'He had quite a few girl friends, if that's what you mean. He was pretty thick with a Miss Weston, who lives in the same road. I've seen her, although we've never actually met. But women weren't his whole existence — not by a long way. He was a confirmed bachelor, but he liked feminine company.'

'He wouldn't have known Mrs Laurie, I suppose?' asked Pitt.

Bullet looked surprised.

'Mrs Laurie? I shouldn't think so, Inspector. Neither of them has ever mentioned the other's name to me, anyway. Why? Surely you are not trying to connect Jock Carrington with Laurie, are you?'

'Not necessarily, Mr Bullett. Tell me, did Mrs Laurie ever mention a man who used to hang around Tilnet Close and follow her when she went out?'

'Yes. Yes, she did. But I gather the man never tried to get fresh with her. Didn't even attempt to speak to her. And she said she didn't know — ' He stared at Pitt. 'Good Lord!'

'Yes, Mr Bullett?'

'I see now what you're driving at, Inspector. And you may be right. Some weeks ago Jock told me he'd seen a real smasher in the town. He said he'd followed her home to find out where she lived; he knew she was married, too. But he never referred to her again, and I thought . . . Yes, that's who it was, Inspector, you can bet your life. Jane Laurie, eh? Well, I'm damned!'

He frowned. 'But wait a moment. That doesn't make sense, does it? I mean, why should Jock commit suicide *after* Jane's husband was killed? If he was that keen on her it was a lucky break for him, in a way. Gave him his chance. Unless — ' He paused, and his voice was tinged with anxiety as he went on: 'You haven't got some wild notion that he killed Laurie, have you? Because if so, you can put it right out of your mind. Jock wouldn't do a thing like that. And anyway, he was in London that day. I know. I was with him.'

'You were with him the whole afternoon, Mr Bullett?'

'Well, no. I had to get back here after lunch. But he told me he was going to a cinema. There was a French film he wanted to see.'

Pitt said slowly, 'You may as well know it now. Carrington didn't commit suicide — he was murdered.'

The reporter gasped, and the colour left his face. He sat down heavily in a chair, and his voice was shaky as he said, 'Oh, no. No, I just don't believe it. You must be mistaken.'

'There's no mistake, Mr Bullett. All the evidence points to murder.'

The reporter shook himself. 'But I can't see . . . Have you any idea who did it?'

'Not exactly an idea,' Pitt said slowly. 'Just the dawning of a suspicion, as it were.' And then, more briskly, 'I'm sorry if it has upset you, sir. But you had to know.'

'Of course. I'm grateful to you for

telling me. Poor old Jock. What was the motive, do you think? Was anything stolen? The pictures, for instance?'

'Not the pictures,' said Pitt. 'I wouldn't know about other things — you may be able to help us there. But it doesn't look like a burglary to me. No, I'd say it was a more personal motive. Love, hate, jealousy — something on those lines. Or fear.'

'Well, I hope you get him. Or I suppose it might be her. And of course you can count on me for any help you need. Jock and I . . . '

He shook his head and became lost in thought.

Dick Ponsford had taken no part in the conversation. As he listened he had been rereading in his mind Carrington's supposed confession and remembering the things it left unexplained.

And suddenly he was filled with an inspiration.

'That note you received from Laurie, Mr Bullett,' he said. 'The one asking you to keep an eye on his wife. Remember it?'

The reporter looked at him in surprise.

'Of course. What about it?'

'Laurie couldn't have written it, you know. He was dead.'

'Was he? I didn't know. Not the exact date, I mean. The police don't seem to be very forthcoming these days,' he said carelessly. 'I have to scratch around for what little information I can get.'

'They might be more co-operative if they thought you were on the level yourself,' Dick retorted.

'Here! What the hell are you getting at?' Bullett demanded. 'Who says I'm not on the level? Didn't I bring that blasted note round to you the moment I'd read it? You know damned well there aren't many reporters who would have done that. They'd have hung on to it like leeches, hoping to find Laurie on their own. But not me. I'm the muggins who plays fair with you blighters and then gets bawled out for not doing so. But not any more, blast you. You can muddle along without any help from yours truly in the future.'

Pitt looked from one to the other of the two men. Bullett's indignation did not ring true. Obviously the Sergeant thought the same, for he remained unperturbed.

'You didn't hang on to that note and try to trace it because you knew all there was to know about it,' he said evenly. 'In fact, you wrote it yourself, didn't you?'

Dick had always regarded the reporter as a man who was never caught off balance, was never at a loss for words. Now he knew he had been wrong. If ever a man was flummoxed it was Bullett at that moment. Had he murdered both Carrington and the postman he could not have looked more guilty.

'I . . . I . . . ' he stammered. Then he shook himself. 'Yes, damn you, I did! But how the hell did you find out?'

There was a momentary silence. Then: 'That is a very serious admission,' said Inspector Pitt.

'I know, I know.' The reporter was fast recovering his aplomb. 'But don't try to make too much out of it, Inspector. It's easily explained.'

'I'm glad to hear it,' said Pitt. 'Suppose you explain, then?'

'All right. Only don't keep eyeing me as though I had committed a murder or something. It puts me off. Well — when I got Mrs Laurie's address from the Sergeant here my idea was to get a story from her. You know — sob-stuff, and all that. But I hadn't reckoned on her being such a smasher. I'm a susceptible male, Inspector, not a policeman, and she knocked me for six the first time I saw her. So then I tried to hit on an excuse for seeing her again without her thinking I was taking advantage of her husband's absence. She knew Laurie and I had been friendly, and about him fishing me out of the water, but I didn't think that was strong enough. And then I got it. If I could show her a letter purporting to come from Laurie and asking me to keep an eye on her, it would seem natural for me to drop in regularly. And after all, who else would he write to if not to me?

'So that's what I did; and she fell for it completely. Never queried it at all. But I had to let you see it as well in case she mentioned it to you later. I didn't know her well enough then to ask her to keep quiet about it.'

But you do now, thought the Sergeant.

Pitt's face was expressive. Forestalling the explosion, Bullett grinned at him disarmingly.

'No good getting rattled, Inspector,' he said. 'I'm sorry, of course. But how the hell was I to know the man had been murdered? *You* didn't. I thought he'd turn up in a few days' time. And as long as I didn't mislead you by putting a fictitious address — well, where was the harm?'

Pitt told him. He did not waste words, but he made them strong.

'And did you also send that money to Mrs Laurie?' he asked.

'No fear. I'm broke. And anyway, my regard for her husband didn't stretch that far. No, that's a puzzler, isn't it? If Laurie was dead . . . '

He shrugged his shoulders.

'The ruddy interfering fool!' said Pitt, when the reporter had gone. 'How the hell can one get results with idiots like him gumming up the works? I've a good mind to bring a charge against him. All the same, that was a brainwave of yours, Dick. What put you on to it?'

271

'Just a hunch,' said the Sergeant modestly. 'I know friend Bullett.'

'Well, try and have a hunch about the money Mrs L. received. Carrington might have sent it, I suppose. He seems to have been keen on the woman. Whether he killed her husband or not, he may have wanted to help her.'

'The address on the envelope wasn't typed on Carrington's machine,' said Dick. 'On the envelope the capitals are not in line with the rest of the type. The machine must have been faulty.'

'How about the note Bullett admitted writing?' asked the Inspector. 'Check it with the others. I don't trust that blighter.'

'I warned you. Don't blame me now.'

But it was obvious that the confession purporting to have been written by Carrington, the envelope sent to Mrs Laurie, and the note typed by Bullett had all been typed on different machines.

'Not that that proves anything,' said Pitt.

Superintendent Howard had news of Morris.

272

'The Yard have picked him up,' he said. 'He's well known to them, apparently. And from his past record he doesn't seem to have prospered. Perhaps he moved down here to make a fresh start.'

'His future doesn't look too rosy, either,' said Pitt. 'Not if he is mixed up with Blake and Sullivan. Are they handing him over?'

'Yes.'

As they left the building Dick said, 'Did you mean it when you told Bullett that you had a suspicion as to who killed Carrington? Or were you just stringing him along?'

'I was thinking,' said Pitt, 'of Miss Weston.'

Dick grinned. 'That I can well believe,' he said.

10

Bodies All Over the Place

The sudden eruption of murder in their midst shook Grange Road to the very foundations. Although to all but a few Jock Carrington had been almost a stranger, that did not alter the fact that he had lived in the road and was therefore one of them. The disappearance of the postman the previous week-end — even the news that he too had met a sudden and mysterious death — was almost forgotten in the later tragedy. Most of Grange Road knew nothing of Laurie as a man, had never even seen him. But Carrington — he was different.

Mrs Gill was the heroine of the hour. Had she not been whisked away in a police car from the very scene of the crime? And only a few days before that there had been the identification parade. No doubt, thought the majority of

Grange Road, Mrs Gill and the police were thick as thieves. And if one or two of her neighbours avoided her, the rest flocked to No. 24 for the latest information.

Mrs Gill, glorying in her hour, did her best to uphold her position. She told them all she knew, and much that she didn't. But only to Miss Plant did she voice her own suspicions.

'Didn't I say in this very room, Ethel, that there was trouble brewing for Carrington? And didn't I say that I wouldn't put even murder past Donald Heath? Only last week that was. And now look what's happened!'

Miss Plant admitted that her friend had said all that. 'But you don't *know* it was Donald,' she protested. 'You're only guessing.'

'I wasn't there when he did it, if that's what you mean,' Mrs Gill agreed tartly. 'But I don't need spectacles to see a mountain. Hasn't he said time and again that he'd get even with Carrington? Everyone knows he hated the sight of the man. And then there's that black eye of his. I thought at the time he got it from the postman. Well, I was wrong there, and I don't mind admitting it. It was Carrington gave it him, no doubt of that. And Donald Heath's not the man to lie down under a thing like that. He'd want to get his own back — and so he has.'

Miss Plant was impressed. 'Did you tell all that to the police?' she asked.

'I did, Ethel. And more. They hadn't heard, you see, about it being Carrington that broke into Miss Fratton's house Sunday night. Miss Fratton said not to tell them — goodness knows why — but, of course, I couldn't take any notice of that. One has one's duty.'

'That's true.' Miss Plant was worried. She too had a duty. Only she wasn't like Hermione, she didn't find it easy to tell people — especially the police — things about her neighbours. Perhaps Hermione . . .

'They had a row Sunday night,' she blurted out.

Mrs Gill sat up sharply. 'Who had a row? Carrington and Donald?'

Her friend nodded. 'Quite late it was

— well after midnight. I'd sat up trying to finish a book so as I could take it back to the library Monday morning. Then I had a cup of cocoa, and then I went into the back garden for a breath of air before going to bed.

'They must have had the French windows open in the lounge, I think. I don't normally hear what goes on there. They were shouting at each other fit to wake the neighbourhood. I didn't catch what it was all about — I heard Dorothy's name mentioned, and Carrington said something about spying — but it didn't last very long.'

Mrs Gill was uncertain whether to be pleased or annoyed at this piece of information. It was disgraceful of Ethel that she had kept it to herself — for five whole days, too. On the other hand, here was another titbit she could offer the Inspector. Unless, of course, Ethel . . .

'You ought to have gone to the police at once,' she said severely. 'The very next morning, anyway.'

'But why?' queried the perplexed Miss Plant. 'Mr Carrington hadn't been killed then. It was just a quarrel. And I couldn't know he was going to be murdered, could I?'

'No. Well, you should have told them this afternoon, then. Anyway, there's no time to be lost, Ethel. You must ring them up at once. If you don't I shall.'

She knew how Miss Plant hated the telephone.

Miss Plant leapt at the alternative. 'I really think that would be best,' she said. 'For you to ring them, I mean. You're quite friendly with that Inspector, aren't you? He'll take more notice if it comes from you, Hermione.'

'That's true.' Mrs Gill tried to sound reluctant. 'Very well, Ethel — I'll do it. But I must have it all quite clear in my head before I ring up. The police are so particular about accuracy. Now, let me see. Sunday night — after midnight, you said — and — Good gracious!'

'What's the matter, Hermione?'

'Sunday night. That was the night Miss Fratton said Carrington attacked her. But he couldn't have done that *and* quarrelled with Donald, could he?'

'Well, no. Not at the same time, of course. But one after the other, perhaps. We don't know at what *hour* he attacked her, do we?'

'No. Miss Fratton didn't say. But I expect the police will know. We must just tell them the facts and leave them to sort it out.'

★　★　★

Susan Avery's main reaction to the news of Carrington's death was a certain uneasiness that a murder could be committed in the very road in which she lived. And there would be bits in the papers — particularly the Sunday papers. There might even be a photograph of Grange Road.

It was all rather degrading, she thought. When she expressed this view to her husband he agreed with her; which was so unusual that she regarded him with acute suspicion for the rest of the day.

William Harris was more distressed by the disappearance of his neighbour

Morris than by the murder. Having found a saviour in his hour of need, he had hoped that Morris would continue to act the benefactor. The bills were still unpaid; Christmas was a few days nearer. Although Morris had paid his costs and told him to think no more about it, Harris had thought about it quite a lot. He needed money, and he needed it quickly. If Morris hadn't gone away he could have asked for a loan ... perhaps Morris would have offered ...

When his wife tried to discuss the murder he shied away from it. 'I'm not interested,' he said. 'I didn't even know the fellow.'

'You ought to be interested,' she answered. 'The police called this afternoon. They wanted to know if you were out last night.'

That shook him. 'Oh! And what did you tell them?'

'I said you stayed home.'

He bent to kiss her cold cheek. It was an unfamiliar gesture, and therefore an awkward one. 'Thanks, Marion,' he said.

Donald Heath was worried. So was

Mrs Heath. The police had lost no time. Just a routine check, the Sergeant had said; but the Heaths knew better. The police wouldn't be asking all those questions at the other houses in Grange Road. Everyone knew of Donald's dislike of Carrington and the cause of it, and there were many who had heard him threaten to 'do' Carrington. It would be strange indeed if the police did not get to hear of it. And after that dust-up with the postman . . .

Miss Fratton's dislike of Carrington was equally well known; but Miss Fratton wasn't worrying. Everyone, including the police, knew how she chivvied and rated the postman; but no one, to her knowledge, had so much as hinted that she might have had anything to do with the postman's untimely end. If you were eccentric enough you could get away with anything, even murder. And Carrington's death meant that she now had no rival for Dorothy's affections. Dorothy might marry that impossible Donald Heath, but Miss Fratton knew that the girl's affections would not be involved. They would live in the same road, and she and Dorothy could be together as much as they pleased.

A slight cloud crossed her horizon as she recalled her last meeting with the girl. Dorothy had certainly resented her announcement that it was Carrington who had attacked her Sunday night. Perhaps, now that the man was dead and no longer a menace, she could afford to retract that. After all, she wasn't *sure*. It *could* have been Carrington — and after her following him and Dorothy Sunday afternoon it *should* have been him — but she wasn't really sure. And it didn't matter now, anyway. The main thing was to win back Dorothy's affection.

The Archers behaved as normal middle-class people usually behave when a murder takes place in their vicinity. They rubber-necked at the bungalow, asked innumerable questions of anybody who knew anything, discussed it between themselves, and then forgot it until someone or something reminded them of it.

But Sam Archer went off to the local a

little earlier that evening. It wasn't every day that a man had such red-hot news to impart to his fellows.

It was on Dorothy Weston that Carrington's death had the greatest impact. She had felt sick when they had brought the body out of the bungalow. As the stretcher was borne down the garden path and hoisted into the ambulance she could see, under the blanket that covered it, the outlines of the body that had once been Jock's; a body that had always been so full of vigour, had so often been intimately close to hers. And the crowd outside the bungalow — they were all looking at her, discussing her. But she could not bring herself to leave; not until the police had gone and she knew the bungalow was empty again.

Later, at home, she tried to be philosophical. Since she had already decided to break with Jock, what did it matter to her whether he was alive or dead? Better dead, really, since he could no longer arouse her jealousy.

At which reflection she burst into tears. But she was composed and dry-eyed when the police arrived.

The Inspector's first question was inevitable. When, he asked, had she last seen Mr Carrington?

'Last night.' Was it really only last night? 'About seven o'clock, at the bungalow. I left then to come home for supper.'

It was usually supper in the Weston household. Jock always had dinner — when she was with him, anyway. He was quite a good cook; better than herself. Some of the dishes he used to prepare . . .

At the Inspector's request she described that last evening she had spent with Jock. Yes, she said, she had repeated to him her conversation with the police; that had been the reason for her visit. And he had told her they had called on him, and then they had dropped the subject. It had been like any other evening they had spent together, except that Jock had gradually grown more and more preoccupied — and hadn't asked her to stay.

'He could have been expecting another visitor?' the Inspector suggested.

'Perhaps. He didn't say so.'

'You stayed at home that evening? You didn't go out again?'

'No, I didn't go out. Mum and Dad went to the pictures after supper, but I didn't feel like it.'

For some moments there was silence in the room. Pitt's attention was focused on the tall hedge that separated the garden of No. 13 from the road. And as he looked he realized that something was wrong. Very, very wrong.

Had the girl been lying, he wondered, or had she been genuinely mistaken? If she had lied . . . Well, he had considered the possibility of her having murdered Carrington. But that other business . . .

He could not deal with it now, he decided; it was too vague. He needed time to sort it out, to consider the implications.

'Did you know Mr Carrington pos- sessed a shotgun?' He asked the girl.

She shuddered. 'Yes. It was in the hall cupboard, along with the hats and coats. I often asked him why he kept it — he never used it. But he said it was just one of those things one *did* keep. I think it had belonged to his father.'

No one had noticed a visitor at Carrington's bungalow the previous evening, and no one except Miss Plant appeared to have heard the shot. But then the Alsters were away and the house on the other side of No. 5 was empty. And even Miss Plant had not been certain that it *was* a shot. It had been just a noise in the night, she said, that had woken her up. And she had turned over and gone to sleep again without looking at the clock.

He questioned her about the alleged quarrel between Carrington and Heath that she had overheard on the previous Sunday, but she could add nothing to the information with which Mrs Gill had already supplied him. Heath would probably deny it, he thought; he was the denying kind. He would leave Heath to stew for a little while. There was no real evidence against him, and motive in itself meant nothing.

Pitt was surprised at Miss Fratton's changed attitude. She was just as fearsome to look at, but the bark and the bite had gone out of her. Yes, she said, she *had* told Miss Weston that it was Carrington who had invaded her house Sunday night; but now she was not so sure of it. She still *thought* it was him; she just couldn't swear to it, that was all.

'This torch that was stolen?' asked Pitt. 'Where had you put it?'

'On the hall-stand,' said Miss Fratton.

The Inspector cursed himself roundly. He remembered now that he had seen the torch on his first visit to the house; it had been lying in an oval pewter dish. And Miss Fratton had certainly mentioned that the postman had dropped it. But she had *not* mentioned that she had picked it up. If the old horror had behaved more like a human being he might have got round to that. As it was . . .

There had been no sign of the torch at No. 5. But they had not searched the bungalow, it might be hidden away somewhere He did not think they would find it there, however. If they did it would add to the complexity of the case.

Sam Archer was passing the house as the Inspector left it, and greeted him with his customary geniality

'Crime's looking up — eh, Inspector? Bodies all over the place. If they pay you at so much a corpse you will soon be in the super-tax class.'

Pitt frowned. He considered the remark to be in rather bad taste.

'Were you playing darts last night, Mr Archer?' he asked.

'I was. Why?'

'I wondered whether you noticed a light at No. 5 on your way home?'

Archer considered this.

'Come to think of it, I believe I did. About a quarter to eleven, that'd be.'

So the murderer had not left by then; might not even have arrived. But what could be gleaned from that?

'Did you notice anything suspicious or unusual, sir? Meet anyone you know?'

'Aren't those questions rather opposed to each other, Inspector? It isn't suspicious or unusual to meet an acquaintance, is it?' The man paused, and added thoughtfully, 'Or is it? Come to think of it, meeting him like that *was* unusual.'

'Meeting who, sir? And like what?'

'Harris, Inspector. My neighbour once removed. He's a bit of a stay-at-home, you know. I've tried to get him along to the Goat of an evening, but there's no shifting the fellow. Maybe he's got wife trouble, eh? He ought to be able to afford the odd pint, even in these hard times.'

'What was unusual about meeting Mr Harris?' Pitt persisted.

'Well — just meeting him, you know, at such a late hour. And he wasn't going home; coming away from it, in fact. In this direction.'

'Did you speak to him?'

'Just goodnight. But I don't think he heard me. Didn't answer, anyway. Seemed in quite a hurry.'

★　★　★

When Pitt got to the police-station the next morning Dick was waiting for him with a letter. 'Just arrived by hand,' he said. 'I haven't opened it, but it interests me more than somewhat. And if you don't know why, I'll tell you when you've read it.'

'Your natural propensity for poking your nose into other people's business, I imagine,' said the Inspector, slitting the envelope.

The letter was from Avery. It was a restrained epistle, congratulating the police on their handling of a delicate situation. Perhaps the Inspector would be kind enough to telephone him at his office when they had recovered the missing letters? And if the police could see their way to drop the charge of blackmail against the two men involved (he understood there were quite a number of other charges to be brought against them) he would be extremely grateful.

A cheque for ten pounds, 'for police charities,' was enclosed.

'Scared of having to give evidence,' said Pitt. 'I don't blame him, either. Well, we can't drop the charge, but I imagine his name can be kept out of it. As for the letters, God knows what has happened to them. Perhaps Blake has destroyed them.

Now — what are you all het up about, my lad?'

'Call yourself a detective!' scoffed the Sergeant. 'Look at the typing!'

'I've already looked,' said Pitt. 'If we are not both mistaken, it matches with another specimen in our growing collection. Capitals out of line. Which is it? I've forgotten.'

'The money sent to Mrs Laurie,' answered Dick, somewhat crestfallen.

'H'm! Friend Avery likes his women wholesale, it seems.'

'They never learn,' said the Sergeant.

'Only by experience — and Avery is getting his share of that. But I wonder if Mrs Laurie was lying? I wonder if she knew it came from Avery? It may not have been the first instalment, you see.'

'That's true. But she wouldn't tell Bullett and she wouldn't tell us. You know, Loy, it could be that Avery's been playing us up good and proper.'

'How do you mean?'

'Those letters from his girl friend. Both Blake and Sullivan denied all knowledge of them; and they've never been found.

You say Blake may have destroyed them. But why should he? In fact, we've only Avery's word for it that they ever existed. We can't even trace the woman, because she's supposed to have left the country. I had my doubts about that gentleman when he first came to us with his troubles — remember? Now it's beginning to look as if I was right.'

'There's the note,' Pitt pointed out. 'The blackmailing epistle from Blake. You saw that.'

'Who says Blake wrote it?' the Sergeant demanded. 'Not Blake, anyway. Nor Sullivan. Avery could have written it himself.'

'And the hold-up out at Rawsley? How does that come into it?' asked Pitt.

'I don't know. But I do know that Avery's behaviour on the evening Laurie disappeared warrants further investigation. By his own admission he was out that evening. Not only out, but in the right place and at the right time. Laurie left Harris's about five o'clock, Avery left his house at just after five. Mrs Gill saw him.'

'On foot.'

'Yes, I know. Well, there they were, with about two hundred yards between them, walking (or I suppose Laurie may have been cycling) towards each other. And then Avery says he never saw the postman! It's unbelievable.'

'No. It's not that. Not if Laurie was whisked away in the car that Avery said passed him just as he left his house.'

His brother-in-law snorted. 'Avery said! There you go again. Who else saw the car? Harris saw one going down the road, so did Mrs Gill. But we've only Blake's and Sullivan's word for it that it stopped to pick up Laurie. And a nice reliable couple of witnesses *they* are.'

'You think Avery and those two birds are in cahoots?'

'I think they damned well could be. And with him sending money to Mrs Laurie, it shows us a possible motive for Avery wanting to get rid of her husband. If you ask me, it's time we put a few simple questions to that gentleman.'

'Let's put them, then,' said Pitt.

But Avery appeared flabbergasted at

the suggestion that he had sent money to Mrs Laurie. 'I've never either seen or heard of the woman,' he declared indignantly. 'So why the hell should I send her money? I've had enough trouble of that sort, as you damned well know. And I certainly wouldn't foul my own doorstep. What made you pick on me, anyway?'

Pitt showed him his own letter and the envelope addressed to Mrs Laurie. Avery examined them carefully.

'You're right. It looks like they were typed on the same machine,' he agreed. 'But not by me, Inspector. I didn't type that envelope.'

'What machine did you use for the letter, sir?'

'One in the general office. It's the room next to this. Normally my secretary takes down my letters, but you will appreciate that I preferred to type that one myself. I wrote it last night after the staff had gone home.'

'Who has access to the general office, Mr Avery?' asked Pitt.

'Practically everyone. Everyone on the

sales and service staff, that is. And probably others.'

'That would include most of the employees living in Grange Road? Heath, Harris, Archer?'

'Yes. All of them.'

The Sergeant was standing by the window. Pitt, in the centre of the office, heard a faint click as though someone had closed the door very quietly. And he remembered he had shut it firmly on entering the room.

He moved quickly, but there was no one in the passage outside. From the general office came the hum of voices and the clicking of many typewriters. There were other doors, other offices. The eavesdropper could have vanished into any one of them. Or he could have disappeared down the passage. There would have been time for him to turn the corner before the Inspector was even out of the office.

'Somebody is mighty interested in our visit,' Pitt said to the Sergeant, who had joined him. 'I wonder who? And why?'

'I can guess,' said Dick. 'And so can you.'

They went back to Avery, who was still seated at his desk. 'What was all that in aid of?' he asked.

Pitt explained. 'I dare say I was mistaken,' he said. 'Now, sir — I'd like a word with each of those three men. Can you arrange it?'

'Certainly. They should all be here this morning. We close down at midday for the Christmas holiday, you know. I'll get them for you — you can use this office, if you wish.'

Archer treated it as a joke, Harris was scornful. Was it likely, asked Harris, that he would be in a position to send money anywhere? He could not even pay his own way, let alone provide for the needs of a perfect stranger. 'I wouldn't have borrowed that money from Morris if I'd had four quid to chuck away,' he declared. 'You chaps want to use your loaf a bit more.'

'It might be a good idea to use yours, come to that,' Pitt retorted, nettled. 'Getting your wife to give you an alibi for

Thursday night wasn't such a bright idea, was it? Not when you were seen and recognized by a neighbour.'

The man was startled. For a moment he appeared undecided how to answer. Then: 'Who says it was an alibi?' he demanded. 'Why should I need one, anyway?'

'A man was murdered Thursday night,' Pitt reminded him. 'In Grange Road. Or had you forgotten?'

'Oh!' Harris was still truculent. 'So it's murder now, is it? A chap goes for an evening stroll, and that makes him a murderer, eh?'

'It could do,' said the Inspector. 'And it wasn't just a stroll, Mr Harris. I understand you were in quite a hurry. Would you mind telling me why?'

'Yes, I would mind. But that doesn't cut any ice with you, does it? The trouble with you, Inspector, is that you lack imagination. Why do *you* suppose a chap would rush out of his house at half-past ten at night?'

Pitt shook his head. 'As you said, I lack imagination. So suppose you tell me?'

'Because he'd had a row with the wife, of course. Here am I snowed under with bills — and she asks for money to buy a ruddy pram. A pram!' He pursed his lips in disgust. 'Just like a woman — no sense of proportion. And then, when one of your brave boys in blue comes knocking at the door the next morning, she gets all worked up and starts lying. But does that make sense to you? Of course it doesn't. It's too far off the end of your nose.'

'Nice, friendly chap,' said Dick, when Harris had gone. 'Well, now for Heath.'

But Donald Heath was not in the building. After a search Avery contacted a workman who had seen him leave the yard in one of the firm's vans.

'It could only have been a short while ago.' Avery was apologetic. 'I was talking to him a few minutes before you arrived.'

'It must have been Heath, then, who was listening in on us,' said Pitt; 'and something he heard has put the wind up him. Can you let me have the number of the van, sir?'

'I should think so. There can't be many out this morning.'

Pitt telephoned the Superintendent, giving him the particulars. 'There's no indication which way he is heading,' he said.

'I'll put out a general call,' said the Superintendent. 'What's the charge?'

'There isn't one. I want him held for questioning.'

'All right. By the way, they've located that schoolmaster of yours. A man named Stilby. He's living in Guildford.'

Blake and Sullivan had been lodged in Lexeter Gaol pending trial. Pitt paid them a visit. Carrington's supposed confession had stated that he had persuaded Laurie to get into the car, and it was the word 'persuaded' that puzzled the Inspector. Obviously that part of the document was based on fact, if Blake and Sullivan were to be believed. Yet both these men, when first questioned, had said that as soon as the car pulled up the postman had dumped his bicycle and hopped into the car. That did not sound as though much persuasion had been needed, or used.

Blake was of the same opinion. Gaol, apparently, had softened him. He was more than willing to talk.

'He didn't need no persuading,' he declared. 'Soon as he saw the car coming he was on the grass with his bike. Then, when the car pulled up, he just got into the back seat and they was off.'

'How long was the car stationary?'

'Only a few seconds, Inspector. Looked to me as though it was a fixed job. I'd swear the postman was expecting the car to pick him up.'

That was how it looked to the Inspector. 'Would you be able to recognize the man who passed you on foot before you picked up the mail?' he asked.

Blake shook his head. 'He was all muffled up,' he said. 'Collar round his face, hat jammed down on his head. I couldn't pick him out in a month of Sundays.' He hesitated. 'Er — how's the chap what got it in the stomach, Inspector? Will he be okay?'

'He'll pull through, with luck,' said Pitt. In fact, Hennessy was making a remarkably rapid recovery, but he saw no reason to relieve the gunman of all anxiety on this score.

Sullivan was as loquacious as Blake, and equally unhelpful about Avery. And both men reiterated their denial of blackmail.

Pitt was puzzled by this, and a little worried. Sullivan, he thought, could well be speaking the truth. He was a simple fellow, and obviously under Blake's influence. Since he could neither read nor write, it was possible that Blake had written the note to Avery without Sullivan's knowledge. It was Blake who had been watching the Averys' house on the Saturday, it was Blake whom Mrs Gill had seen from the top of the bus on Wednesday. And no doubt Blake had had every intention of pocketing the whole of the blackmail money if it materialized.

That was straightforward enough. But why should Blake deny it all? Perhaps he thought the police would be unable to prove the charge, might even decide to drop it in view of the other charges. Yet those damned letters written to Avery's woman had never been found; and why should Blake have destroyed them?

There was no I-told-you-so air about

Sergeant Ponsford when his brother-in-law confessed to him this nagging doubt. The Sergeant had a headache, and his stomach was misbehaving. 'A chill, I expect,' he said. 'I always did have a delicate tum.'

The van in which Heath had escaped had been found two miles west of Durnbourne. Heath himself was still missing. They thought he was probably hiding in the woods that fringed both sides of the main road at that point, and a police cordon had been thrown round the area. 'And they are watching all the bus termini and railway stations, just in case,' added Dick. 'He can't have got far; he didn't have a long enough start.'

The Inspector nodded absently. There were so many odd facets, so many contradictions.

'How deeply do you think Heath is involved?' asked Dick. 'Did he kill them both, or only Carrington, or neither?'

Pitt shook his head. He was not really listening. He sat at his desk doodling on the blotting-paper in front of him. The events of that morning had allowed little time for thought. Now, with Heath looming large in his mind, he was considering the possibilities of the vague idea which had occurred to him the previous afternoon.

The Sergeant eyed him curiously. 'What's on your mind, Loy?' he asked.

'Miss Weston's hedge,' said Pitt.

'Eh?' Dick was startled. 'They're a nice pair, I'll admit that. But I wouldn't have thought a girl's legs could — '

'Not her legs, you fool. Her hedge.'

'Oh. That's different. What's wrong with her hedge?'

'It's too tall.'

'Is it, though? Well, maybe we can persuade her to have it cut. How much do you want taken off?'

'You're an ass, Dick,' said his brother-in-law, 'but I'll have to bear with you. What I'm getting at is that Miss Weston's hedge is too high for her to have seen Laurie passing the house yesterday week — as she said she did.'

'Oh!' The Sergeant was sobered. 'How high it is, then?'

'Five foot six exactly.'

'But that's fine!' exclaimed Dick. 'Laurie was five foot six, and she only saw his cap. What's wrong with that?'

The Inspector stood up and walked over to the window.

'It isn't fine,' he said. 'What you've forgotten — I overlooked it myself until yesterday — is that — Come in!'

The knock was followed by an excited young constable.

'That chap Heath, sir,' he said. 'They've got him. He's here now.'

11

A Dose of Bicarb

It was blind panic that prompted Heath to run. He had no real hope of evading the police for long; sooner or later, he knew, they would catch up with him. But he wanted time to think. He had heard the questions they had put to Avery — the questions that later they would put to him. If he could get away, stall them off for a while — well, maybe then he could work it out. But he had to have time.

He drove fast, heading east along the coast road. The direction did not matter; all he wanted was to put as many miles as possible between himself and the police. Hands gripping the wheel, he urged the van on with his body, swaying backward and forward, steering mechanically. But the windows were down, and the cold air steadied his panic-stricken brain. He began to think, to search for the right answer. The time he was borrowing might be short. He must not waste it.

As he neared Durnbourne he realized that they would probably be waiting for him. There would have been time to alert the police in the area. But he was not ready for them yet, and the woods offered a sanctuary. He would sit in the woods and think it all out; and then, when he was ready, he would go home — if they would let him.

He was in the woods for two hours. It did not seem very long to him, and it was only the sound of voices that made him look at his watch. He knew it was the police, searching the woods; and still he wasn't ready. His mind had gone round and round the problem. It seemed to him that there was only the truth; and the truth spelt disaster.

He began to move silently through the woods, away from the voices. But presently there were other voices ahead, and he turned right, going faster, thinking speed more important than silence. They were all round him, he thought. He would have to get out of the wood.

When he heard the voices again he lost his nerve and began to run; blindly, with no thought to direction. He was deep in the wood now, and the undergrowth was thicker. Brambles and low branches impeded him, and sometimes he fell. But always he picked himself up and ran on, a hand shielding his face, another stretched out to move the foliage aside where it was thick. The very act of running added to his fear, so that his mind was now obsessed with a wild desire to escape. He no longer tried to reason.

They heard him coming and waited. And to Heath the hand that caught him was at first just another bramble, so that instinctively he fought to release himself from its clutches. But then there were other hands, and he came to his senses and saw them. And at that he ceased to struggle and was suddenly calm.

'What are you arresting me for?' he asked, panting. 'I've done nothing wrong.'

'We are not arresting you, sir,' said a tall sergeant. 'But I must ask you to accompany me to the police-station for questioning.'

His trousers were torn and his jacket was frayed where the brambles had caught and loosened the threads. His face was scratched and dirty. To Inspector Pitt he looked a rather pitiable object.

'Why did you run away, Mr Heath?' he asked sternly.

It was funny, thought Heath, how you could try to escape from something, fight like hell to fend it off — and then, when it caught up with you, find that it wasn't nearly as big or as terrifying as you had imagined it to be. All that time in the woods had not been able to supply him with the right answer. And now it didn't seem to matter. Not so much, anyway.

Even so, he wouldn't succumb meekly. He wasn't done yet. If they didn't know . . . if they were only guessing, hoping to frighten him into the truth . . .

'I was browned off.' His throat was dry, his voice not quite under control. 'You fellows seem to haunt me. Seeing you at the works again this morning — ' He stopped. Wiser not to enlarge on that. 'What am I supposed to have done, anyway?'

'We'll come to that later,' said Pitt. 'But if you get yourself involved in a murder — two murders — you must expect the police to ask questions. Had you been more co-operative at the beginning — '

'You can cut out the sermon, Inspector. What is it you want to know?'

'That's better,' Pitt approved. 'Well, now. To begin with, how well do you know Mrs Laurie?'

This applied assumption by the police of a knowledge at which they were only guessing had the desired effect. Heath, uncertain of how much they knew (he had caught only fragments of the conversation in Avery's office), dare not deny it. He shook his head in a negative manner, hoping that the Inspector might yet give him a lead.

Pitt looked at him sorrowfully. 'Still running away, Mr Heath? Then I'll be more explicit. Why did you send money to Mrs Laurie?'

The Inspector's confidence was disturbing. 'Oh, that!' He tried to laugh. 'It's not a crime to send money to a person, is it?'

But Pitt had no intention of being baulked at this stage. Heath was going to talk, and talk turkey. 'You know Mrs Laurie is the wife of the postman who was murdered yesterday week?' he asked.

'I'd *heard* he was murdered,' Heath said cautiously. 'But of course that was only a rumour. There are a good many rumours floating around Grange Road at present, Inspector, and most of them aren't true.'

'It was in the papers,' said Pitt.

'Was it? Well, that still doesn't make it true. At least . . . ' He paused, and looked from one to the other of the police officers. '*When* did you say he was murdered?'

'Yesterday week. Friday, the day he disappeared.'

To their astonishment, he laughed. It was a genuine laugh, tinged with contempt. 'If you believe that then someone's been fooling you,' he said. 'The postman may be dead, but he wasn't killed yesterday week.'

'And why are you so sure of that?' asked Pitt.

'Why? Because he spoke to me on the telephone Monday evening. That's why.'

Has he gone crackers? wondered the Inspector; or is it another of his lies? 'You're wrong, you know,' he said. 'Laurie died on the Friday, as I said. If someone spoke to you on the telephone it wasn't Laurie.'

It was Heath's turn to look puzzled. He scratched his head.

'I can't understand it,' he said. 'The voice was the same. What's more, he *told* me he was the postman. And it seemed reasonable. That was how he got hold of the letter, I thought.'

It wasn't until he had said it that he realized he had given himself away. He looked fearfully at the Inspector. But it was the Sergeant who spoke.

'Why are you so sure it was the postman on the phone?' he asked. 'You heard his voice only once before, and I gathered that wasn't a lengthy conversation.'

'He happened to use the same words,' said Heath, relieved that they had taken him up on that point and not on the other. 'He's got quite a distinctive voice, too. But I agree that I may be mistaken. As you say, he didn't have much to say the first time I heard him.'

'Would you recognize him if you saw him?' asked Pitt.

Heath shook his head. 'No. I didn't see him properly.'

'And this letter you say he got hold of? What's all that about?'

His heart sank, but he tried to bluff it out. 'It was a private matter, Inspector. I don't wish to discuss it.'

'I don't think you quite realize your position, Mr Heath.' Pitt's voice was icy. 'On your own admission you and Laurie had a fight on the day he disappeared — only a few minutes, in fact, *before* he disappeared. On Tuesday you sent money to his wife. Taken together, those two facts need a lot of explaining. And if you cannot explain them satisfactorily . . . '

He thought it better to leave the sentence unfinished. The implication should be sufficient.

Heath was really worried now. He knew very little about the law, and he thought it quite likely that, should he continue in his refusal to explain, he stood a good chance of being arrested for the postman's murder. And as yet they had said nothing about Carrington!

He began to walk nervously up and down the room.

'I'll tell you this,' he said. 'About a fortnight ago I was desperately in need of money. I'd committed a . . . an indiscretion. That's the part I can't explain, Inspector — but I swear it has absolutely nothing to do with Laurie.'

'Go on,' said Pitt.

'Well, I wrote to an aunt of mine, telling her what had happened and asking her to help me out. I needed two hundred pounds, I told her, and I needed it before last week-end. I thought she might send it because — well, that's bound up with family affairs that wouldn't interest you. But it was this money I was expecting when the postman called Friday afternoon. I had made sure it would come that day if it was coming at all. And when it didn't I — well, as I told you, I chased after him.'

'That was when he knocked you down?'

'Yes. Of course, afterwards I realized what a fool I'd been; but that didn't alter the fact that the money hadn't turned up. When you told me next day that there should have been a registered letter for me I guessed it must have been from my aunt. But I still hadn't got the money, so I wrote again, asking her to cancel the cheque and send another.'

'Did she do that?'

'Yes.'

'And how does the postman come into all this?' asked Pitt.

'It was on Monday evening that he rang me up,' said Heath. 'He told me he'd got my aunt's letter, with a cheque for four hundred pounds enclosed.'

Dick Ponsford whistled softly. Some aunt! he thought.

Heath heard the whistle. 'Yes,' he said. 'It staggered me, too. But then came the shock. Laurie said that Aunt Ellen had replied to my letter by writing on the back of it — that's a habit of hers — and he therefore knew all about my — er

— indiscretion. He said he would return the cheque; but as I had only asked for two hundred I could pay him the balance in return for his silence.'

'I see,' said Pitt. 'And how does Mrs Laurie come into it?'

'I was to send the money to her. Not all at once, but in weekly instalments. If I sent her four pounds a week, he said, it would keep her for a year. After that he would be able to provide for her himself.'

'So you sent the first instalment?'

'Yes. I couldn't do anything else, could I? If I'd refused he would have sent my letter to the — to the people concerned.'

'You could have informed the police,' Pitt suggested. 'We know how to deal with gentry like that. Did he return the cheque?'

'Yes. But I already had the second one by then, so I burnt it.'

'And the envelope?'

'I burnt that too.'

The Inspector sat silent for some time, thinking over what Heath had told him. And with the silence Heath himself grew more nervous. At last he could stand it no longer.

'I didn't kill the man, Inspector,' he said earnestly. 'I've told you everything now, honest I have. I know I've acted like a damned fool, but it's no worse than that.' He wanted to refer to Carrington, to make them come out into the open; but he could not bring himself to speak the man's name. 'What are you going to do? You're not going to keep me here, are you? The sergeant said I wasn't under arrest.'

'No, you're not under arrest, Mr Heath.' Pitt was uncertain how to act. He could not detain the man indefinitely. Yet if he let him go . . .

'There's another little matter we may as well clear up while you're here,' he said. 'The quarrel between you and Carrington.'

Now for it. 'You couldn't really call it a quarrel,' he said slowly. 'We happened to be in love with the same girl, that's all. The gossips in Grange Road will have told you that; it won't be news to you.'

'I wasn't referring to the general state of affairs between the two of you, Mr Heath. I want to know about the row you had on Sunday night.'

Heath shook his head. 'I don't understand, Inspector. I haven't spoken to Carrington for weeks.'

Pitt lost his temper.

'Good God, man!' he said angrily. 'Don't you ever come out into the open without being pushed? I've got witnesses who heard you — can you understand that?'

'They're lying,' said Heath. 'I wasn't there.'

'Where?' snapped Pitt.

'Well — wherever they said I was.'

The Inspector looked at him in disgust.

'All right,' he said. 'Have it your own way. But let me tell you this. From now on we'll be watching you all the time. You won't get away from us. One false move . . . '

He snapped his fingers expressively and turned away.

'Bloody young fool,' he said, when Heath had gone. 'Lies, lies, lies. It gets him nowhere. Worse, it gets us nowhere also.'

'Self-preservation, I suppose,' Dick suggested.

'Lying won't help him. Nor the others, either. Avery, Harris, Morris, Bullett, Mrs Laurie — the whole flaming lot of 'em have lied right and left. They have no more moral sense than a bunch of — of — of stoats,' he ended lamely.

'Why stoats?' asked Dick.

'Well — why not?'

The Sergeant did not press the point. 'You were suggesting, before Heath arrived, that Dorothy Weston was also a candidate for the Ananias stakes,' he said.

'Ah, yes. Miss Weston.' The Inspector's mood changed. He sat down at the desk, picked up a pencil and began to draw. 'Look, Dick. It's a matter of simple geometry. The Westons' hedge is five foot six high and at least a foot thick. The snag lies in the fact that the house lies below the level of the road and is fairly close to the hedge. So Miss Weston, standing in the front room downstairs, was looking *up* at the hedge. There.' He drew in a diagonal line. 'That's roughly her line of vision. See what I mean?'

Dick nodded, calculating rapidly. 'According to this the postman would have had to be over seven foot high for her to have seen his cap.'

'Yes, I know. I'm a bit out somewhere. Probably the house stands higher than that. But the fact remains that she couldn't have seen a man only five foot six inches tall on the other side of that hedge. Not even his cap. Not from that angle, anyway.'

'So she was lying, eh?'

'Yes. But the point is — did she know she was lying?'

The Sergeant considered this. 'I don't think I quite get it, Loy,' he said. 'You couldn't make it plainer, could you?'

'No,' said Pitt. 'I can't. The idea is there, chasing itself round my head. But don't ask me to put it into words. Not yet. What I need is — well, something that will make it click. Blow up all the bits and pieces, mix 'em thoroughly, and have them fitting neatly into place when they settle again.'

'A dose of bicarb, same as my stomach. That's what you need,' suggested the other.

'Perhaps.' Inspector Pitt stood up and reached for his hat. 'Have Heath tailed, Dick, in case he bolts. I'm going in search of that bicarb.'

As the police car threaded its way through the town the Inspector admitted to himself that he had not been entirely frank with his brother-in-law. The idea was not as vague as he had pretended; it was just that he needed confirmation before putting it into words. He *must* be right — there was really no alternative.

The sight of a familiar figure carrying a shopping-basket caused him to lean forward and speak to the driver. The car drew into the kerb and stopped.

'Can I give you a lift, Mrs Gill?' asked Pitt. 'I'm on my way to Grange Road.'

Mrs Gill was flustered and flattered.

'How kind of you, Inspector. I've missed the bus, and this basket really is quite heavy. And the evenings do draw in, don't they. It's almost dark already, and I must say I don't fancy walking down

Grange Road after dark these days. Silly of me, I know. But there it is.'

It was inevitable that they should talk of the murders.

'Of course, I know it's none of my business, but I think I'm speaking for the whole road when I say that we'll all sleep a lot easier when you decide to arrest him, Inspector,' she said, enjoying the comfort of the car and the sense of importance it gave her. 'You can't rush these things, I know. It's all bound up with evidence and witnesses and suchlike, isn't it? You have to have a case that will convince a jury, don't you? But all the same — well, I think you should know that you will have our full support when you decide to act.'

'Thank you, Mrs Gill. That's very comforting,' Pitt assured her gravely. 'Er — arrest whom? Were you referring to any specific person?'

'Not by name, Inspector. I'll not be caught again.' Mrs Gill's voice was arch. 'But I don't think we need to mention names, do we, to know that we're talking of the same person? Even to an amateur like myself it's obvious enough.'

Pitt's reply was non-committal. He was back to his problem again.

'How well did you know Mr Carrington?' he asked.

'It so happens, Inspector, that he was the one person in Grange Road with whom I've had absolutely no contact at all,' Mrs Gill told him regretfully. 'Both he and Miss Fratton did not mix with the rest of us. Except, of course, with Miss Weston. They were both very partial to *her*.'

'Ah, yes. Miss Fratton. Would you call her a truthful person, Mrs Gill?'

'I don't know, I'm sure. Perhaps not. But then, it's only since these dreadful things have been happening that I've really got to know her. I think she exaggerates, certainly. All that fuss about postmen, calling them thieves and liars and goodness knows what else. She can't really believe it, can she?'

'It does seem bigoted, certainly,' the Inspector agreed. He was glad that they were rapidly nearing Grange Road. A little of Mrs Gill went a long way.

'I stood up for them, of course, when she started on *me*,' Mrs Gill continued. 'They're always such nice men, I said, and a uniform does something to a man, there's no denying it. Of course, I didn't see this Mr Laurie, so I couldn't argue when she spoke about him. Slovenly, she said he was, with oilskins several sizes too small for him. And Miss Plant, when she passed him outside Carrington's bungalow, did think he was rather surly. Just grunted at her, she said.'

'Probably fed up with the weather,' suggested Pitt, leaning forward to open the door as the car slowed and came to a stop in front of No. 24. Then he stiffened. Still grasping the handle, he turned and looked at the woman.

'You said they were too small, Mrs Gill,' he said. 'The postman's oilskins, I mean. But you made a mistake, didn't you? What Miss Fratton actually said was that the oilskins were too *big* for him. Isn't that it?'

Mrs Gill was surprised at the tension in his voice.

'Oh, no, Inspector. She was quite

definite. Too small, she said, as though he'd grown out of them years ago. Those were her very words, I assure you.'

He got out of the car and helped her on to the pavement.

'Goodbye, Inspector, and thank you so much for the lift. It was a real treat,' Mrs Gill said gratefully, as she took the shopping-basket from him.

Inspector Pitt almost bowed over her hand. 'Thank *you*, Mrs Gill,' he said fervently.

Mrs Gill watched the rear-light of the police car diminish and disappear down the length of Grange Road. Then she sighed and turned to open the gate.

I've quite misjudged him, she thought guiltily. He really has *charming* manners. The way he said 'thank you,' it might have been *me* who'd done *him* a service.

12

You Would Be the Corpse

Inspector Pitt thought Eric Stilby a rather seedy individual, and hoped he was not representative of his profession. As a schoolmaster the man seemed unlikely to inspire the young. Although he was not much over thirty, his hair was thin and wispy and he walked with a stoop, his body bent forward from the waist. His face was long and lean, and he appeared not to have shaved that morning. He wore a faded sports jacket, frayed at the cuffs; the seams were splitting at the back of the shoulders, and foodstuffs marked the lapels. His flannel trousers were old and baggy, and there were eggstains on the grey pullover. But his hands were clean and well cared for, with long, tapering fingers. Artistic, probably, thought Pitt; although that hardly seemed sufficient excuse for his general appearance.

The name Laurie meant nothing to him. But at the mention of Jane Abbott, Mrs Laurie's maiden name, he nodded. Yes, he admitted, he had known her in the past.

'About two years ago, wasn't it, sir?' asked Pitt. 'When you were living in Tanmouth?'

'I wasn't living there,' said Stilby. 'Had a job there, that's all. At a prep school. I lived in, of course, but I came home to Guildford for the holidays.'

'How well did you know Mrs Laurie, sir? Or should I say, Miss Abbott?'

He did not answer this at once. Instead, he said, 'Why have you come to see me, Inspector? What has Miss Abbott been up to? And what's it got to do with me, anyway?'

'We'll come to that in a minute, Mr Stilby. It may have nothing at all to do with you. At present I am searching for something that may clear up a point which is worrying me, and I've come to you because I believe it may be connected with her life before she was married. You knew her then, you say.'

'Yes. We were engaged; but not for long. She was a damned good-looker, but too flighty for me. Headmasters would have thought twice about giving me a job if I'd had Jane Abbott for a wife.'

At the Inspector's prompting Stilby told what he could remember of the girl. It fitted well enough with the impression Pitt had already formed. She had been a good-time girl, thinking of nothing but dances and clothes and parties. And men. There were always men, said Stilby; she never seemed to have a girl friend. Her mother had died many years before he knew her, and her father had married again. Jane lived with an indulgent uncle; although, thinking it over afterwards, the young man said darkly, he had wondered just what sort of an uncle the fellow was. 'I never met him; but he certainly gave her her head. She could stay out half the night, and never seemed to care what the old man might say when she got in. She never asked anyone back to her home; not to my knowledge, anyway. Perhaps he wasn't as indulgent as all that.'

'And how long were you engaged?' asked Pitt.

'Oh, not long. Just over a month. I got paid at half-term, and was able to take her out in the car a bit. Taught her to drive, as a matter of fact. That was something new for her, and it took her fancy. Maybe that's why she stuck to me for a few weeks. And with her being such a good-looker, and sex rearing its ugly head, I — well, I asked her to marry me. And, much to my surprise, she accepted.'

I wonder why? thought Pitt. You can't have been such a good catch. Schoolmasters are not liberally paid, and you're no Apollo.

'And then you quarrelled?' he said.

'Not exactly,' said Stilby. 'It takes two to make a quarrel. I just told her I was through, that's all. That was at the end of term. And as I was packing up at the school I never saw her again. You say she's married?'

'Yes. To a man named Laurie. A postman. You never met him?'

'Never even heard of him, Inspector. A

postman, eh? That was a bit of a come-down for Jane, with all her big ideas. How are they getting along?'

'Her husband is dead, Mr Stilby. He was murdered nine days ago. That is why I am here.'

Eric Stilby leaned forward excitedly. 'Murdered, eh? Good Lord! And who did it? Jane?'

'We don't know,' said Pitt. 'Not yet. I wonder if you can recall the names of any of her previous friends or acquaintances, sir? That may help. I have an idea her husband died because she was mixed up with another man.'

'I should say that's a pretty safe bet, knowing Jane,' Stilby agreed. He rattled off a few names, and then, at longer intervals, a few more. None of them meant anything to the Inspector, but he made a note of them.

'Of course, there must have been dozens I never met,' said Stilby. 'She sort of collected them, you might say. For instance, there was this chap that caused all the trouble. I didn't think highly of him at the time, but afterwards I realized he had saved me from making an ass of myself.'

'And who was he?'

'I don't know. Neither did she. We just kind of picked him up.'

'Perhaps I might have the details,' Pitt suggested.

'Certainly. It's a sordid story, but no doubt you're used to that. We had gone out in the car to some village or other a few miles out of Tanmouth. I was in the money, so we had a good dinner. After that we did a bit of pub-crawling, and then we came across this snake in the grass. Quite a decent-looking bloke — I rather took to him at first. He was propping up the bar, and we had a few drinks together. Then we had a few more, and a few more after that — not Jane; drinking wasn't one of her vices, I'll say that for her. She came in about every fourth round, just to be matey — and in no time at all I was pretty near being whistled. No, let's be truthful — I *was* whistled. Tight as a drum. So I just settled myself in an armchair and left them to it.

'I'm somewhat hazy as to what happened immediately after that. I've a faint recollection of them shoving me into the front of the car, and Jane getting in beside me and driving off. And then I passed out again.

'About an hour or so later I struggled back to consciousness to find myself still in the car, which had been parked in the entrance to a field. Jane seemed to have disappeared, and I wondered what the hell had happened to her and what I was doing there. It was raining, too — not the sort of night one picks for star-gazing. But I was feeling lousy, and not too inquisitive. So I just sat there, hoping my stomach would stay where it was and my head wouldn't split.

'There was a sort of rustling noise in the back of the car, and after a while I got around to noticing it. Then I heard them murmuring to each other, and I realized what was going on. It hurt like hell to turn my head, but I managed it; and talk about a necking party!

'They were so engrossed in each other that they didn't notice I'd come to; and, being somewhat uncertain as to the correct procedure, I didn't disturb them at once. I couldn't just say something like 'Hi, you! Leave my fiancée alone'; it was a bit too late for that, anyway. And I was in no state to take physical action. But I knew I had to do something. To sit there and say nothing would be most undignified. And I'm a great one for dignity, Inspector.'

You're a great one for talking, thought Pitt. He was getting rather bored with this long rigmarole, and hoped it would lead somewhere eventually. But he had asked for detail. He could hardly grumble now that he was getting it.

'And what *did* you do, sir?' he asked.

'Well, I sat there a bit longer, trying to think of the appropriate words. Then I heard Jane say, 'You'll have to marry me now,' and the man laughed and said something about not being the marrying type. And at that I made a great effort and turned round and said, 'Then you'd better change your type, because it looks as though somebody ought to marry her, and I'm certainly not going to.' Then I managed to open the door of the car and got out — and promptly fell flat on my face.'

The Inspector laughed. He asked, 'And what happened after that?'

'Oh, they picked me up and dumped me back in the car, and Jane drove me back to the school. I never saw either of them again. When I looked in the car the next morning the ring I had given her was in an envelope on the front seat. And that was the end of *that* little romance.'

'Most unfortunate, sir,' said Pitt. 'But if you don't know the man's name it isn't much help to me. Could you describe him, perhaps? I know it means going back two years, and that you only saw the man for one evening. But if you could give me a sort of thumbnail sketch, as it were . . .'

Stilby stared at him. 'Why, yes, Inspector. I think I could manage *that*.'

⋆   ⋆   ⋆

On his way back to Tanmouth the Inspector had to change at Lexeter. Michael Bullett was on the platform, waiting for the same train. Pitt was sure the reporter had noticed him; but when the train came in Bullett moved farther down the platform before entering a carriage.

What's biting him? thought Pitt. He's not usually so shy. He walked down the swaying corridor until he found his quarry. Bullett was alone in the compartment.

'Why so coy, Mr Bullett?' asked Pitt. 'You don't usually avoid us. It tends to be the other way round.'

'I wasn't avoiding you.' If he had not known that to be untrue Pitt would have believed it. The man was certainly convincing. 'In any case, you may recall that our last meeting was rather strained.'

Pitt nodded. 'I remember all right. As I said at the time — in my righteous anger — you acted like a fool. I even dallied with the idea of arresting you for obstructing the police. But we all have our foolish moments. Don't let it burden your conscience, Mr Bullett.'

The reporter grinned. 'Thanks, I won't. How's crime, anyway? Have you found out who sent that money to Jane Laurie?'

'Yes. It appears to have no connection with her husband's murder.' He was not anxious to enlarge on this, and said hastily, 'You haven't given us much of a write-up, Mr Bullett. Carrington's death was splashed, of course — you couldn't avoid that, him being a fairly prominent figure in the world of art. Though I noticed you didn't say outright it was murder. 'The police have not ruled out the possibility of foul play,' I think you said.'

'Something like that. I was trying to be kind.'

'Kind? Kind to whom?'

'To you. You and the Sarge. You never want to plump for murder, Inspector, unless you're dead sure you can make an early arrest. Just hint at suicide. The public lap it up, wonder a bit, and then forget it. But murder — that's different. They look forward to an arrest. And as the days pass and there's nothing about it in the papers, they begin to wonder what the police are up to. Soon they start writing to the papers; and I suppose it is about then that the Chief Constable begins asking you awkward questions, eh? No. Take my advice, Inspector, as a man who knows the public. Stick to suicide. They just think you're extra smart if you turn it into murder later. So you win both ways.'

'I'll bear it in mind,' Pitt promised.

'My editor thinks that either you or I have fallen down on the job,' said Bullett, taking up his paper again. 'If you don't make an arrest soon we'll *both* be in the soup. How about one of those reconstruction scenes they have in books? That would make good copy, if nothing else.'

'Perhaps,' said Pitt. 'They always seem rather pointless to me. One can't depend on the two chief actors, you see. The corpse is unable to play his part, so you have to get a stand-in for him. As for the murderer — well, you can hardly expect him to enter into it whole-heartedly, can you? He is far more likely to throw a spanner into the works when he gets the chance.'

'That's true,' Bullett agreed. 'Well, perhaps the good old-fashioned police methods will bring results in due course.'

For a while, as the reporter read his paper, Pitt ruminated on his interview with Eric Stilby. He knew most of it now, and what he didn't know he could guess. The difficulty was to prove it. He had a case, of course; but was it good enough to put before a jury? Would he get a conviction?

Presently he said, 'You know, perhaps that's not a bad idea of yours, Mr Bullett.'

'What isn't a bad idea? I've lost the thread.'

'Sorry. I was referring to your suggestion that we reconstruct the crime. It wouldn't help us with Carrington's death — we don't know enough of the circumstances — but we might be able to clear up a point about Laurie's disappearance that has been worrying me. Something — several things, in fact — happened to him while he was in Grange Road. I want to know — ' He looked speculatively at the other. 'You wouldn't care to take part, I suppose?'

Bullett raised an arm across his face in mock alarm.

'I most certainly would not. Not after last time. Sitting at a ruddy attic window with my eyes glued on a blasted pillar-box, waiting for it to be cleared by a postman who had been dead for days. No, thank you, Inspector. Never again.'

'We didn't know then that he was dead,' Pitt reminded him. 'Anyway, it wouldn't be like that. This time you would be the corpse.'

'Oh, would I! Well, that's different, of course. Promotion — star billing, eh? But the answer is still no, Inspector. I'm not cut out for an actor. Get one of your own bright boys to play the part. What's wrong with the Sarge, for instance?'

'Gastric flu.'

'Really? I'm sorry; I didn't know. Still, you've got a large cast to choose from. Let me know when the play is to be staged, Inspector, and I'll give you a write-up in the *Chronicle*.'

Pitt thanked him. 'We could do with a little publicity of the right sort,' he said.

★　★　★

Dick Ponsford was in bed and far from cheerful. 'A nice time I choose to fall sick,' he groaned. 'How's it going, Loy?'

Pitt told him. When he heard of the proposed reconstruction the Sergeant groaned even louder. 'It can't wait, I suppose?' he pleaded. 'I'll be up in a day or two.'

'You know it can't, Dick.'

'No, of course. Who's going to take Laurie's place?'

'I haven't fixed that. I asked Bullett, but he turned it down.'

The Sergeant was surprised. 'Did he though? And him always grumbling about the scoops he doesn't get.'

'He's going to attend in his official capacity,' said Pitt.

'What about Carrington?'

'I don't think we'll need a substitute for Carrington,' said the Inspector.

'Well, I hope it's a success. What exactly do you expect to learn from it?'

'Nothing much,' lied Pitt, remembering his sister's instructions. 'But you never know.'

Inspector Pitt spent a busy and varied

afternoon; but when he returned to his sister's house that evening he considered he had done everything possible to ensure the success of the experiment fixed for the morrow. The Superintendent had promised him the needed men; the inhabitants of Grange Road had been advised and instructed. Yet he knew well that the odds against his plan succeeding were heavy. 'I'd say you have enough evidence without this; but if you want the murderer to hang himself there's no harm in trying,' had been the Super's comment. Pitt was not so sure he had been right there. It might well be that if the plan failed it would provide evidence for instead of against the killer. But he felt he had to take that chance. He had a fair case, but he wanted a perfect one.

'How's Dick?' he asked his sister, as she prepared a hot drink. 'I could do with his support tomorrow.'

'You won't get it,' said Wendy. 'He has a high temperature, and it isn't improved by his fretting over this wretched case. He feels he's letting you down.'

'That's rot. Let me talk to him.'

'Not tonight, Loy. Tomorrow.'

Tomorrow. As he sipped his drink the Inspector once more reviewed the arrangements he had made. Grange Road had shown little enthusiasm for his plan. Perhaps they were reluctant to be dragged back into the realms of murder. There were, after all, only four more days to Christmas. It was a time for festivity, not for inquests; although there had been a lack of the usual seasonal decorations in the houses he had visited that afternoon. Only the Archers had done the thing properly: paper streamers and balloons, holly and a candle-lit Christmas tree. But then there were children at No. 19, and the Archers seemed essentially a united family. A happy one, too. But though there were also children at No. 17, no one could call the Harrises a happy family. There was nothing there to compensate for poverty. Mrs Harris had no doubt done her best: holly, and a few tattered decorations which had done service on previous occasions. But it would have taken more than this sop to festivity to dispel the dreary atmosphere pervading the house.

Pitt felt sorry for Mrs Harris and the children. But Harris himself was all wrong. Although he had not refused to conform to the police arrangements for the morrow, he had been extremely surly. No doubt he had suffered a shock when he had read in the newspapers of Morris's arrest. The vision of easy money had been rudely dispelled.

Archer's welcome had been typical. 'Come in, man,' he had said heartily; and then, to his wife, 'Maisie, here's the Inspector. The one that thought I was keeping another woman. Me — with my stomach!' He had made no demur at the rather unusual request Pitt had made of him, had shown no surprise and had asked few questions. And as the Inspector was leaving he had said in a loud whisper, 'Just write down the address, will you? Who knows, I might get fed up with darts.'

Robert Avery had shown little enthusiasm. 'What use can I be?' he had asked querulously. 'I never saw the damned postman, as I told you. And I bet we get another of those filthy evenings.' Pitt thought that the man's charm was something he turned on only when it could be of use to him, but that otherwise he didn't bother. He began to feel some slight sympathy for Mrs Avery. 'You will probably be entirely superfluous, sir,' he had said blandly; and had added, hoping it did not sound too much like blackmail, 'I think you owe us a little co-operation.'

Avery's bubble of discontent had burst like a balloon at that.

Mrs Gill, on the other hand, was only sorry that she had no proper part to play; and Donald Heath had seemed eager to help. 'I'm glad I don't have to sport another black eye,' he had said, with some attempt at humour. 'I suppose I couldn't give the postman one, for a change?'

There had been a bunch of mistletoe hanging in the hall of No. 9, and Pitt had wondered whether it was there for Miss Weston's benefit. If so, he doubted whether it would be brought into use. Miss Weston herself had made it quite clear that she had no intention of observing Christmas. 'I don't want to be morbid,' she had said to the Inspector, 'but Jock Carrington was a special friend, someone out of the ordinary. It wouldn't seem right to be celebrating so soon after his death. At least, that's the way I feel. And Mum and Dad agree with me.'

I wish I understood women, thought Pitt. If she wasn't in love with Carrington, she certainly wasn't indifferent to him. Yet she had referred to the man without a tremor in her voice, and had spoken of her plans calmly and easily. And, if he had not expected to find her in mourning, he also had not expected the bright attractiveness that she had displayed for his benefit. Either she's a cold-blooded fish, he decided, or she's a better actress than one would expect a chorus-girl to be.

He had saved Miss Fratton until the end. Despite her less bellicose attitude on his last visit, there was no knowing whether or not she had reverted to her former frame of mind. As he knocked at the door of No. 14 he had been glad that he was alone. To confront Miss Fratton with a uniformed officer would not have been a tactful beginning.

She had been grudgingly suspicious, but she had not refused him admittance. To his surprise, however, she had been most reluctant to re-enact her former rôle of Postman's Nightmare. Only an assurance that in so doing she would be benefiting her neighbours had made her consent. 'I still don't like 'em,' she had said as he was leaving. 'They're a thieving lot, as this business only goes to show. But telling them so doesn't make 'em any better, it just puts them on their guard.'

I wonder how much of her former ferocity was an act, Pitt thought sleepily, as he got into bed. If she ever looked in a mirror she would know how well it suited her. Benevolence in the guise of Miss Fratton would be difficult to recognize.

13

So It Was You

As Avery had predicted, it was raining again. Not the cold, driven sleet of the afternoon on which John Laurie had disappeared, but a fine drizzle that had been falling all day, blotting out the cliffs and the sea and much of the golf-links; appropriate weather for the play about to be enacted, however inappropriate for Christmas. But few adult minds in Grange Road were properly attuned that afternoon to Christmas. The police arrangements had reminded them — if reminder were necessary — that two men had died a sudden death, and that the reckoning was yet to come. It might be very near now. For some the fear had lessened, for others intensified; but all were filled with a common curiosity, a common sense of impending drama.

At twenty minutes past five Ethel Plant

left her house and turned left. It was dark in the road, and she shivered as she hurried on. The postman's red bicycle was propped against the gatepost of No. 5, a man in postman's uniform, with cape and leggings, beside it. She could not see his face, but he gave a curt grunt as she bade him good afternoon. And suddenly her spine no longer tingled with the apprehension that had formerly possessed her. For the postman was taller — much taller — than the man she had seen that fateful Friday. That was a mistake, she thought. The police should have chosen a man nearer Laurie's size if they wanted to create an air of reality for the performance.

But as she plodded down the road in her sensible shoes some of the excitement returned to her. She saw curtains pulled aside and faces pressed against the glass panes. Some of the houses were in darkness. Miss Plant imagined the silent watchers, and wondered at their thoughts.

It was, she thought nervously, unusual to take part in a play and know nothing of how it would end.

Footsteps behind her made her quicken her pace. There was no cause to be frightened, she told herself; there must be dozens of policemen in the area. All the same, it was a little unnerving. That dark stretch between Nos. 19 and 20 — she wasn't looking forward to that. But she *was* looking forward to the shelter of Hermione's house and the tea which she hoped Hermione had not forgotten to provide.

Inspector Pitt watched her go, heard her footsteps fade into silence. Then he sat back and waited.

Donald Heath stood in the front parlour of No. 9, his mother beside him. The room was dark, and occasionally he took his eyes off the white blur of the garden gate to glance at the luminous dial of his wrist-watch. Mrs Heath watched his nervous, jerky movements until the darkness hid them from her. He had told her nothing of his flight, of his enforced visit to the police-station; but she sensed he was in danger, and wished she knew exactly whence the danger might come. He had not been a good son; he had brought her many worries in the past. But he *was* her son, and she had no one else.

Each time she tried to talk he silenced her. His nerves were too taut, his mind too preoccupied for conversation. But now she could stand the dark and the silence no longer.

'If only you'd tell me, Donald,' she pleaded, harping on the same theme as before.

He shook his head, forgetting that she could not see the action. 'For God's sake, Mother! Can't you leave me alone? I've told you all there is to tell. I don't know what they're up to any more than you do.'

'But they suspect you, don't they? You must know about that.'

'I don't know what they suspect.'

He moved away from her, farther into the bay-window. But she would not leave it at that.

'Is it Carrington?' she asked haltingly. It was the first time she had dared to put her fears into words. 'You — you didn't, did you, Donald?'

Something of what she had gone

through in the past few days communicated itself to him. He said, his tone more gentle than it had been previously, 'Of course I didn't. You don't have to worry, Mother. It isn't what I've done but what the police may think I've done that worries me. I told you, I don't know what they suspect. I only wish I did.'

'What will you do?' she asked.

'Do? What they want me to do, of course. There's no alternative.'

His gentler mood calmed her. She could not help saying, a note of bitterness in her voice, 'None of this would have happened if it hadn't been for that Weston girl. You wouldn't have stolen the money, you wouldn't have had to write to your Aunt Ellen, you wouldn't have had that fight with the postman. If she hadn't got her claws into you *and* Carrington there would have been no reason for the police to suspect — '

'Shut up!' he said, his gentleness gone. Would she never learn? 'I've told you before — Sh! Listen!'

The click of the garden gate, the faint crunch of feet on gravel. Now for it, he thought, as he went into the hall. There must be no mistake. I don't know where they are or what they're up to, but I know they'll be watching. If I make a mistake . . .

He hardly saw the envelopes that slid through the letter-box into the wire cage; but as the metal flap snapped back into place he opened the door.

The torch was moving away down the path. He tried to shout, but his throat was dry.

'Hey, postman!' The words sounded cracked, detached from himself. He cleared his throat and tried again. 'Hey, postman!' That was better. 'There ought to be a registered letter for me. Are you sure you haven't mislaid it?'

It sounded all wrong. There wasn't the urgency in it that had been there that other time. It was uncertain, half-hearted.

'Sorry. That's all,' came the postman's muffled voice.

Donald stood petrified as the beam moved on down the path, shone on to and through the white gate, and disappeared. His brain urged his feet to move, but they would not respond.

Behind him came his mother's anxious voice.

'Go on, Donald! What are you waiting for?'

The tension snapped. He started off at a run. Faster even than on that other occasion, so that the water shot from under his flying feet as he splashed through the puddles.

Out on the road the beam was moving steadily away.

'Hey!' he shouted; and this time there was no lack of urgency in his voice. 'Hey, you! I know — '

Dark figures moved from the shadow and grabbed at him, holding him back. He struggled furiously.

'Let me go!' he shouted. 'Let me go, damn you! I — '

'That's all right, sir,' came the calm voice of a constable. 'We know all about it. Just you come along with us, Mr Heath. The Inspector'll want to see you.'

Down the road the postman turned, shone his torch for a moment on the struggling figures, and then went on with his task.

In the front room of No. 13 Miss Weston and Inspector Pitt stood in the dark. 'My sister was here with me that afternoon,' she had told him. 'You'll have to be like a sister to me, Inspector. And sit yourself down in that chair. That's what she did — I was the one who was restless.' He had done as she directed, glad for once that Dick was not present. Dick, he knew, would have made some crack out of that bit about the sister.

But after a while he had got up and walked over to stand by her at the window. 'I'm here to watch what happens,' he said. 'I can't see anything from the depths of an armchair.'

The street-lamp at the corner of the hedge shone mistily. He could sense the tension in the girl beside him, despite her pleasantries. Or maybe because of them — they sounded forced. She's all keyed up, he thought. Well, I hope there is at least one other who is feeling the same way. I am, for one.

For some reason he could not explain,

her nervousness pleased him. She wasn't so hard-boiled as he had thought. Though why that —

Her hand gripped his arm. 'There it is,' she whispered.

The postman's cap glistened in the rain as it passed under the street-lamp and glided along the top of the hedge. Pitt nodded to himself.

'Was it like that?' he asked.

'Just like that,' the girl said. 'But it didn't seem so eerie before. Only rather odd.'

He ran from the room and out of the house. From the garden path he could see the postman's torch shining on Miss Fratton's doorstep, heard the clang of the knocker. As the front door opened he had already joined Sergeant Roberts inside the gate of No. 14.

Although Miss Fratton had previously expressed reluctance to lecture the postman in the manner she had been wont to use in the past (that Friday had been no isolated instance, as Gofer had testified), she showed no reluctance now. Her voice was as shrill and as strident as ever; her tongue dripped venom. The two officers, concealed by the darkness, listened entranced.

'Atta-girl!' whispered the Sergeant joyously.

The postman did not stand it for long. He wrenched himself free and ran down the farther arm of the path, his figure outlined faintly by the light from the street-lamp. And as he ran Pitt snapped his fingers in grim exultation.

'He didn't drop the torch,' said Sergeant Roberts.

'I expect he forgot. It doesn't matter.'

Miss Fratton was down the path, a stick upraised in her hand. But this time the postman did not stumble, was through the gate before she could reach him. For a moment Miss Fratton stood irresolute. Then she turned and went back to the house.

As the knocker sounded on the front door of No. 17 William Harris got up and went into the hall. 'Play-acting!' he scoffed, as he returned to the kitchen with the letters. 'Play-acting, that's what it is.'

'But you're going out, aren't you?'

355

asked his wife. 'You said you would.'

'I suppose so. When I'm ready.'

Marion Harris had never had any dealings with the police before the trouble started in Grange Road. Her husband's arrest for theft had been a great shock to her. All her life she had been poor; but always, as she said, her family had kept themselves respectable. And although Will had escaped so easily, she no longer felt clean. There were the neighbours, too. To leave the security of her house was now a torment to her. Every eye, she imagined, was watching, every finger pointing at her in scorn. And, above all, they would never be free of the police. There would always be that black mark against Will. The smallest slip . . .

Well, there would be no slip. Not if she could help it.

Normally a quiet, unassuming woman, she jumped up and gripped her husband's arm. 'You go out now, not when you're ready,' she said fiercely. 'I'll not have you bringing any more disgrace on us. You go out now, as the police said.'

'All right, all right!' His complacency

was shaken by this unexpected assumption of authority. 'I said I'd go, didn't I?'

As the door closed behind him she ran to the front room and peered out into the night. She could see Will standing by the gate. But it was a policeman he was taking to, not the postman.

Marion Harris watched them nervously.

The postman walked past the dark and untenanted house of Wilfred Morris, leant his bicycle against the low hedge of No. 19, and shone his torch on the one envelope left in his hand. Then, with a shrug of the shoulders, he pushed open the gate and walked up the path.

As the knocker sounded the door opened, and a flood of light bathed the glistening figure of the postman. In the doorway, his bulk almost filling it, stood Sam Archer.

'Thanks,' he said. 'I'll take it.'

Mechanically the postman held out the letter. But Archer ignored it. Instead he peered down at the outstretched hand.

'Blimey!' he said. 'So it was you? You're the chap that brought the letters that night!' And as the postman stood irresolute Archer leaned swiftly forward and grasped him by the arm. 'That scar on your thumb — I couldn't get that wrong. It was you all right.' Raising his voice, he shouted, 'Hey, Inspector! I've got him! This is the bloke you're looking for.'

'You bloody liar!' shouted the other, struggling to free himself. 'You couldn't have seen it. I didn't call at this house — there weren't any letters for you that afternoon!'

The police were through the gate, were running up the path towards the struggling figures on the doorstep. Archer was a big man, but the postman was no weakling. Exerting every ounce of his strength, he wrenched himself free, raced across the small front lawn and, clearing the hedge in one leap, landed heavily on the pavement.

As he disappeared eastward into the night police whistles shrilled, men came running. The road was suddenly bathed in light as head-lamps were switched on, catching the figure in their beam. For a moment he pounded on. Then, swerving left, he was lost in the darkness of the golf-links.

★   ★   ★

Mrs Gill had prepared tea. She was not one to neglect her meals, not even on such an occasion as this. But it was not the fine spread that had greeted Miss Plant on that memorable Friday. Bread and butter, jam, and a rather stale Madeira cake. But the tea was hot, and the butter was butter and not margarine, and Miss Plant was ready for both. She made a comfortable meal.

Mrs Gill was too excited to eat heartily, but she drank several cups of tea and nibbled at the cake. And all the time she watched the clock.

At ten minutes to five she said, 'I can't stand this any longer, Ethel. I must know what's happening. I'm going out.' And she stood up determinedly.

Miss Plant was alarmed. 'You can't do that, Hermione,' she protested, gazing up at her friend with troubled eyes. 'The

Inspector would be furious. He'd think you were interfering; you know he would. He said we were to do just as we did that other afternoon.'

'But if we stay indoors we won't see a thing, Ethel. Whatever happens, it will be the other side of the gap. The postman didn't get as far as this. If we go just a little way up the road . . . '

'But you'll know afterwards,' said Miss Plant, who was not at all anxious to leave the shelter of the house. 'And probably nothing *will* happen, anyway.'

'Yes, it will. I know it will.' Mrs Gill went out into the hall and returned with raincoat and umbrella. 'It's no good, Ethel. This is something I absolutely refuse to miss. Hearing about it afterwards wouldn't be the same — you know that. I'm going out.'

'The Inspector will be furious,' Miss Plant said again, harping on the one argument she hoped might prove a deterrent.

Mrs Gill hesitated. She knew this was true. 'Very well,' she said. 'I'll go the back way, on to the golf-links. They won't be able to see me from there.'

She had her raincoat on and was in the hall, with Miss Plant risen from her chair (uncertain whether to stay where she was or to follow her friend), when the whistles shrilled and Grange Road was suddenly light. They acted on Mrs Gill as a spur. Any fear she might have felt was swamped by her curiosity. Without another word she hurried from the house, threaded her way through the familiar labyrinth of the back garden, and out through the gate on to the links. It was only then that she realized she had no torch to light her over the rough ground between the houses and the fairway.

She could see the lights on the road and began to feel her way westward, striking away from the houses the better to improve her view. The whistles were silent now, but she could hear men shouting. I wonder if they've got him? she thought, prodding with her umbrella at the uneven ground as she went.

She did not see the fugitive; he did not see her, until he was on top of her. Mrs Gill's scream of terror was cut short as the running, stumbling figure crashed into her, knocking the breath out of her body. They fell to the ground, the postman uppermost.

It was Mrs Gill's umbrella that foiled him. Somehow, somewhere it had become hooked into his clothing She was aware of his struggle to free himself, of his feet and hands searching desperately for purchase on the wet and slippery ground. She was bruised and shaken, and convinced that her end was near. As his weight shifted and he scrambled to his feet she screamed again; and then there were others round them, and the lights of torches, and men struggling.

A constable helped her gently to her feet and put a strong arm round her trembling body. Mrs Gill was glad of the support. She could not have stood alone. She wondered vaguely whether she was going to faint. She had never done so before; but then she had never before done personal battle with an escaping criminal.

'All right, ma'am?' asked the constable.

'I — I think so,' she answered. She put

up a hand to push the hair away from her face. There was a pain in her back, and her foot ached where the man had kicked it. But at least she was whole — and alive.

A tall figure came from behind the ring of torches. 'No bones broken?' asked Inspector Pitt.

'I don't think so, Inspector. Did you — have you got him?'

'Yes, ma'am, we've got him. Thanks to you,' said Pitt. 'Looks as though you ought to join the Force. You've taken quite a hand in this business, one way and another. But I think you'd be wiser not to tackle escaping criminals single-handed. You might not get off so lightly the next time.'

Was it possible, wondered Mrs Gill, that he didn't know it was an accident? Did he think she had tried deliberately to stop the man? Good heaven! What would Grange Road say to *that*? Fame would indeed be hers.

'I think perhaps you're right, Inspector,' she said, almost purring. Forgotten were the trembling limbs, the aching body. 'But then, one doesn't stop to consider the consequences to oneself on such occasions, does one?'

Curiosity came once more to the fore, and she moved a few paces nearer to the tall figure flanked by two policemen. They stood just outside the circle of light.

'Oh, Donald!' she said, peering forward to look at him. 'How could you — '

'Donald?' A foot shot out, missing her by inches. 'Go to hell, you ruddy interfering old crow!' said Michael Bullett.

14

All Very Clever

'Did you *know* it was Bullett?' asked Dick. 'Or was it just a lucky hunch, the same as I had had about that letter?'

'It was a hunch until I went to Guildford,' said Pitt. 'That more or less settled it. Or perhaps 'hunch' isn't the right word. Whatever it was, its birth was delayed over-long.'

'Whatever it was, you kept it to yourself,' chided Dick.

'I know.' The Inspector looked guilty. 'But twice before, when the pangs of detection first started, you scoffed at them. I may not look it, but I'm a sensitive creature; I like my brain-children to be admired, not ridiculed. This time I meant to be sure. I'd have told you yesterday, Dick, if your temperature had been lower. But I knew damned well you'd never stay in bed if you thought an arrest was in the offing.'

Wendy Ponsford smiled at him gratefully.

'We got off to a bad start,' mused the Sergeant, leaning back against the pillows. 'Blake and Sullivan confused the issue properly. Even after Laurie's body was found I never suspected that everything that happened in Grange Road that Friday hadn't happened to him. What made you rumble it, Loy?'

'I don't know exactly. Right from that first interview with Mrs Laurie I had a suspicion she knew more than she admitted. She spoke of her husband in the past tense, as though she *knew* he was dead — or gone for good, anyway. But the note to Bullett seemed to contradict that. Even after we found he wasn't concerned with the Rawsley hold-up, the money sent to Mrs L. indicated he was still alive.

'I suppose it was the theft of the torch from No. 14 that first put me, however insecurely, on the right lines. Why should the man be so eager to regain it? Fingerprints, I thought; and then realized the absurdity of that, applied to Laurie.

He wouldn't worry about leaving finger-prints if he were engaged on lawful business. I'd have dismissed the idea altogether if it hadn't been for the attack on Heath. If Heath's account of that was true — which was doubtful, of course — it was an odd way for a postman to behave. And he'd behaved oddly from the start; delivering some letters and not others, abandoning the mail so casually.

'I began to think more about the postman as a *person*.

'Heath had said the man was tall. I wouldn't have accepted your explanation of that, Dick, if I hadn't thought of Miss Weston's hedge from the *outside* — as you did. So her remark about the postman's cap indicated a small man; and it wasn't until I looked at the hedge from the right angle — *her* angle — that I suspected Heath might be right. And then, when Mrs Gill repeated Miss Fratton's remark — that the postman's oilskins were too small for him — I began to see daylight. Laurie had borrowed Gofer's, and Laurie was five inches shorter than Gofer. They should have been too big for him, not too small.'

He paused to light a cigarette.

'As you say, Dick, we got off to a bad start. It never occurred to us that the postman wasn't Laurie, and so all our inquiries dealt with his actions — not with his appearance.'

'Would it have made much difference?' said Dick. 'The only one of that bunch to see him at all clearly was Miss Fratton. And how much attention would we have paid to her? Damn all, if you ask me. Personally, I wouldn't have believed her if she'd told us straight out that the man was Bullett. What put you on to him, by the way?'

'Miss Weston's information about the gun,' Pitt said promptly. 'She said it was kept in the hall cupboard, along with the coats. If that was so Bullett must have seen it there; he was a frequent visitor, actually lived in the bungalow for a few weeks. Yet he denied all knowledge of the gun. Why?'

Dick nodded. 'It's the sort of stupid and unnecessary mistake they often make,' he agreed.

'That's what I thought,' said Pitt. 'Unfortunately, Miss Weston was figuring rather prominently in my mind just then — stop grinning, you ape! You know damn' well what I mean. There was Heath, too. With two such hot favourites, I didn't give Bullett the consideration he deserved. But I got around to it gradually. I remembered how shaken he had been when we told him Carrington's death was murder, not suicide. He hadn't expected us to rumble that, you see. It seemed odd, too, that as a reporter he should have made no effort to interview any of the people in Grange Road — neither after Laurie's disappearance nor after Carrington's death. I don't think he *expected* to be recognized; he just wasn't running any unnecessary risks, that's all.

'Then there was the note he wrote himself, purporting to come from Laurie. At the time his explanation seemed fair enough. But I reasoned that, if he *had* killed Laurie, Mrs L. was likely to be behind it. That meant Bullett had lied to us when he said he had never met her. If he was to live up to the lie he either had to keep away from the woman or account to us — not to her, as he pretended — for his frequent visits to Tilnet Close.'

'So he wrote the note, eh?' said Dick. 'Neat. Very neat.'

'Yes. It was safer than keeping away from her. It enabled him to deal with any awkward questions we might put to her. And the most awkward of all, from their angle, was our inquiry into her previous engagement. Stilby, you see, was the one man who could disprove Bullett's statement that he did not know Mrs Laurie prior to her husband's disappearance.'

'And I thought you were exploring a dead end!' said his brother-in-law.

'I wasn't too confident myself,' Pitt admitted. 'It was only her reluctance to talk that made me persist. But I didn't suspect then that it would lead me to Bullett. That came later. Just as well it did, too. Stilby didn't know Bullett's name, and his memory of his last evening with the girl was hazy. But I jogged his memory by asking for a thumbnail sketch. That did it. He couldn't forget that scar.'

'I never suspected Bullett,' Dick admitted. 'In fact, my suspicions were as inconsistent as Miss Weston's affections appear to be — begging your pardon, Loy. Apart from Donald Heath, of course. But then he practically asked to be arrested, the way he carried on.'

'He's a frightened fool,' said Pitt.

'How did you persuade Bullett to take over the rôle of postman this afternoon?' asked Dick. 'I thought you said he'd turned it down?'

'His editor persuaded him. I saw the old man and explained that I wanted Bullett because he'd known Carrington. (I was very mysterious about that. I didn't want him asking how Carrington came into it, as I didn't know the answer to that one myself.) No editor could refuse a scoop like that, I thought. And how right I was! He almost went down on his knees to thank me.'

'I bet Bullett didn't feel that way,' said Dick.

'No. But he couldn't refuse.'

'I know it's none of my business,' Wendy said plaintively; 'but since you insist on discussing this in front of me, couldn't I be told what happened? I don't know about Dick, but I'm positively seething with curiosity.'

'It could be a little clearer,' her husband admitted.

The Inspector laughed. 'Sorry; I forgot. Well, where shall I start?'

'At the beginning,' said his sister. 'And don't skip.'

'The beginning, eh? Well, I suppose that was the night Stilby and Jane Abbott picked up Bullett, and Bullett seduced the girl. She was scared of the consequences. And since Bullett refused to marry her, she took Laurie. Laurie was an old stand-by; he wouldn't make too much fuss, she thought, if a child happened to be born out of turn. Although how right she was in that respect I wouldn't know. The feared consequences didn't arrive.

'Marriage to Laurie only made Bullett appear more attractive. Consequences didn't matter now, and the two continued to meet. Very much in secret, however; Bullett saw to that. An angry husband and a possible divorce suit were not in his line at all. And their favourite rendezvous — latterly, at any rate — was Carrington's bungalow. Not when Carrington was there, of course — although I dare say Carrington guessed something of what was going on, even if he never met the woman. But Carrington was often away, and Bullett had the key. He could come and go openly. Mrs Laurie, however, met him there after dark, via the golf-links and the back door. And no one in Grange Road seems to have seen her.'

'Mrs Gill would have rumbled them if *she'd* lived down that end,' said Dick.

'Yes, I imagine she would. Well — last Friday week Bullett knew Carrington would be staying in Town fairly late, so he caught the early train back and met the girl at the bungalow as arranged. When Laurie rang the bell, having a registered letter to deliver, Bullett, who was in the hall and had no reason to hide his own presence there, opened it. To find the postman was Laurie came as a shock — he knew the man normally worked over at Cambersleigh Park — but he couldn't shut the door in his face. They were, as he had said, old acquaintances. It was even true that Laurie had saved Bullett's life — which goes to show what a nice type Bullett is!

'All might have been well had not Mrs Laurie, who hadn't heard the bell, chosen that moment to emerge from a bedroom in her underwear and call out some affectionate remark to Bullett. Laurie recognized the voice, pushed his way past Bullett into the hall, and naturally disapproved of what he saw. One can't blame him if, as Bullett asserts, he started the fight.

'Anyway, there *was* a fight. Bullett says he was merely trying to hold the other off; that he had a hand at Laurie's throat and didn't realize he was throttling him. Not until Laurie sagged and collapsed, and they found he was dead.'

'They?' queried Dick. 'Did Mrs L. join in?'

'No. But she helped Bullett to conceal the body afterwards. They had to get rid of it and clear out before Carrington returned. But Bullett knew the police would start their inquiries from where the

374

postman was known to have made his last call. He must make it appear that Laurie got well past the bungalow before ceasing delivery of the mail. He put on the man's leggings, cape, and cap, and together they got the body into the Austin (the keys, remember, were kept in the hall). Then he set off, arranging with the girl to pick him up in the car farther down the road.'

'He was taking a big risk, wasn't he?' said Wendy.

'No bigger than the occasion warranted. It was dark, and raining hard; the road would be deserted. Only a few people in Grange Road knew him by sight. If he avoided direct contact he was unlikely to be recognized.

'The first snag came at No. 9, with the registered letter for Heath. He couldn't risk obtaining a signature for it, and if he delivered it without one the police would smell a rat. So he put it in his pocket.'

'I bet Heath's behaviour shook him,' said Dick.

'It shook him to the core. When Heath came bellowing after him he thought it was all up. Knocking the man down was an instinctive action. After that he took to his heels — until he realized that Heath had had enough, that he wasn't following.

'Bullett still wasn't far enough away from the bungalow to be safe. He knew that. So he pulled himself together and went on with his self-appointed task.

'He had to bypass No. 13. Miss Weston was one of the few who knew him by sight. Her brooch went into his pocket along with the letter for Heath.'

'And then came shock number two, eh?' said Dick. 'He couldn't have anticipated anyone like Miss Fratton. Nobody could.'

Pitt smiled.

'Miss Fratton ditched him in more ways than one,' he said, ignoring their groans at the pun. 'She made him drop his torch; and a metal torch takes a nice clean fingerprint. That was why he had to break into her house on Sunday night to recover it. And it was the loss of the torch that caused him to misread the address on Morris's letter and deliver it to Harris instead.

'However, it was plain sailing after that.

He cycled past the Vauxhall (I wonder if that gave him any qualms?), and Mrs Laurie picked him up in the car as arranged. (Incidentally, it was Mrs Laurie who lifted the receiver when Miss Weston phoned. She was standing by it, and acted without thinking. But she realized her mistake in time.) They drove out to Coppins Point, put the cape and leggings back on the body, and pushed it over the cliff. Then, after dropping Mrs Laurie near Tilnet Close, Bullett took the car back to the bungalow, made sure that everything there was as it should be, and went home.'

'He certainly kept his wits about him,' the Sergeant commented. 'I wonder how he felt when you invited him out to Rawsley to identify Laurie?'

'Pleased as Punch, I imagine, after the initial shock,' said Pitt. 'He realized we were right off the track. Maybe it was because he felt so safe that he slipped up over the brooch. Carrington knew he was going to Town on Tuesday, and asked him to get another. But Bullett was broke, and he had found the original in his pocket; so he gave that to Carrington and kept the money. And it was because he was broke that he blackmailed Heath. Having killed Jane Laurie's husband, he now had to provide for her. Heath's indiscretion, whatever it was, appeared to solve that problem.'

'Was it Bullett who sent us the letter about Heath?'

'Yes. Trying to muddle the issue, presumably.'

'What about Carrington?' asked Wendy.

'Ah, yes, Carrington. He suspected Bullett before I did. The brooch, the telephone call, our inquiries about the Austin — I've no doubt that, with his own knowledge of Bullett, they added up very easily to Carrington. He telephoned Bullett that evening, asking him round to the bungalow; and because he knew he might be dealing with a killer, he kept the shotgun handy.

'Bullett tried to bluff it out, but Carrington remained unconvinced. It was a matter for the police, he said. And when Carrington reached for the phone Bullett made a grab for the gun. There was a struggle, in the course of which the gun went off, and — well, we saw the result, Dick.'

'We certainly did,' said his brother-in-law, grimacing. 'But that bit in the confession, hinting at Carrington having been keen on Mrs Laurie? That was all bunkum, I suppose?'

'Absolutely. Bullett had to invent a reason for the supposed quarrel between Carrington and Laurie; and the girl was primed to recognize the photo if confronted with it. But she mustn't be too deeply involved — hence the mild tone of the supposed infatuation. They didn't want to suspect *her* of Laurie's murder.'

'Did you get all this from Bullett?'

'Partly from him, partly from the girl. They both talked.'

'I suppose Bullett didn't blackmail Avery as well?' Dick suggested. 'We never sorted that one out, did we?'

'No. But Bullett says he didn't, and I believe him. He threw the mail away before getting into the car with Mrs Laurie. It would have been an amazing coincidence if he had happened to pick out that one particular letter to keep. No, that was Blake's handiwork. No doubt about that.'

'Well, I think you're all very clever,' Wendy declared. 'And you seemed to know so much about this man Bullett that I wonder you bothered with this evening's performance.'

'As the Super said, I wanted him to hang himself,' said her brother. 'Do the job for us, so to speak. There was no mail for Archer the afternoon Laurie was killed; but there was today. Bullett must have wondered at that change in the routine, but he couldn't question it. He'd had a harrowing time, what with Heath and Miss Fratton doing their stuff. Archer's accusation was the last straw — as I'd hoped it would be.'

'Would you have arrested him if he hadn't reacted?'

'Oh, yes. I had a strong case without that. Heath, for instance, said he recognized the voice. A good defence counsel could pull Heath to pieces, I've no doubt; but it would be bound to influence the jury to some extent.

'Then there was his mistake at No. 14. As he ran down the path to escape from Miss Fratton he remembered the ditch that had tripped him before, and jumped to clear it. Only the ditch wasn't there — it had been filled in. And he had told us that he had never called at the house.'

'How fitting that it should have been Mrs Gill who stopped him,' said Dick. 'She's taken quite a hand in this business.'

'Ah! Dear Mrs Gill! How I love that woman!'

'Oh, you do, do you? I thought it was the fair Dorothy who commanded your affections. Bought her a Christmas present?'

'You're a fool, Dick, as I've told you before,' said Pitt.

'Why, Loy!' His sister was laughing. 'I do believe you're blushing!'

We do hope that you have enjoyed reading this large print book.

Did you know that all of our titles are available for purchase?

We publish a wide range of high quality large print books including:
Romances, Mysteries, Classics
General Fiction
Non Fiction and Westerns

Special interest titles available in large print are:
The Little Oxford Dictionary
Music Book, Song Book
Hymn Book, Service Book

Also available from us courtesy of Oxford University Press:
Young Readers' Dictionary
(large print edition)
Young Readers' Thesaurus
(large print edition)

For further information or a free brochure, please contact us at:
Ulverscroft Large Print Books Ltd.,
The Green, Bradgate Road, Anstey,
Leicester, LE7 7FU, England.
Tel: (00 44) **0116 236 4325**
Fax: (00 44) **0116 234 0205**

Other titles in the
Linford Mystery Library:

THE SISKIYOU TWO-STEP

Richard Hoyt

John Denson, a private investigator, goes to Oregon's North Umpqua River to fish trout but, instead, he finds himself caught up in a net of international intelligence agents and academics. It all starts when the naked body of a girl with a bullet hole between her eyes goes rushing past Denson in the rapids. He embarks on a bizarre search to find the girl's identity and to bring her killer to justice. Strange clues lead to three more corpses, and only the Siskiyou Two-Step saves Denson from being the fourth . . .

THREE MAY KEEP A SECRET

Stella Phillips

The proudest citizens of Dolph Hill would not deny that it was a backwater where nothing ever happened — until, that is, the arrival of handsome, secretive Peter Markland disturbs the surface. After his shocking and violent death, old secrets begin to emerge. Detectives Matthew Furnival and Reg King are put on the case. As they delve through the conflicting mysteries, how will they arrive at the one relevant truth?